Text Classics

T0359168

AMY WITTING was the pen name of Joan Austral Fraser, born on 26 January 1918 in the inner-Sydney suburb of Annandale. After attending Fort Street Girls' High School she studied arts at the University of Sydney.

She married Les Levick, a teacher, in 1948 and they had a son. Witting spent her working life teaching, but began writing seriously while recovering from tuberculosis in the 1950s.

Two stories appeared in the *New Yorker* in the mid-1960s, leading to *The Visit* (1977), an acclaimed novel about small-town life in New South Wales. Two years later Witting completed her masterpiece, *I for Isobel*, which was rejected by publishers troubled by its depiction of a mother tormenting her child.

When *I for Isobel* was eventually published, in 1989, it became a bestseller. Witting was lauded for the power and acuity of her portrait of the artist as a young woman. In 1993 she won the Patrick White Award.

Witting published prolifically in her final decade. After two more novels, her *Collected Poems* appeared in 1998 and her collected stories, *Faces and Voices*, in 2000.

Between these volumes came *Isobel on the Way to the Corner Shop*, the sequel to *I for Isobel*. Both *Isobel* novels were shortlisted for the Miles Franklin Award; the latter was the 2000 *Age* Book of the Year.

Amy Witting died in 2001, weeks before her novel *After Cynthia* was published and while she was in the early stages of writing the third *Isobel* book. She was made a Member of the Order of Australia and a street in Canberra bears her name.

SUSAN JOHNSON is the author of eight novels and two non-fiction books, variously longlisted and shortlisted for awards including the National Biography Award, the ALS Gold Medal, the Commonwealth Writers' Prize and the Miles Franklin Literary Award. She is working on a ninth novel, *From Where I Fell*. She lives in Brisbane.

ALSO BY AMY WITTING

I for Isobel
Marriages (stories)
A Change in the Lighting
In and Out the Window (stories)
Maria's War
Isobel on the Way to the Corner Shop
Faces and Voices (stories)
After Cynthia
Selected Stories

The Visit
Amy Witting

Text Publishing Melbourne Australia

textclassics.com.au
textpublishing.com.au

The Text Publishing Company
Swann House
22 William Street
Melbourne Victoria 3000
Australia

First published by Thomas Nelson (Australia) 1977
This edition published by The Text Publishing Company 2017

Cover design by Imogen Stubbs
Series design by W. H. Chong
Typeset by Midland Typesetters

Printed and bound in Australia by Griffin Press, an accredited ISO/NZS 1401:2004 Environmental Management System printer

National Library of Australia Cataloguing-in-Publication entry
ISBN: 9781925498134 (paperback)
ISBN: 9781925410471 (ebook)
Creator: Witting, Amy, 1918–2001, author.
Title: The visit / by Amy Witting ; introduced by Susan Johnson.
Subjects: Women—Fiction.

CONTENTS

Becoming Witting
by Susan Johnson

THERE ARE MANY visits in Amy Witting's first novel, published in 1977. At its centre is the mysterious visit to Bangoree of the celebrated Australian poet Roderick Fitzallan—but, this being a Witting novel set in a fictional town in small-minded rural Australia, a poet uncelebrated in Bangoree, where 'a poet would be a vagrant, by definition'.

She was very good at the coruscating but uncomfortable truth, was Amy Witting, in both her prose and her person. Take *The Visit*'s intelligent central eye, Naomi—too good for Bangoree and possibly too good for herself—who escorts Fitzallan's biographer, Maurice Ellman, to dinner on his own visit to Bangoree. In less accomplished hands Ellman might be reduced to Naomi's 'love interest' but in Witting's clever grasp he is a man with an unoccupied heart. Witting knows that love, if you're lucky, is always an embattled journey to the centre.

Then there is Naomi's son, Peter, on his eye-opening visit to Sydney, to girls, to sex, to emerging life and—more disappointingly—to his newly found father. Witting knows, too, life's hard lessons in family romance—how rarely love conquers all—revealing the shabby truth in all its squirming pity. Love is often wanting, or else it speaks in the wrong words, and Witting in her genius lets us down gently.

Everywhere in *The Visit* is evidence of Witting's formidable intelligence and heart. Glorious, frustrated Barbara, hemmed in by a bitch of a mother-in-law, secretly loved by Phil Truebody, himself hemmed in by an alcoholic wife and despair. Poor Phil and Barbara, playing Nagg and Nell in Beckett's merciless *Endgame* as part of Bangoree's amateur play group, Phil wondering how Barbara's 'incongruous words open a door suddenly on an enchanted landscape'. If Witting knew bitter truths—and she did—she also knew the endless human capacity for hope. We keep turning up for more, battering our hearts again and again, unable—or unwilling—to believe our cherished romances are myth.

If one definition of superior intelligence is the ability to keep two opposing ideas in the mind at once, then Witting knew romance is myth but also that it's the gold standard we keep aiming for our whole lives long. Always with Amy Witting: the possibility of redemption through love. Hope runs ceaselessly through *The Visit*, like the river running through Bangoree, the river of Fitzallan's famous poems. Here are Naomi and Barbara, sitting by its banks:

> In the silence, as they looked after the lovers, the persistent undertone of the river was audible. Naomi thought about Phil Truebody and wondered whether a hopeless love was better than nothing at all. The river insisted quietly that to live, love, live was better. Not much better, yet better.

*

The most renowned author in the world today working under a non de plume is Italy's Elena Ferrante. Ferrante has written widely about her choice to remain anonymous and her readers respect that choice, rounding on the attempt to unmask her by a journalist in the *New York Review of Books*.

Ferrante chose invisibility in the way Italo Calvino chose disguise in his fiction ('Ask me what you want to know, but I won't tell you the truth, of that you can be sure') yet, in adopting her pseudonym, Amy Witting chose freedom. *I for Isobel* was also J for Joan. Witting's second novel was published in 1989, more than a decade after *The Visit*. It is regarded as her breakout novel, even though her agent (and mine at the time), Margaret

Connolly, had to approach every publisher in the country with the manuscript. Despite critical acclaim for *The Visit*, it was *I for Isobel* which proved to be Witting's announcement to the world that she was here.

But it was the decisive earlier act of turning the hand to the page, the imaginative eye to the everyday world, which announced to the girl born Joan Austral Fraser on 26 January 1918 (hence the middle name) her full existence. In declaring that existence on the page, in poetry—her first love; Fitzallan's marvellous poems in *The Visit* are all hers—and later in prose, she named herself. Witting was a born writer, in that she wanted to speak the unspoken, to write her truth—which turned out to be a lot of other people's truths—which is not to say she merely wrote down her diary.

She wrote the everyday awful truths of existence: that sometimes parents don't—or can't—love their children, that often people marry the wrong partner, that some of us wake to find ourselves in the wrong life. Witting knew the power of the transformative act, the power of imaginative will. Throughout her life she kept in contact with former students—who became her friends—because, I believe, she most identified with those on the brink of becoming. Amy Witting wrote about becoming because she was once Joan Fraser, who became her fullest self through an act of imaginative will.

*

I always knew Amy as Amy. We met through our mutual agent, not long after I published my first novel, *Messages from Chaos*, in 1987. I devoured *I for Isobel* in a matter of hours. As when I read *Little Women* and identified with Jo, or *Jane Eyre*—joining millions of girls across centuries imagining themselves like Jane, brave and shining—I imagined I knew Isobel as I knew my own self.

I was nervous about meeting Amy. Within moments, however, my nervousness vanished and I felt charmed. She lived with her husband, Les Levick (she had long been Mrs Levick to the girls to whom she taught French and English), in what looked like a country cottage in Epping but which I later learned was once a small farm when outer Sydney was still partly rural.

She was used to younger women. She was used to mentoring, to being magnanimous, to showing the way. She was a smoker—from memory there was no nonsense about smoking outdoors; she sat inside in a comfortable chair puffing away. Her voice was deep, gravelly, a true smoker's. She did a good turn in cracking one-liners, she was the sort of person who used 'one' a lot instead of 'I', and she was fond of aphorisms. I saw her as a kind of antipodean Dorothy Parker.

We met a few times at her house and for meals in restaurants. I was quick with the questions—about life at the University of Sydney in the 1930s and '40s, when she was part of the bright young crowd which included Donald Horne and the poets James McAuley and Harold Stewart.

I knew she was supposed to be exceptionally modest and that writing under a pseudonym was possibly her way of hiding her light under a bushel. I didn't find her like that at all—I found her forthright, ambitious, proud, a writer who wanted her work to be known and celebrated. It was clear to me she enjoyed her delayed literary acclaim. She was already gravely ill when *Isobel on the Way to the Corner Shop*—the long-awaited sequel to *I for Isobel*—won the *Age* Book of the Year in 2000. (She died the following year.) Anyone who saw her take the stage at the prize ceremony could not fail to see how much she enjoyed being seen, being chosen—having *become*.

*

The period when I got to know Amy best coincided with some dark years in my marriage. In 1999 I had two small children under three, a temporary colostomy because of childbirth injury, no money, and I was trying to finish my memoir of motherhood, *A Better Woman*. My husband thought I should put aside my book—he did some calculations and worked out I was earning fifty cents an hour. I should have been a better cook, a better mother (I know! I know!); I should have been a better woman and put aside my neurotic, vainglorious desire to write.

Life is so much messier than books. There was a terrible scene: I fled with my children to a friend's house, where we all bunked down on the floor. I had *no money*. I spent hours on the phone to Centrelink; my parents transferred some cash to my account. I was forty-two years old, ashamed, the author of many books, sleepless on someone's floor in North Carlton.

I was scraping by on titbits from publishing's table, on freelance journalism, on teaching writing at RMIT, and unaware of the tsunami about to break over journalism and publishing. I was forty-two and I had run away from home.

My agent came to Melbourne on business. I had sworn her to secrecy—the colostomy, the marriage break-up, the scene in which I fled the house, the struggle to write my book, to *become*—none of which found their way into *A Better Woman* exactly as it happened. Memoir—like fiction—is a crafted thing, which is why I never mistake Isobel for a replica of Amy or Joan.

Margaret and I met for coffee somewhere. Where were my children? Perhaps my friend was minding them; perhaps they were with their father. Suddenly Margaret was pressing a rolled-up wad of fifty-dollar notes into my hand—five hundred dollars' worth, in fact—a gift from Amy. 'She doesn't want to hear another word about it,' said Margaret.

I'm telling it here. Amy Witting stood for becoming. Amy Witting was an exceptionally fine writer. Does it matter that she was also an exceptionally fine human being? Great artists can be shits. Arseholes can make great art. But when great art meets a great soul, something miraculous happens: the transformative act transforms every one of us who reads her. I envy anyone reading *The Visit* for the first time.

The Visit

CHAPTER ONE

On Monday morning at half past nine Robert Somers set off for his office in the main street and for once his wife Barbara walked to the gate with him. Feeling a need to speak to him, not knowing what she wanted to say, she followed him up the rough stone steps that led through the rockery to the road. On the second-last step Robert bent down, put two fingers under a dark-blue flower and drew it clear of the sheltering leaves, saying, 'Barbara's eyes', in a remote voice that went well with his severe, handsome looks, though he reserved it for the idiocies of love.

Barbara looked without enthusiasm at the flower. She had heard so much about her eyes in thirty-one years that she saw herself as the hireling who carried them about. Barbara Somers – Barbara MacFarlane . . . who? . . . the one with the lovely blue eyes. A time came when one had to answer that 'who?' for oneself, and it was no use talking about blue eyes.

Now her eyes had come between her and whatever it was she had to say to Robert.

Instead she said, 'Will you be late?'

'I shouldn't think so.' He kissed a fingertip and pressed it on the tip of her nose. 'Have a good day.'

The thought came clear then, but Robert was gone.

Barbara turned and paused to look at the house before she started down the steps again.

'Your poor house,' Naomi Faulding had said once, 'sitting there longing with all its soul for Paddington.' She had spoken affectionately, longing for Paddington herself. 'But then it has a soul. I like that in a house.'

Barbara liked it too and was proud of the fluted pillars, the cast-iron balcony, the long windows opening onto the tiled veranda – shabby elegance imbued with melancholy, evoking old ambitions. It was older than any other house in Bangoree except perhaps the Prescotts' over in the west, and much grander than Prescotts'.

Now she stood gazing at it and felt like a trespasser, reluctant to go in. She went down the steps, passed the open front door and walked round the side of the house towards the kitchen door, loitering among the dahlias, the habit of beauty smoothing her face in spite of her uneasiness. A tall, thin woman with a complexion of acid gold and dust-coloured hair drawn into a knot at the nape of her neck, she owed her beauty to her extraordinary eyes; yet, once they had pronounced her beautiful, nothing in her appearance contradicted them. As she picked off withered

4

flowers, she wondered how Robert could have lived so long with his mother and come through in such good condition. Had he been born with a better character than she? That was what she feared. Or was there a secret, an attitude to be taken that would protect against corruption? If there was, it was urgent that she should know it, for in six days with her mother-in-law she had developed the manners of an affected fool, covering sordid rage.

'She's only a sick old woman,' she told herself.

Sick my foot! said her anger, in her own mother's forthright tone. Bloody spiteful old malingerer.

In haste, she rejected the words. They were vulgar, unsuitable for young Mrs Somers, Robert's wife. She strangled a wilting dahlia and dragged its head off its torn stem.

A boy ran down the steps calling, 'Parcel from Foster's, for Mrs Somers.'

'Thank you.' She came to take the bulky, soft parcel, went through the front door to the living-room, sending her voice ahead of her like a nervous scout.

'The rug's come, Mother.'

The old woman was sitting in the armchair she had made her own, beside one of the long windows, facing the dead screen of the television set. She had Robert's features. Though the mouth had withered and the noble nose and chin now inclined towards one another, the likeness was plain enough to trouble Barbara. It was a caricature of Robert, drawn by an enemy. The settled malevolence of the old woman's expression and the upswept, glittering silver hair made her look like a hanging judge wearing an astonishingly fashionable wig.

She watched severely as Barbara opened the parcel and said in a voice much gentler than her expression, 'Dear me. Is that the best they had?'

'But it's the only one they had, remember? I rang them yesterday. You didn't want mohair because you didn't like the feel of it, and they said they had one pure wool rug, so I asked them to send it.'

'But it's so drab!' She spoke clearly and patiently, as if this disposed of Barbara's argument, as any fool could see.

'Would you like mohair, after all? I'll get Robert to change it.'

'No, thank you. I would not want to be a trouble. I suppose I should be thankful that it isn't vulgar.' She allowed three seconds to pass before she studied the curtains, on which stripes of hot pink and white formed a background for wreaths of lavender.

Barbara, who had kept her eyes from the curtains but not the colour from her face, said courteously, 'How is your hip today? Is it any better?'

'No better at all. I shall have to sit here all day again. Alone as usual, I suppose.'

Barbara tried to sound regretful but heard herself whining instead.

'I can't sit down all day, you know. I'd never get my work done.'

'Your work! I don't know what you have to do. When I was your age,' she added complacently, 'I had two children.'

Clutching the rug as if there were some support in it, Barbara said in a thin voice, 'You were lucky then, weren't you?' She bent to pick up the wrappings with a shaking hand and added while her face was hidden, 'I'll bring your tea in a minute. I'm going out.'

Her hands were steadier when she came back with the tray, which she put on a low table beside the old woman's chair.

'What's to become of me while you're out?'

Barbara looked at her, absent-minded with pain and indifferent for the moment to her anger.

'Is there anything you want me to get you before I go?'

'No, thank you.' She spoke with bitter contempt.

'I'll be off, then.'

When she had shut the back gate behind her she was standing on the river path, facing the tall, empty boathouse. At the path's edge, close to her feet, a wooden step led to a landing, then to a flight of steps which gave access to an upper room. She stood looking down at the flat, muddy verge below her, focusing her anger on its fringe of lolly papers, bottle caps, and drink cans. 'Disgusting,' she snapped to herself, and felt a little better. The silky surface of the water creased as it slid past the piles of the boathouse and wrapped a sodden sheet of newspaper round one of them, while it licked the others with an idle, peaceful sound that suited the nakedness of wood and earth and the neglected look of the place. She breathed steadily, getting control of anger and pain. A line of verse slipped through her mind and was gone with one of the ripples . . . something . . . loving and dissolving . . . moulding, never holding . . .

She walked along the river path and climbed the wooden steps that led to the bridge. On the other side the path began again, passing humbler backyards. She stopped at the third one, lifted the sagging gate, and looked with anxiety at the upstairs balcony. Smiling with relief at the open door, she propped the gate shut behind her, hurried up the steps, and tapped at the door-frame.

Naomi looked up from the ironing-board, noted her expression, switched off the iron and set it upright.

'Barbara. What's the matter?'

Her harsh deep-carved little features being set in a natural scowl, anxiety made her look ferocious, but her voice was gentle.

'My dear, what is it?'

Already she was talking to the back of Barbara's head as she huddled in the big chair sobbing and gasping, beating its arm with her fist.

Naomi, at a loss, stood and watched, till the roaring outburst of weeping died down to a comfortable snivel.

'My mother-in-law. Oh, what a bitch! What a bloody awful woman!'

'Oh, dear. She hasn't improved then?'

'No, she hasn't. My God, I think she's worse than she used to be. And I can't . . . I don't seem to be able to stand up to her. So it all got bottled up, you see.'

'Well, it's better out of the bottle, at least.'

'Oh, yes. That was such a relief. It wouldn't be so bad, you know, if I could ever get away from her.'

Naomi was filling the electric jug at the sink. She turned round to say with astonishment, 'You can't get away at all?'

8

'She can't get about much. She's got arthritis in her hip. And the journey made it worse. We just about had to carry her off the train. I felt sorry for her. *Sorry* for her,' she raged, then sobered. 'She was in a black sulk about the journey, but under it, you could see . . . puzzled and a bit frightened. The move must have been so sudden for her. Well, now I'm the one that's frightened.' She began to cry again, on an angry note. When the jug came clattering to the boil, she stopped, abashed. 'It sounds just like me.'

Naomi switched it off.

'I don't blame you.' Angry herself, she added, 'Now you can't, you absolutely can't, be put in that position, no matter what. Not for any length of time. How long is it going to go on?'

'Grosvenor gave her some tablets, but she won't take them. She says they upset her. And, he said, activity, not to sit still all day but to force herself to exercise it.' She grinned faintly. 'Dear me, what a look she gave the poor man!' The grin gave place to the look of dignified astonishment with which the old woman had quelled the doctor.

Naomi refused the invitation to laughter.

'How long is she going to stay?'

'Well,' Barbara grew serious, 'we don't know. As far as we know now, for ever.'

'Oh, my God! I thought it was temporary. A temporary crisis.'

'So did we. That's what we were told at first. But Lionel rang again, he rang Robert at the office. The old woman thinks Ivy has gone to look after her sister while

9

she's sick; but the truth is that Ivy has left him, and she won't come back till the old woman is out of the house for good. I suppose at first he didn't believe her, he thought he could cover up; but she rang him from Sydney to ask what he was going to do and he's begun to see that she means it.' Her delivery was steady and listless: this had already become an old story. 'He's in a bit of a state.'

'Nothing like a trunk call, in the circumstances, if you want to be convincing.' Naomi took a cigarette out of the packet, looked at it and put it back.

'When he asked Robert to take her, what could we say? They've had her ever since we were married, eight years. It's our turn.' She winced with reluctant pity for the old woman. 'She keeps telling me what a wonderful housekeeper Ivy is, what a marvellous cook. *Et cetera*. Everything shines in Ivy's house, floors, windows, silver . . .'

'Ivy uses Wondo, the friend of every housewife.' Naomi's voice was sprightly with resentment.

'That's right.' Barbara drooped in comic dismay. 'Oh, Lord! She has this sweet little laugh, and she looks round her and says, "Oh, my poor house."'

Looking round at Naomi's big, unclassified room: sink, stove, refrigerator, dining-table and chairs, books, posters, calico curtains dyed patchy russet, she reproduced the expression of gentle despair, the little laugh like a shattered sigh, with such accuracy that Naomi was forced to laugh briefly.

'That's all very well. Laughing gets us nowhere. Have you told her it isn't her house?'

'Oh, yes. Pulled myself together, drew myself up, and told her it was in my name as well as Robert's and I'd gone back to work to pay off the bank loan.'

'What did she say to that?'

Barbara reproduced a tranquil and reserved expression which indicated that the wearer would not stoop to dispute such nonsense. Its tranquillity was suddenly distorted by misery.

'I don't mind that. I don't mind it that nothing suits her and she's always picking about my housekeeping. But this morning she said –' she paused to get control of her working mouth – 'she said, "When I was your age, I had two children."' Tears rolled down Barbara's face again as she cried, 'Why can't I have children? Why can't I? It's so unfair. It's so bloody unfair.'

'I know. I know.' Naomi came to rub her shoulder. 'Have a cup of coffee.'

She hated herself at once for her ineptitude. Have a healthy eight-pound cup of coffee – instead.

'And I tell you what. I wish there was a reason. So that I didn't have to go on hoping.'

Her way of pronouncing the word struck Naomi painfully. She wanted to be rid of this subject on which there was only one thing left to be said.

'She probably didn't mean anything by it, you know.' She had removed herself from the source of pain and was putting coffee powder into cups.

'I know.' Barbara wiped her eyes. 'I'm touchy on the subject, I suppose.'

'Barbara, don't you ever think about adoption?'

Seeing resentment come and go on Barbara's blubbered face, she thought, No, not for our Barbara. Robert's son, the old family mansion, only the best.

'It wouldn't stop you having one of your own, you know.'

Barbara was astounded. 'I never thought of that.' She began to laugh, quietly, shaking her head at her own stupidity. 'I always felt that adoption would be the finish. Giving up.'

It had been known to work the other way, Naomi thought, but she did not say so because of the tone in which Barbara had pronounced the word 'hoping'.

'Come and drink your coffee on the balcony and look at the river. It's looking beautiful.'

Barbara followed her onto the balcony, where they stood at the railing watching the smooth-running stream.

'I was thinking when I walked past the boathouse how sordid and dirty it looked.'

'Like life, dear. Sordid in detail, but overall you must admit it has something.'

Barbara said, teasing, 'I thought life was a poker machine rigged by a bastard to pay out just enough to keep you from giving up.'

'Did I say that? I must have had my eye on the details then. Though you might almost call it an optimistic view. My God, do you see what I see?'

On the other side of the river, below River Street, a slope covered with tufts of tough shining grass descended steeply to the water. It was threaded with narrow paths. On one of them a tall young woman had been walking

12

carefully. Now, having reached a piece of level ground, she set down her handbag. Even at this distance they could read a heavy playfulness in the gesture, as if it was a dog she was ordering to wait or to stand guard. Then she squatted, skirt pulled up and pants round her knees, and began to urinate, her head poised arrogantly as she looked about her with the self-righteous dignity of the drunk.

'She must have made an early start today.' Naomi's voice was dull with horror.

'How can she do it? I feel so sorry for him.'

'So do I. I get tired of his silly wisecracking some-times, then I remember what he has to put up with and I'm ashamed of myself.'

Barbara was shocked. After all, Phil Truebody was a doctor. She didn't think Naomi ought to criticise his wisecracks.

'She came to Red Cross again the other day. She hadn't been for ages, to everyone's relief, after the dreadful business of the speech. She didn't do anything this time, just sat there looking boiled until her bag slipped off her lap and fell open, and she said, "Oh, f—." Well, she swore, loud and clear. People scrabbling on the floor for her belong-ings, keeping their heads down so she wouldn't see them laughing. It was so embarrassing.'

Barbara talked steadily, weaving words into a screen against the scene across the river, while Naomi watched it with anguish.

'You didn't tell me about the speech.'

'I suppose I couldn't bear to talk about it. She just got up suddenly and started on it in the middle of the meeting.

13

It didn't make a word of sense, and she sounded so convinced, and so pleased with herself. It was like one of those mad plays you read at drama group: if you weren't listening to the words it sounded more like a speech than any speech you ever heard.'

'She must have had something in mind when she started.'

'Oh, yes. The iniquity of organised charity. And its ubiquity. Then she looked round the room and said, "– and I must add, propinquity." And other words kept coming in and getting hold of her.'

'The chairman should have stopped her,' Naomi said angrily, entertaining an unjust vision of sly smiles behind manicured hands.

Now Eleanor Truebody was on her feet again and was pulling up her pants.

Barbara had guessed Naomi's thoughts correctly. 'I suppose Mrs Braddon didn't dare, for fear of worse. Nobody wanted to talk about it; it was too dreadful. When she realised . . .' Eleanor's growing doubt and horror looked out through Barbara's eyes. 'She just sat down and stared in front of her for the rest of the meeting. I don't feel sorry for her often, but I did then.'

Naomi breathed deeply with relief as Eleanor started up the slope.

'We don't know how we might be if we had a mongol child.'

Barbara said bitterly, 'She could have more children if she wanted to, I suppose. He loves it. I've seen him carrying it into the kindergarten, laughing and talking to it.'

'He's a nice fellow. Barbie, you will come back to the drama group, won't you?'

Barbara stared into her empty cup.

'Oh, come on, do. You're so good! How can you have such a talent and not want to use it? I wish I had a talent for something.'

'Why, Naomi! You're a very talented person.'

'Here lies Naomi Faulding, librarian of this town.' Her tone was comic-sour. 'What has she left behind her? Well, this tombstone . . .' And Peter. She said hastily, 'Actually, I know what I'm going to have on my tombstone. I think of it every time some old duck hands in her books and says, "I'd like something a little bit different this time." The librarian's epitaph. I can see it carved in stone. "I'd like something a little bit different this time."'

Barbara laughed, but not heartily. She had said those words to Naomi herself. It had been the beginning of their friendship.

'I like the play-readings. It's those discussions. They frighten the life out of me. And Brian Milson asks me all the hardest questions, I'm sure. Or perhaps I'm imagining that.'

'No, you're quite right, he does. He's jealous because you act so much better than he does.' A grin drifted across her mind at the thought of Barbara exchanging the privileges of beauty for the penalties of talent. 'I'll protect you from him, cross my heart. But do come back. The readings aren't half so good without you.'

Barbara tried again. 'You've just got a false idea about me and my acting. That first thing we read. *The Lesson*. That girl was in a trance because the whole thing was beyond her, and that's exactly how I felt myself. No acting about it.'

What a beautiful voice she has, thought Naomi.

'When are we going to talk, if you don't come back to the drama group? I could come to your place, but your mother-in-law will be there. And if you can't get out . . . Do you mean you really can't get out? Is she helpless?'

'Oh, no. She can get to the bathroom, and upstairs to bed. Robert has to help her up the stairs.'

'Um. Well, you can get out in the evenings, and I think you should if you can. We're not reading nonsense, it's only Brecht. *The Caucasian Chalk Circle*. It's quite straightforward.'

Barbara reflected and found Brian Milson less terrible than her mother-in-law.

'All right. I suppose it is better to get away when I can. I'd better go now. How's my face? Is it bleary?'

'You'll pass. I'll drop the Brecht in to you. And Barbara – don't be frightened of her.' At Barbara's bleak expression she said, 'Oh, all right. I know you are. But don't give in to it. Fight it off. If you give in to it, you're done.'

Barbara gave her the empty cup and started down the steps, nodding sadly in agreement.

'Remember,' Naomi called after her in an encouraging tone, while mentally she rearranged her day. The cataloguing she had meant to do would have to wait now till after the evening session – late home again, damn it; nothing made for Peter's afternoon tea yet – she would have to make some biscuits and eat a sandwich while they were cooking. A familiar sharp pain stabbed at her intestine,

16

where fatigue, anxiety, and fear of the public, all turned habitually to tormenting flatulence.

Naomi's final word influenced Barbara till she reached the garden gate. Then she thought with fear, 'But I don't know what to do. If only somebody would tell me what to do.'

As she approached the house, a complex murmur of sound reached her and brought comfort. It was the midday movie. She was not quite alone.

She was like a child who had sneaked out without permission and was scared to go home. Ridiculous. Naomi had said, 'If you give in to it, you're done.'

She walked along the tiled veranda to the long windows, stepped in with a show of calm, and stood beside the old woman's armchair, watching the screen: Paulette Goddard smiling up, intimate, impudent, in charge of the game, at Edward G. Robinson – I run a licensed escort service, strictly legit, my girls wouldn't go out with anyone like that. You know that, Barney. Pencilled eyebrows, shining flowing hair, a scanty satin blouse with bootlace straps like honeymoon underwear; she sat with a mink coat collapsed around her like an emperor's tent. Always a pleasure to see you, Barney. Edward G. looked at her with a bitterness that had reached its limit and verged on tenderness, or perhaps it was only fatigue.

The old woman watched with a greedy and contented air.

Paulette and Edward G. withdrew their protection; angelic girls in chiffon drifted through a misty dawn singing of toilet paper.

'Is it a good film?'

'Rubbish,' the old woman answered in a tone that matched her rapt expression, then changed both, suddenly. 'You've been long enough.'

'It was so long since I'd seen Naomi. You've been all right, haven't you?'

'No thanks to you.' She was in a full-blown rage at once. 'Anything could happen to me while you're out gallivanting.' She exchanged anger for pathos with an indecent lack of plausibility. 'Nobody cares for you when you're old.'

I wish Edward G. Robinson would come back and shoot her, thought Barbara, staring at the screen, refusing to retreat, at least for five minutes.

When the film began again, it passed like a roller over the harsh face, obliterating rage and bitterness. She puts feelings on and off like hats, Barbara said to herself as she went away to get the lunch ready.

CHAPTER TWO

Four o'clock was peak hour at the library. Naomi was working quickly, stamping books and filling in borrowers' cards, unaware that the pain in her bowel was twisting her face into a deeper scowl than usual. There were a few people waiting at the desk; looking up she saw among them one of the reasons for her persistent stomach-aches. Mrs Latter. Oh . . . God! She hadn't noticed her come in. Calm as a goddess, carrying her great bulk with dignity – funny, Mrs Latter did look like a Greek goddess from the chin up, the fat which had engulfed her figure having preserved the beauty of her face – she had a book under one arm, another in the other hand with a finger marking the place, a sinister sign. And that well-fed look was another. She was coming, coming. Brian Milson came to stand behind her. That heartened Naomi, though she did not look on Brian Milson as a friend. A human being, just the same. Besides, she might hear some praise of Peter, Brian being his English teacher. She wouldn't fish for it, much as she hungered for it.

'I should like your opinion of this, Mrs Faulding.'

Mrs Latter laid the book under Naomi's cringing gaze, her fat, smooth, white hand marking the beginning of a paragraph. A hand like a naked, voluptuous, sprawling woman.

'I'm a little busy just now, Mrs Latter. If you'd just let me know—'

'I think you'll understand my meaning when you have read the paragraph.'

'Out of context it wouldn't mean much. If you don't mind . . .'

Naomi held out her hand for this week's choice. Mrs Latter withheld it.

She picks the moments when I'm busy, blast her.

'You have not read the book yourself then?'

Naomi closed it and pretended to read the title.

'Yes, I have.'

'And you think it is a suitable book for this library?'

'That isn't altogether for me to decide,' said Naomi, showing strain and wondering if her intestine was about to burst. That would be an answer to Mrs Latter. But socially disastrous. 'It wouldn't be much of a library if it reflected only the librarian's tastes.'

'I should like to know your personal opinion of the book.'

'Marvellous thing.' Brian Milson leant forward and picked it up. 'Magnificent bit of realism, didn't you think?'

20

'I found it a bit rough in spots,' said Naomi. 'But I'm a self-indulgent reader.'

'Absolutely true to life,' said Brian.

Mrs Latter drew a breath that straightened her spine even further and caused her great bosom to expand dauntingly. 'I think the book should be banned. I think it disgraceful that such things should be left where they may fall into the hands of young people.'

Brian was a bony, loose-fleshed man, fair as a baby. Under narrow, bright eyes his cheeks folded towards a fine hooked nose and a knowing mouth, disguised at this moment by an expression of innocent interest.

'Why is that?'

'You have read the book and you ask me why?'

'Well, yes. That's the situation. I've read the book and found it a true and valuable presentation of certain aspects of human behaviour; but what I liked most about it I must say was the subtle underlying reference to some most interesting generalisations about human fate. You didn't think so? I'd really like to hear what you think of it.' He was so earnest that he sounded almost loving. 'There's nothing so valuable as an exchange of views.'

'If you wouldn't mind stamping my card, Mrs Faulding – I'm in rather a hurry.' As she passed she gave Brian a contemptuous stare to which, showing no mercy, he returned a friendly smile.

'That was marvellous,' Naomi murmured, smiling too, but more discreetly.

Brian stood back while she dealt with the other borrowers. When they were alone, she took his books. 'I wish you could be around whenever Mrs Latter attacks.'

'Does she make a habit of it?'

'Oh, yes. And she has such a nose for porn.' Carried away by an impulse of friendship, she added. 'I'm terrified of her. I tense up whenever I see her coming.' She regretted that when he raised his eyebrows in unsympathetic surprise.

'Have you thought any more about *Endgame*?' he asked. The tone was casual; the question was not.

Oh dear, here we go again. Naomi was resisting Brian's attempt to turn their play-reading group into a dramatic society.

'I've sent for the scripts and asked if we can hold them for an extended period. There's no harm in a reading, I suppose. I still think you're being too ambitious.' She leant back in her chair, sighing with fatigue. '*Endgame*.' She shook her head. 'I think Beckett is just too difficult for amateurs.'

'Well, the kids have to study it. It's not supposed to be too hard for them.'

'Yes, that's true. Pete loves it. You've certainly got him in. I should think it would be a difficult play to get across to the young – all that sameness and boredom and hopelessness.'

'They know more about that than we tend to suppose.'

All of them? She found the thought consoling.

'Look, Naomi. There are only four parts, after all, and Cec Prescott would be marvellous as Hamm.'

'It was a loss to the stage, all right, when Cec took to pharmacy.'

'You are dodging.' He looked firmly at her. 'If we don't do it, how are the kids going to see it? It's so visual – the clown make-ups and the set movements – so much that doesn't get across in a reading.'

How nice of him not to bring Peter into it, she thought, and in that pause lost the initiative.

'By the way, Barbara is coming back. But you're not to ask her hard questions in the discussions.' She repaid his firm look. 'She isn't Mrs Latter, you know.'

He was startled, then grinned suddenly. Now and then she saw in him the teacher Peter loved.

'She'd be good as Nell. And Phil Truebody could play Nagg.'

Hoping to sound authoritative, she said, 'We don't have anyone to play Clov.'

'I don't mind playing Clov myself.'

That was the very thing Naomi had feared. If only he was a complete stick, like young Neil, he might make a possible Clov; but Brian did it all with enthusiasm, with authority, and he did it all completely wrong. Never on the stage had Naomi seen such self-confidence combined with such an astounding lack of talent. Oh, well, she thought, I suppose Beckett will never know.

She tried again. 'Who's to direct it? It's a play that needs good direction.'

'I was hoping you would do that.'

'Oh, hell!' Then she would be the one to tell him what a bad actor he was. 'What about Cathy?'

'Cathy's not up to it. She doesn't have the authority for a job like that. She can be your assistant.'

She said Yes, finally, out of ego, wanting to do Peter credit and impress the other Sixth-Formers who cold-shouldered him. Not fair, that. He and his friend Rick had

23

lived to themselves; now that Rick was gone, Peter was isolated. Nobody's fault; but how tough young society was! How tough all society was.

Time to close now, and the pain in her bowel was easier. It was the talk about the play-reading group that had caused the improvement. And how unwillingly she had taken it on when Cec Prescott had urged it – only because she had understood he was seeking some distraction for Phil Truebody, and expecting dullness, incompetence, embarrassment. It had not happened so. Thinking of the group and of Barbara's return, she smiled to herself – a rare occurrence. Usually Naomi kept her smiles for others.

CHAPTER THREE

At four o'clock Peter left his bike under the steps, climbed them, and unlocked the balcony door with the latch-key he had carried since he was ten years old. He put his brief-case on the table and looked sourly at the biscuits Naomi had left to cool there under a tent of wire and gauze, seeing and disliking their connection with the latch-key. He felt inclined to write a notice and leave it speared like an explorer's flag on top of the pile, showing the message, 'Symbols of maternal solicitude are no longer relevant to my situation.' There were areas where such polysyllabic facetiousness was the only language they had in common, though they talked easily enough about politics, economics, literature, the possible extinction of the human race, the origin of species and its connection with the idea of ineradicable original sin. In the matter of the biscuits, even facetiousness failed him. She would be hurt. Two castaways, saving each other's feelings. Morosely he ate two of the biscuits and drank a glass of milk.

Lately he was troubled by the thought that his mother was pathetic. He could not shake it off. It enraged him, made him surly, prompted remarks that she tried to turn into jokes in a way that made her more pathetic than ever.

Fringe-dwellers. That's what he and Naomi were, fringe-dwellers. A tall, gaunt boy wearing an air of abstraction as confining as a tight coat, he would at this stage of his development be a fringe-dweller in any society that was not itself a fringe; but he did not know that. He longed for family life, a house with a living-room; like the Milsons' or the Somerses'. The old brown Genoa velvet armchair in juxtaposition with the refrigerator made him squirm.

He had said to Naomi once, 'I wish we had a proper lounge-room.'

'Not lounge-room, darling. Living-room.' She had looked quite shocked for a moment. That had offended him terribly. They didn't have one, whatever it was called. That was Naomi. Words were what she took most seriously. Then she had looked round in a way that had made him regret his own, seeing the naked sink, the stove, the bookshelves, the equipment of cooking, eating, reading, writing: 'If this isn't a living-room, I'd like to know what is.' He saw the hurt look and remembered how proud she was of the cedar table she had bought at an auction and stripped and polished. One of the ghastly moments.

He had muttered, 'I'm not blaming you.'

She had answered, with precise and delicate articulation, 'Thank you very . . . bloody . . . much.'

They had both laughed. There was always that out.

He was blaming her. For the first failure, about which he knew nothing. Mystery and confusion. Once he had thought his father was dead. 'When did my father die?' he had asked, in the casual voice one kept for the urgent question.

'He isn't dead. We just don't get on so we don't live together.'

How could she be so calm about it? He isn't dead, he isn't dead, isn't dead. That thought was still intact in his mind, without development or comment.

Then the divorce. A woman's voice saying to Naomi, 'What will you do if he tries to get custody?'

'I'd have to fight it, I suppose.'

He had looked up custody in the dictionary: guardianship, care, (parent has ——— of child, child is in the ——— of father). He had fitted the word into the blank (the child is in the custody of father) and was excited because it made sense. He waited to hear the word said again, but it never came.

He had nothing against Naomi; only a sense of life's bleakness and a keen interest in what was beyond his little scope of living. After they came to the country the thing had lain lightly buried till Ricky Lodge his best friend, went away to Sydney.

Fringe-dwellers don't get girls. He went into the bathroom and looked in the glass, studying his face with a gloomy concentration that made it utterly unlovable. Was he intolerable? A figure of fun? If he asked Fran Dennison to the end-of-term social, would she refuse? Would she report his offer, giggling, to the other girls? She seemed all gentleness, but was mysterious. Girls who were not mysterious were not of interest. A dilemma. He tried three-quarter face – a bit better. Nothing wrong with the features. But the condemnation was mysterious too, as mysterious as the choice. For example Stephen Grant – why, why? The thought of Stephen Grant turned the image in the glass so sour that he turned away from it in haste and dropped it from his calculations.

No getting away from it – his situation was peculiar, and peculiarity was social ruin. Living alone with his zany, wordy, loud-voiced, shabby mother and liking her – well, loving her, then. If only she looked a bit more like other people's mothers . . . no, that wasn't what he wanted at all.

He wanted a situation where he and Naomi were less important to each other. And he wanted to take Fran Dennison to the end-of-term social. What made him so sure she'd say No?

He got out of the bathroom before the looking-glass captured him again, spread out his books on the cedar table, and started his homework.

Naomi got in at five o'clock and smiled at the sight of him.

'I'm all she's got,' he thought. That was the worst of it. Momentarily he disliked her for the incompetence that implied, then said remorsefully, 'You look done in, Mum. Sit down and I'll get you a sherry.'

Sadness weighed on Naomi. She knew that when he was gentle and considerate his depression was at its worst.

'I'm not really done in, but if I look tired I'm prepared to trade on it.' She dropped into the armchair, bent forward and massaged the muscles at the base of her neck, then sat up, accepted the sherry, and set about cheering him up.

'Brian Milson was in this afternoon, and dealt most beautifully with a wowser who was complaining about a book. Marvellous. He made this long, impressive speech about nothing and then asked her seriously for her opinion. Left her for dead. I never saw what you could see in Brian before.'

'Brian's terrific. I don't know what you've got against him.'

'A bit of an ego. It's just my impression. He's always trying to dominate the situation at play-readings.' Naomi expected to dominate such situations herself. 'He wants to put on a performance of *Endgame* for the seniors.'

'Oh, ripper!'

'Do you think so? I thought Beckett in Bangoree might be rather sad.' She sipped sherry and frowned. 'The Bangoree University Extension Board! But Cec Prescott is marvellous, and so is Barbara, and Phil Truebody would be good as Nagg if we can get him to do it. Brian wants to play Clov, and he wants me to direct it. I think it's taking on a lot.'

'You have to see a play. It'll be a whole lot better than watching kids do it.' Slowly, he took the measure of Brian Milson's respect for her. 'I wish you had something for yourself, Mum. Writing or painting or something.'

Naomi pursed her lower lip in a funny-sad look of resignation. 'You're not the only one who wishes that. Meanwhile I'll apply my talents to peeling the potatoes.' The rest period was over: she had to be back at the library by seven. 'Will you water the garden for me?' Oh, damn, I forgot to take Barbara the script. We're doing some Brecht – *The Caucasian Chalk Circle*. I'll leave it in her letterbox on the way to work.'

'Leave me the washing-up. That'll give you time to go in.'

She hadn't cheered him up then to the state of careless selfishness she aimed at. She usually washed up after dinner so that he could watch television for a while before he started work, but half an hour's television was so small an offering she refrained from making it.

'Thanks. I will then. I'm dying for a diagonal squint at her mother-in-law. She sounds like a proper old bitch.'

An hour later she was thinking, 'Looks like one, too.' She had gone round to the kitchen door, and, finding the kitchen, then the dining-room, empty, had walked into the sitting-room where the Somers family was drinking sherry, Robert standing in front of the marble fireplace with its clinging cherubs, Barbara sad and ghostly in the nearer armchair, and from the farther one a malevolent beam that announced itself far in advance of its producer. Not allowed, Naomi thought in astonishment.

'I just dropped in to leave the script,' she said, and put the book on the arm of Barbara's chair.

The beam had switched to Barbara.

'Do you encourage people to walk into this house without knocking?'

Barbara looked faint and was silent.

'Only the back door,' said Naomi. 'I'm hoping to be promoted to the front door in time.' You silly old goat – glare away. And how was Robert taking it?

'Mother, this is Naomi Faulding. A very dear friend of ours. A drink, Naomi?'

Robert was smiling, perhaps from politeness, perhaps from amusement at what she had said. Politeness seemed fantastic in the circumstances.

'Sorry, no. I'm on my way to work.'

At the word 'work' a sneer stirred, expanded, and came to its perfect form on the old woman's lips. Naomi stood fascinated, like a lepidopterist watching a rare butterfly stretch its wings. Then with the painful start that played a great part in her life, she remembered the clock and said, 'In fact, I'll have to be off at once' – catching Robert's eye and shaking her head to ward off an offer to drive her to the library. He was better off there, protecting Barbara.

Pleased with her own stand against the old woman, she scurried across the bridge grinning, muttered, 'Silly old goat', and sobered up suddenly. The gap between those who talk to themselves in the street and those who don't. No gap greater. Looking round you furtively makes it worse.

Poor Pete. No father and an odd-ball mother who muttered to herself in the street – no wonder he was gloomy. One more year and he could get away, have his own life. A commune. Girls.

31

You didn't do so well with Mrs Latter, did you? she asked herself with hostility.

'A very dear friend of ours.' That was the phrase that had caused her elation. She was like a dog wagging its tail at a kind word. If they knew . . . Don't think of that.

She did think of it, in bed that night, lying tense and wakeful, seeing herself, hearing herself. Rejected once, she said to herself, you had to act it out, didn't you, over and over again? Make a hobby of it. Here I am, gentlemen, anyone else feel like kicking the dog? The bitch?

Nobody else remembers this but you. You're the one who keeps it alive. Who else cares what you do?

In that car . . . unbuttoning her shirt . . . the look on that man. Done on purpose.

Why did you go back that day? You had left him, he didn't leave you. Why did you go back? That mean, complacent face. Without a word he waited for you to go. His wordlessness came into its own at last while he waited.

Why did you marry him? Because he looked like a husband. My big moment . . . down the aisle, taratantara. Pretending to be somebody else. The story of my life.

Why did he marry me? Because I was articulate, the very thing he couldn't endure.

'You married me,' she said to him furiously, 'in the spirit of a cannibal eating his enemy's liver to acquire his qualities.' Preserved in her hatred, that fountain of youth, his smooth, handsome face showed no reaction, the lips did not stir from the gentle smile that was not a smile at

32

all but their state of repose. 'And when you found out that it wouldn't work (the gloom, the silence), you started to devour a small child I had so considerately provided as your victim. After making him love you, you bastard.'

Peter had cried for his father, had walked about every house she took him to, investigating strange rooms with a worried frown, muttering, 'Daddy, Daddy', breaking into a wail when he gave up hope, or into a neurotic elderly whimper that was worse than the crying. When that stopped, was something else gone, too? Something essential? He was so depressed. Gloom and silence again.

'For that I hate and despise you. A three-year-old child who loved you. Just your fighting weight. Your division.' For relief she whispered the words.

The image did not stir. No wonder. Naomi had never said any of that to him, nor anything like it. She repaired the omission on sleepless nights, with words as unvarying as prayers. Naomi's book of hours.

Was Peter like him?

Stop that. Gloom was gloom. Adolescence. Everybody got depressed. Worrying about girls, sex, careers.

The cardboard box, the worst thing the past could serve up in its horrible, indigestible meal, the Old Gold chocolate box that had *Peter Faulding* printed carefully, with curlicues, inside the lid – a box for treasures and in it Peter's loot: worn rubbers, chewed pencils, a little ink-stained ruler, all with names or initials, and a tin beetle with a clapper underneath.

Not stealing, Mrs Faulding. We mustn't think of it as stealing, the teacher had said kindly.

The teacher had put the box back where she had found it under Peter's desk without a word to him about it – that had shown, as if Naomi did not know, how serious it was.

It was stealing all right, stealing little bits of other children's lives.

My poor little boy. Wordlessness, I caught up with it then. Those pathetic little children with legs like sticks and sores on their faces, and my boy envied them. We're getting out of this town, Pete. It's nicer in the country.

And now I'm trying to fool him that it's nicer in the city. Well, he has a friend there. Rick's there. Try to get him away for a holiday.

The money. Worry about money soothed her with familiarity. She switched on the bed-lamp and lit a cigarette, thinking, 'Whenever I start to worry about money I spend some.'

She stubbed out the cigarette, put out the lamp, and drifted away at last from the hostile shore.

CHAPTER FOUR

The play-reading group met every Friday night in the
School of Arts, in the committee room opposite the library.
Tonight it was Brian's turn to take the chair at the head
of the table. As soon as he took his place, arranged his
papers and looked about him, the rest of them became a
class, and Naomi, handing out scripts of the next play,
took the air of a monitor willynilly. (Indeed, she reflected,
decidedly nilly.) Cathy Bates, Brian's junior on the English
staff, was wearing an eager-beaver, best-pupil look on the
bright round face she had turned towards him already. (And
what did Neil Dunn think of that? He sat beside Cathy
as usual and also as usual wore a bored, impatient look.
Boyfriend or not? Did Cathy wonder, too?) Cec Prescott
looked amused – that was the inward-turning squint in
his right eye, which gave him the air of dwelling without
malice on a secret joke. Phil Truebody's troubles were so

great and so widely known that he could never afford to look otherwise than self-possessed. There was something adolescent about him – thin frame, sharp, dark eyes, acne scars, and of course the dreadful puns. (Take that nervous, placatory smile off your face, Barbara dear. Brian can't bite you, not while I'm here.)

'You'll have noticed with this one,' Brian said as he opened his copy of *The Caucasian Chalk Circle,* 'that the form is threefold. First the parable, which is pretty simple on the face of it: two women claim the child, the judge puts the child into a chalk circle and says that only the real mother can draw it out easily . . .'

'No marks at all for mentioning Solomon,' murmured Naomi.

Neil showed his annoyance more plainly. He yawned out, 'We can just about struggle so far for ourselves. It's simple, as you say.'

'Except for the nature of the chalk circle itself.' Brian was calm. 'You notice that it's presented as a magical device for revealing the truth, and though everyone plays along nobody really believes in it. The false claimant knows it won't hinder her, the true mother knows it won't help, and that's why she refuses to pull. And the judge knows they won't accept it – that's why it works. It suggests that Brecht is exploring the nature of convention.' He cleared his throat, a faint authoritative sound. 'Nothing much to the prologue. Two lots of people claim the valley. There's your correspondence. One lot call it home, the other lot can put it to better use. Is that a fair summing-up?'

36

The captives nodded, except for Neil, who looked at Brian with dreamy dislike.

'Then the main play develops the parable and brings an answer to the problem of the valley. OK? Now casting . . .'

They stirred to life.

'I want to be the fat prince,' said Cec Prescott, who was stout and princely, 'and order fifty strokes on the soles of the doctor's feet.'

'You're taking it for granted that I'll play the doctor, aren't you? It happens to be my night off.'

'Quite right, Phil. Damned if I'd play a librarian, either.'

Brian had been waiting for them, a little too quietly.

'Cec, will you play the judge and Barbara Hai-Tang? Then, in the prologue, Cec the old man right, Phil the old man left, myself the delegate, Cathy Kato, Barbara the girl tractorist, Naomi the peasant woman, Neil the soldier. . . .'

'What about the directions and the rhubarb-rhubarb? Neil and me?'

'Is Barbara to play the singer?'

'Yes.' 'Yes.' A specially earnest and enthusiastic 'Yes' from Cathy, who had been expecting that part. If they gave her Grusha as well . . . really most unfair.

Cec and Barbara began to read. Peace descended far below the surface.

When they had finished Naomi came back refreshed to the fret of reality, marvelling at her luck. In this bare little room in a country town, an amateur play-reading group, everything promising absurdity, and then . . . Cec had some professional experience, having, as he said, carried a spear in his youth. Barbara's talent was mysterious to everyone and alarming to herself.

Brian closed his script and said, 'Any comments?'

Phil opened his writing-pad and raised his ballpoint pen, holding it ready to harpoon the passing phrase, but no phrase passed.

Barbara sympathised. 'Are you doing the report on this one?'

'I have . . . er . . . copped it. It ought to count for two.' As Brian looked quelling, he said, 'Would you mind giving us that bit again, about the chalk circle and convention?'

'I think the chalk circle is a symbol of convention, in that the two women accept it without believing in it, and I think Brecht is discarding convention to look for a reality.'

Neil placed his thigh along Cathy's and muttered, 'So am I.'

She gave him a sketchy, troubled smile and turned her head towards Brian. Like Pavlov's dog, summoned in two directions at once, he thought, delighted by her confusion, thinking with joy of the forces that drew her towards him.

It was anger that troubled Cathy's smile. Why did he do it? He had plenty of opportunity to make his advances when they were alone. She would like the approach to be different, too. He was shy and awkward, found it hard to communicate. Surely when he felt really at ease with her . . . It was taking a long time. She had to remind herself of his virtues: intelligent, serious, good looking, alone on the horizon . . .

'You've seen it played, I suppose, Neil?' Brian added cheerily, 'In East Berlin?'

Cathy's sympathy turned at once towards Neil. If only Brian wouldn't tease him so. It brought out the worst in him.

'No,' he answered faintly. 'I haven't been in East Berlin. You may have heard there's a wall. And for Brecht . . . I don't think I would have bothered.'

'There is the progaganda element, of course,' Brian answered furiously; 'but if you dismiss Brecht as a propagandist you're being too simplistic.'

'Always the same with the ideas men,' said Naomi. 'You make the idea your own and begin to look down on the man. When I see something of Shaw's again I'm surprised at how good it is.'

Brian said with pleased astonishment, 'I wouldn't have minded saying that myself.'

Naomi bent her head quickly over her script, guessing rightly that the look on her face was comic.

'He doesn't actually dismiss convention, does he, Brian?' Cathy asked. 'After all, if they didn't accept convention, the chalk circle wouldn't work at all. Convention plays a part in revealing reality.' She mumbled the last word and hoped Neil would keep his knee to himself.

'Just the same' – Naomi was ready to attack – 'he may not be a propagandist but he does a wonderful job of selling the idea that the orchardists get the valley.'

Brian defended, tense with love of Brecht, while the dogs of criticism snapped skilfully at him.

Barbara, daring for once, could not see why the old inhabitants didn't correspond to the real mother.

Phil began to move his pen like a conductor's baton.

'How much of this am I expected to write down?'

Cec turned a page of the script. '"All pleasures are rationed. Tobacco is rationed, and wine. Discussion should be rationed",' he read to them.

They laughed. Brian shook himself easily into calm and said with approval, 'That was a very good discussion. Look, before we go, there's something I want to say. You notice that the next play we're reading is Beckett's *Endgame*. Well, Sixth Form are studying it for the exam this year and I want to put on a performance for them. It would only involve Cec and myself, and Phil and Barbara to play Nagg and Nell, if they're willing. And Naomi to direct it.'

'You mean really stage it? Set the scene and learn the parts and all?' Phil was alarmed.

'Learn the parts,' murmured Cec. 'Ay, there's the rub. But I'm game. I don't know the play, however.'

'You've got the script there. Yours is the only long part.' (Liar, thought Naomi.) 'You'd play Hamm, of course. Nagg and Nell don't have much to learn.'

'Barbara and I aren't going to sit in garbage tins all night,' said Phil. 'The refuse refuses.'

As always when he made a pun, he looked round at the others with a quick, worried look like an apology. When the look reached Barbara, who was still living in the wake of the reading, she said in a sleepy, puzzled voice. 'Did you say garbage tins?'

How could incongruous words open a door suddenly on an enchanted landscape? *Truebody, Truebody, be your age.* There was what her voice did to those garbage tins, of course, turning them out in solid silver, incorruptible.

'It all happens inside a man's head,' said Naomi. 'The windows are two eyes looking out at the end of the world. Don't you have anybody stowed in a garbage tin inside your head?'

It seemed that Barbara had not. The silence informed Naomi that the others had not, either.

Brian said, 'The two characters, Hamm and Clov, are trapped in a situation with no way out. Hamm is physically helpless, dependent on Clov, but he has Clov in his power, too. He has the combination of the larder. And besides, he dominates Clov. Every move they make has been made before, countless times, and will be made again. They are two pieces moving in and out of check without any hope of an outcome.'

'The opposite of a suspense drama,' said Cec with too serious and attentive an expression.

'Oh, wait till you read it, Cec.'

Brian looked put out. 'I thought Barbara wanted to know.'

Naomi looked for the play in her memory. 'They do try to contrive change, don't they? That toy dog . . . I forget now. You just get the impression of unending sameness, no escape, a dialogue repeating itself endlessly inside a head. Come to think of it, Beckett's the first person to put boredom on the stage, in full bloom, without dropping a petal. It's a very delicate flower, boredom.'

Phil said, 'I thought it was more in the nature of onion-weed.'

'The setting,' said Naomi. 'I saw it done, ages ago, at the Old Bondstore. They did that very well, with windows

41

like eye sockets. You were aware all the time it was voices in a head. Or do you think that's too obvious?'

No, they chorused.

'Nothing is too obvious for our mob.' Thinking of the mob, Brian smiled affectionately.

Naomi felt kindly towards him. 'You ought to direct it, Brian. I really don't think I'm up to it. You're the one who's teaching it.'

'Then who is going to play Clov?'

'Phil. And put Neil in the garbage tin.'

'Not for me, thank you,' said Neil.

'Well, let's try the reading first. Then we can see where we stand.' Cec got up, yawned, and said, 'Garbage tins', in a reflective tone that made them all laugh as they broke up the meeting.

'A fine mess he's going to make of Clov,' Neil said to Cathy as they walked together down John Street to River Street and the Bluebird Cafe.

But you could have stopped it, she thought uneasily. 'It's not that Brian is so bad. The others are so remarkably good that it's hard to live up to them.'

She had not done badly, reading Grusha, and would have liked him to tell her so.

'He's bloody terrible. You can see Naomi Faulding thinks so, too.'

Cathy didn't answer. Usually she was eager to talk about the play and the discussion; tonight she walked on in silence, till at last she said, 'Why didn't you read Simon Shashava? You would have been good.' She tried to keep her voice light but she couldn't help showing a trace of the discontent she felt as she reviewed the episode: Brian had cast her straight away as Grusha, then had said, 'Simon Shashava . . .' and paused, hoping for nomination. Naomi had said, 'Oh, Neil, of course', thinking, Cathy was sure, of her and her prospects, which made it worse when Neil said, hastily and smoothly, 'Too much for me, I'm afraid.' So the part had gone to Phil Truebody.

Now he said, 'I don't really care for Brecht', thinking, 'Read that romantic twaddle to Cathy? No way.' Just the thing to give a girl the wrong idea, which girls were apt to get, anyway.

God, it was hard to get one's meaning across. Women had sexual needs, didn't they, like men? His own were driving him crazy, roasting him on a slow fire. Why couldn't he satisfy them without putting his neck in the old noose of romance? Other men did, while he (handsome, intelligent, well-read and travelled) had had only a few encounters, after parties, with girls so cold, so vulgar, or so hostile, that he had found the experience chilling. Two adults satisfying each other's needs – what was wrong with that? Why was it so hard to achieve? His whole sex life so far had been a matter of lowering his standards, from his first confident approach to a reigning beauty, whose reaction he tried to forget, through ever less confident approaches to less attractive girls, always meeting rejection. It occurred to him that if he didn't succeed with plain, eager, simple little Cathy the injury to his self-esteem would be serious.

When they came near the Bluebird Cafe, he said, 'Are you coming for a cup of coffee?'

43

'Oh, yes.'

It must have been easier, Cathy was thinking, in her mother's time, when men earned more than women and could be allowed to buy one's supper. There was no question of that between her and Neil, because she earned more than he did. One had known where one stood, then. It was a sign that the man was courting.

'You're glum, tonight,' he said, while they were waiting for their coffee and cinnamon toast.

'No. Just thinking about the play. What have you got against Brecht? Don't you like *The Threepenny Opera*? I think that's wonderful.'

Neil shrugged. 'It just doesn't speak to me. Too long, untidy, unwitty.'

'He isn't witty, but he's pithy. I agree with Mrs Faulding. You don't expect wit on the level where Brecht operates. You don't send Oscar Wilde on a route march.'

Neil had been set down once already this evening by that remark, and would have liked to send Naomi Faulding on a route march.

'Route march is the word for that play. I like the background, though. I wouldn't mind seeing Russia.'

His face grew lively as he set off on remembered and projected travels: in two years he'd have enough money to resign and be off again, a course at the Sorbonne, then a year of wandering till the money ran out . . .

In a breath pause, Cathy said, 'I'd like to see Russia, too', but perceived that her voice was reaching him faintly across an ocean.

The plate was empty. She was finishing her cup of coffee.

'Neil, there *is* something upsetting me. It's such a little thing that you'll be surprised, I suppose, at my mentioning it; but it's best to be open about it. I hate that teasing and muttering you go on with when Brian is talking. Or anyone. But mainly it's Brian. I really don't like it at all.'

And rubbing legs like a dirty old man in a railway compartment.

It wasn't a small thing to Neil. He stared at her, thunderstruck and angry, looking for words.

'Good Lord! You haven't got much sense of humour, have you?'

'Well, I don't know. I don't think that's very funny.'

Rude, in fact, she added silently.

Neil stared furiously at his plate.

I don't like him, she thought. Not at all.

'They bring out the worst in me, I suppose, that lot. Rather a gang of stuffed shirts, aren't they?'

'Why go there, then?' Cathy was offended. The group had captured her ready affection.

Neil studied the question and found no answer that did him any credit.

'Well, as you say, it's a small thing. Hardly worth mentioning. As you object, I'll cut it out. Simple.'

'Please do. It isn't at all like you.' Looking for money in her purse, she added, 'You never do that sort of thing when we're alone.'

Oho, lady! I think I take your meaning.

When Cathy looked up she saw that his mood had changed completely and he was smiling.

They walked to Cathy's boarding-house in silence, but at a different pace, and at the door he stooped and

45

kissed her, hard and awkwardly, on the corner of her mouth. She ducked away, but laughing, and went inside fluttered and bright-eyed, amazed at the sudden change in him. She had forgotten that she didn't like him.

'Well,' said Marlene (telephone exchange) to Bonnie (Foster's electrical department), 'did you get the passionate love scene, last night at the front gate? Such goings on!'

'Well I never! Who was that?' Bonnie asked.

'A certain party not very far from here. With her highly intelligent gentleman friend. Schoolteachers too!' She lifted her eyebrows and her cup, crooking her little finger to show that she was too refined for such behaviour.

Cathy kept her eyes down and went on quietly chewing her mouthful of fried egg. She was accustomed though not resigned to the teasing of the other boarders at Mrs Martin's.

'The things you see when you're out without your gun!' said Mrs Martin, who was cheerful, ribald, and uncharitable. She grinned cruelly as she set her breakfast at her place and sat down.

Marlene was a thin girl with a large bony face and crooked teeth. Her face had not so much prettiness as broken and distorted beauty, but she wore it with confidence. Bonnie was a stalwart with a small blunt face flushed pink and dusted with pale gold freckles. Having a beautiful neck, shoulders, and bosom, she twisted her bright gilded hair into a topknot that did not obscure the view. Cathy did not think either of them much prettier than herself and could not understand why they spent so much time laughing

46

away the idea that she was a normal female. The word 'quiet' summed it up for them.

Sure enough, Marlene said, 'You can never tell with the quiet ones. Worse than the rest, sometimes.'

'Be seeing them at the Sailing Club Ball, next,' said Mrs Martin, winking at Fred Allen (post office), who remained unaware of the joke, being interested only in the morning paper.

Cathy wished she was a man and could read the paper at the breakfast table. Since she couldn't concentrate on an empty plate, she took refuge in abstraction and looked at the wall.

After all, she thought, I am a woman, in spite of them, and last night's kiss appeared in retrospect less awkward and more earnest.

'Oh, look!' said Marlene. 'Who's got starry eyes?'

'Who wouldn't have if she could?' Cathy was tired of standing at bay.

Marlene looked indignantly round the table for support.

'Dear me! There's no need to be nasty. Some people can't take a joke.'

'I was trying to make one. Sorry.'

That was the first attempt she had made to defend herself against their teasing and it had done no good at all, only shown her the real dislike that inspired it.

The maid Gladys came in with Mrs Martin's small teapot.

'Some green eyes around here, I'm thinking,' she said, turning a bright, bold stare on Marlene, who looked back steadily, saying nothing.

Cathy was grateful to Gladys, but Marlene's words had more effect on her.

'I shouldn't stay here,' she thought, as she got ready for school, and once more considered the alternatives: the hotels, too dear; Elsmere, no vacancies (besides, Neil lived there, and might think . . .); no flats to be had at a price she could afford.

'I mustn't let them upset me, that's all.'

But they did just that.

After the play-reading, Naomi and Barbara had stayed to tidy the room and shut the windows.

'Now,' Naomi said. 'Tell me about your mother-in-law. Get it off your chest.'

The answer to that was a walk down John Street in company with a woman and a ghost. Light from street lamps and milk-bars shone in turn on Barbara's face, where disembodied malice, bitterness, insolence, and contempt, held for a moment and dissolved in time with her hallucinating changes of tone. The old woman emerged, demure, spiteful, complacent, outrageous. Naomi, who had been reminding herself urgently that it was nothing to laugh about, was obliged to laugh at last, when Barbara ran her finger along an imaginary skirting-board, stared at it sadly, then wiped the imaginary dust away, giving first a fastidious shudder, then a sad sigh.

'I'm sorry, Barbie. I know it isn't funny. In fact, it's appalling. I can't help laughing at the way you do it.'

'But it is funny.' They stopped on the bridge and looked down into the black onyx water. 'I ought to be laughing about it, too. They are all such little things.'

'They may be little things but they come under two very large headings. All that fuss about washing chandeliers and polishing banisters – that's meant to convey that it's her house, not yours, and that's no joke. Then the bad hip and the complaints about being left alone . . . that's worse. She's after your freedom, she's out to control your movements. I'd fight that one first. A house is only a house, but freedom is freedom.'

'I don't know. The house means a lot to me. I suppose it is dirty. I didn't even know you were supposed to polish banisters.'

'All houses are dirty,' Naomi said, though hers was not. 'It depends where you're looking. And yours is such a big house – can't you get anyone in to help?'

'Cleaning ladies only do what I don't mind doing myself. They don't wash walls or cope with high-up windows. I'm not going to have Robert doing it when he has to bring work home and go back to the office at the week-end.'

'Why doesn't Robert take a clerk?'

Barbara hesitated, feeling that what she had to say ought to give pleasure but would not. At least it must be said with some care.

'He intends to. But old Mr Graves only retired last year and he's been waiting . . . as a matter of fact, in case Peter would like the job. Do you think he might want to do the SAB exams?'

Naomi stared at the river, trying to distil the gratitude this kindness demanded from the sadness and humiliation that rose in her like bile.

'It's very kind of Robert.'

'No kindness really. If Peter wanted the job, Robert would think himself lucky to get him.'

'It was kind of him, just the same. Only I think Pete wants to get away, and I think he should. He's been a bit depressed since Rick went.' Sounding more than a bit depressed herself, she changed the subject quickly. 'About the old lady – I've been thinking. You have to be either a whole lot worse or else a little bit better. I mean, come down to her level and tell her off slap-bang whenever she annoys you.'

'Oh, no! I couldn't do that!'

'I didn't think you could.' Because of Robert. Imagine having all the time to live up to being the love object! Like living on tiptoe. 'Then the only thing to do is to give a bit. Make up your mind to sit with her for half an hour in the morning and an hour in the afternoon, and have a clear conscience for the rest of the day, whether she complains or not.' Barbara uttered a caricatured moan.

'For God's sake, Barbara! Don't be so afraid of her! What can she do to you?'

'I know I'm a fool. I just can't help it. It started with my not being good enough for Robert. I fell over backwards trying to please . . .'

'. . . and never found your feet again.'

'That's right. I know I have to get over it. I'm working at it. Go on with what you were saying.'

'It's like my hide, giving moral advice. If it wasn't a desperate situation I wouldn't. I think you have to decide what's the right thing to do and do it. It certainly isn't right for her to take your freedom, bad hip or not; but it isn't really right to leave her alone all day either. So you have to decide in advance what you owe and stick to that, and hope it gets easier.'

She started to walk, as if walking away from this disagreeably righteous speech.

'How would that apply to washing the chandelier?' asked Barbara, carrying it with them.

'Um. That's an awkward one. There's no harm in washing the chandelier, but it's wrong to do it just because she says so. Disastrous, in fact. Tell her you always get it done in March, or something.'

'Lies! Lies!' Barbara was recovering her good temper. She laughed when Naomi answered, amazed and indignant, 'There's nothing wrong with telling lies.' She uttered a soft howl of rage. 'You weren't good enough! What outrageous bloody impertinence!'

From here the house was visible on the river-bank. The sight of its lighted windows made Barbara pause, the smile Naomi's words had brought to her face beginning to fade.

'Hasn't she got any old cronies who could come to visit her? After all, she's Robert's mother, not his grandmother. She can't be so frightfully aged. Some of her pals must still be alive.'

'You would think so, but she doesn't seem to have friends. And it's funny, because when she was young she was a sort of queen in the town. My mother says there were always parties and dances, and she wore marvellous clothes and was a great beauty and broke all the hearts.' She looked fondly at the old house, dressing it in drifts of music and coloured lighting.

51

'That might be what makes her so nasty. It's hard enough for anyone to get old, but for a great beauty . . . Nothing will ever make you nasty, though.'

'Yes,' thought Barbara, forgetting to parry the compliment, 'if I grow old and have no children I shall be destroyed, nothing left but hatred of the lucky people.'

She said, 'When she came back to look after Grandpa Dutton when he was ill, she kept to herself. It wasn't just that she didn't like me; she didn't seem to like anybody. She didn't want anyone to come to the house. She said it was a house of illness; but it wasn't always, and Grandpa Dutton loved company.'

They had reached the end of the footpath, where a narrow flight of steps went down to the river path that led past the Somers back gate.

'Here goes then!' Barbara started down them.

'Best of luck!'

As she watched Barbara go, Naomi said to herself, 'What a lucky night that was for Robert, when he joined the party for the Bankers' Ball and met Barbara!' He must have been past thirty then. It was easy to picture him growing into a courtly, smiling old bachelor, melancholy sometimes but too polite to rebel and too innocent to cast blame. Oh, yes. Mother had nearly had Robert for her own. No wonder she hated Barbara.

CHAPTER FIVE

As soon as Cec Prescott stopped his car outside the Truebody house, three doors from his own, the front door opened and his wife Laurel came out to meet them. Phil, who had let himself believe for the past few hours that life was normal, remembered now that it was not – a sickening trip through time which he recognised as the price of his holiday. Back to unreality with a jolt.

Sad and troubled, Laurel stooped to speak through the car window.

'Phil, she went out. Just got up and went. I couldn't stop her.'

'No, of course you couldn't. Nobody can stop her when she wants to go.'

Because of Laurel's distress he kept his voice calm, then perceived they were looking at him with ill-founded admiration. He was saddled with the nobility of character

53

that imposes itself on the victim: poor fellow, searching the town for his wife after the pubs close, and so calm . . . never a word . . . He felt calm but not noble. He wanted to have a quiet drink, look in on Linda to make sure she was covered, then go to bed and sleep, giving Eleanor every chance to fall in the river and drown.

'It was quite early,' Laurel said. 'Twenty past eight.'

The Prescotts had taken his troubles so much to themselves that she licked her lips without knowing it and frowned in extreme anxiety. Unfortunately their standards of concern were much higher than his own.

'*You were aware, Dr Truebody, that your wife drank heavily?*'

'*Yes, sir.*'

'*You were not concerned at her prolonged absence from the house?*'

No escape. Sullen, he foresaw great effort, fatigue, and tedium.

'It's nearly eleven. She would have been home by now, unless . . .'

Laurel paused and allowed the alternatives to present themselves, gently applying the thumbscrew: Eleanor found tomorrow morning snoring on a bench in the park with a brandy bottle beside her; a phone call from a citizen who had found her unconscious in the garden . . .

'Do you think she was far gone when she left? Would she have got on a bus? At dinner-time I thought she was all right.'

He set out his private map of Bangoree from where they were standing on the western heights, a modest residential

54

area given countenance by the schools, the churches, and the old Prescott house. The railway line separated them from the central town; on the eastern heights beyond the river lived the best people, Grosvenor's patients to a man: green lawns, sprinklers turning and sparkling in a superior brand of sunshine, azaleas foaming over fences of bruise-coloured brick. His concern was with the centre of the town, not the distant daylight of the east, yet he saw John Street curving away from the eastern hill, turning to cross the river, holding the old Dutton house in its elbow. John Street ran through the centre of the town, connecting the river and the railway line. Since they had just come from there he saw it in its present darkness and artificial lighting, except for a muted glow where the School of Arts stood isolated between the baths and the park. On the corner of John Street, opposite the station, was the Railway Hotel, the only one in easy walking distance; farther down, on the other side, beyond the park, the Royal, frequented by the best people – that one would be her last resort. The Commercial and the Albion, in River Street, were out of range, unless she had taken the bus.

'She had a bottle somewhere, I think. She went out of the room a couple of times. There is a bus at half past but I don't think she was watching the time. If she saw it I suppose she might have got on it.'

'She probably went to the Railway, if she walked.'

'Or the Royal?'

'Not likely.'

The conversation came stiffly and painfully. They were all ashamed to be so knowledgeable.

55

Cec started the engine. 'We'd better try the Railway.'

Phil accepted the help without the conventional demur and took it for granted that Laurel would stay with Linda, all night if necessary. How good the Prescotts were! How good and how superfluous, a life support system for a body better dead. They shared his troubles, but the difference was painful: they were living, he was not. Living, exercising choice, serving friendship. Volunteers not conscripts.

The only piece of open ground between their house and the railway line was round the Church of England. Cec stopped the car there and they went into the grounds.

Away from the street lights the dim moonlight announced itself, diffused through a slate-coloured sky brightened with stars. Cec took the inside track round the church while Phil kept to the darkness of the outer fence, stopping to peer under the trees and shrubs that lined it. It was bad enough to be doing such a thing, but to be experienced at it was degrading. Come, it was only the third time after all: but the shock of the first time was still with him. He tripped on a root and swore, softly and passionately. In a clear patch he came abreast of Cec, half-straightened into a comic pose, and shaded his forehead against the moonlight with a stiff hand: Red Indian scanning the plain. Then he was appalled and was grateful to Cec for returning a bow which was comic, though pointless.

The church was small, but looked taller as he stooped, rearing its steep-pitched roof of darker slate against the spiky stars, sober, quietly reproving.

What happened to a man should have more to do with what he was. A disaster like this – he should have been hatching it somehow since he was born. He would like to prove that he had, since innocence spared him nothing. A touch of guilt would take away the feeling that it was all a stage play he had got into by mistake with a part he couldn't handle.

No excess anywhere. Modest, realistic Truebody. No excess even in love. A sober choice (oh, what a word!) guided by character and common aims. Eleanor under a banner GET OUT OF VIETNAM, Eleanor lying down frightened and brave in front of the President's car.

By the time he found her he would be filled with a pity just as real as his hatred.

GET OUT OF VIETNAM, BAN THE BOMB, FREE VOLINSKY — a written guarantee. He hadn't known a damned thing about people, to be wanting a written guarantee.

He met Cec at the front gate.

'Not there. We'd better try the hotel yard.'

Other couples had had a subnormal child and survived. Linda wasn't so bad, as subnormal children went. Even to himself his tone was angry and defensive, since Linda was the joy of his life. All right, so he wasn't alone with her all day. Neither was Eleanor, now; but it was too late.

He had thought it all before. It wasn't the trip round the town that tired him so much as the trip round his mind.

The Railway Hotel was the sort of building Eleanor would have taken a stand about, once, though he wasn't sure whether she would have wanted it condemned as insanitary or preserved as historic. Silent and stark in the light of a street lamp, receiving a dimmer, chillier light from the deserted railway station, waste land stretching behind it as if John Street had expired on the way to the station, the hotel looked like an outpost of desolation.

Cec drove past and stopped outside one of the warehouses that faced the line. They walked back to the double gate and went quietly into the yard where light still fell from the upstairs windows. A stack of barrels made a square of shade, which was empty. Cec tried the door of the store-room, slowly and carefully. It did not open. Phil put his head in the entrance of the rank-smelling brick building marked *Ladies*, listened for heavy breathing, and removed himself quickly. They gumshoed out then without comedy and stood looking blankly at each other.

'I think we'd better try the park.' Phil nodded in resigned acquiescence. 'After that I'll ring Laurel to see if she's come in.'

They walked down to the park which was sunk under the submarine light that welled from eight globes spaced on its perimeter. It was easily searched: a clump of trees in each corner, the War Memorial centre back. They met there and walked back along the central path together, lagging now, and went back to the phone box outside the Railway Hotel. Cec stopped there to ring Laurel while Phil walked back to the car.

Two minutes later Cec got into the driver's seat.

'She's there. In the garden near the back gate. Laurel got an idea all at once and went to look. She's sorry she didn't think of it before.'

'We don't know how long she's been there.'

The thought crossed Phil's mind that a laugh was required at this point, but he could not attempt it.

Cec started the car.

Laurel was standing at the open front door of the Truebody house, looking wretched.

'I just checked that Linda was all right, Phil. I'll go now unless you need me.'

They really suffered, the Prescotts, watching the slow death of his life. When he took Laurel's hand, having nothing to say, he thought she might begin to cry.

They walked through the house and along the path to the farthest flower-bed, where Eleanor was lying huddled in the deep sleep that seemed to be the only aim of her existence. Phil put his hand under her warm, heavy face and lifted it, daubed with dirt, away from the soft earth. He felt for the bottle of brandy she was cuddling and pulled it out neatly, like an expert defusing a bomb. She was so limp that the signs of life in her were disgusting: her breath reeked and snored, the warmth and weight of her body sickened him. Such dead meat shouldn't be warm. As they pulled her clear of the bed her skirt rode up over her thighs, which didn't matter at all. They knelt one on each side of her, each took an arm, then they heaved till her arms were round their shoulders and her torso clear of the ground. They got laboriously to their feet and staggered towards the house. Picture of a group of revellers, Phil thought, swinging the bottle to give himself balance as he tried to take most of her weight. Her face drooped, her hair fell over it. He heard her shoes scraping on the path and thought that the sound would drive him mad.

At last they dropped her on her bed and Cec walked away at once to the kitchen, where Laurel had left the light on. Phil took off her shoes, settled her head on the pillow, and covered her with a blanket, then he took the bottle of brandy to the kitchen.

'In the books they pour it down the sink, don't they? I couldn't afford the gesture, myself. Have a drink. Nothing but water to drink it with, I'm afraid.'

He got two glasses, opened the bottle, and poured them each a drink.

'One has to remember that it's a sickness,' said Cec, when he had at length got control of his breathing. He looked as sad as Laurel.

'Yes. It's a sickness. It's a device for turning money into empty bottles.'

He brought a jug of water to the table and sat down to his drink. Since the Prescotts allowed themselves to look miserable, he let his own face sag.

'You can't get her to try a cure?'

'First she'd have to know there was something wrong with her.'

'She must know that.'

Phil shrugged. 'Perhaps she does, but she's not going to let me know that she knows. That would have to be the first step.' He took a small gingerly sip of his drink and saw that Cec was approaching his with the same caution. Their eyes met and the laugh came at last.

After that, speaking came easier.

'It isn't just Linda, you know. I shouldn't have brought Eleanor here in the first place.' Taken away from her banner-carrying friends, she had begun to die like coral out of water. 'She can't stand loneliness. And then, the practice not being a success . . . apart from the money worries . . . it was a blow to her pride. Not to mention mine.'

'It would have been a success eventually. It took Begg a long time to establish himself. Grosvenor's father was here before him, and that counts for a lot in this town.'

That 'would have been' frightened and depressed him.

'I was just getting on my feet two years ago. Now . . .' He nodded, admitting, 'I might as well give up.'

Oh, my God, he thought in panic, what am I going to do? Six pensioners in the waiting-room and money draining away out of the bank account. He was a good doctor, too. What happens to a man should have more to do with what he is.

Seeing that Cec wanted to leave but was prevented by whatever he read in his face, he controlled it, and said, 'I didn't thank Laurel', shaking his head to show helplessness. 'I hope she understands that I'm grateful' – meaning this for Cec as well.

'Think nothing of it.' Cec got up. 'I'll see myself out.'

Now he had to undress Eleanor, put her pyjamas on her, and clean away the dirt from her face. Then he would be able to fall down in a sleep as deep as hers, but harder earned.

She had not moved at all. When he rolled her over, she stirred angrily, making feeble fighting gestures to defend her peace. He got her pyjama pants on first, avoiding the aggressive arms. Her nakedness neither stirred nor disgusted him; it brought back no memories. He captured one arm at a time and hooked it neatly into a sleeve. Experience.

He brought in a dish of warm water, soap and a face-towel from the bathroom; but as he was getting ready to wash her face, rubbing soap on a wet corner of the towel, he thought of what he had said to Cec: 'First she'd have to know there was something wrong with her.' Twice he had brought her home, undressed her, cleaned her, and put her to bed; twice he had carefully concealed the evidence of what she refused to know. Where was the sense of that?

He'd been wishing she would drown, but that was different. How cold and spiteful, to leave that great smear of earth on her face, like a message from her own underworld!

Things had to change. Linda was growing, the bank account was dwindling. Change was coming, whether they wanted it or not. He didn't have the right to hide evidence from her.

The towel was cold now. He dipped it in the water again and soaped it without looking at her, intending to wash the dirt away without any more thought. The urge to protect her was too strong for him.

But it wasn't from love. It came from the cheerful days when drunkenness was funny, and the drunk was a sacred fool who had to be cared for. When he realised how far away those days were now, he took the basin to the bathroom and poured the water away. As he spread the towel on the rack, he felt an impulse to go back after all and wipe the dirt away, to go on being himself, whatever the cost; but he listened instead to the voice of common sense.

He put out Eleanor's light at the door without looking at her and went to bed in the small back room he had taken for himself.

Now, when they met in the morning, it was he who would be ashamed.

CHAPTER SIX

At half past six Eleanor came wide awake, lay quite still and stared at the ceiling, warily exploring the circumstances that faced her. For a moment she didn't know where she was, an indication that she had not put herself to bed. She dismissed that quickly, since it required no action. At this stage she was expert in taking account only of matters that had to be attended to. She moved her head and decided she might sit up. She raised herself carefully, sat through one swirl of giddiness, then the world steadied and she considered the state of her stomach. She stood up. A whirlpool of sickness seized her and spun her about. She sat down and waited in complete mental silence till it passed, the state of her body being part of the reality she was accustomed to hold at arm's length. Her hair, hanging stiff and heavy on one side, brought a vague memory of something soft, welcoming, and shameful;

64

but she shut the door on that impression with the speed of a conjurer.

Sitting on the bed, she braced her burdened will-power with images of the bathroom, its shining curved surfaces, its promise of comfort: cold water, hot water, the sharp sweet foam of toothpaste and her own serious, responsible reflection in the glass. That first look in the glass was important to her. Mirror, mirror on the wall, who is the worthiest of them all? Drink had not marked her face yet; every day her large shallow-set grey eyes looked back at her, candid, childlike with their long, sparse lashes, entirely reassuring. On the other hand, the question itself was beginning to mark her face with a prim, severe expression of unbending virtue.

The lonely need to see herself in the glass brought her to her feet. She walked to the bathroom and straight to the basin with the glass above it.

They had served the writ she had been dodging for so long.

At first she didn't know who it was. The bedaubed, disgraced face that looked back at her was an intruder where no intruder could be. Then she clung to the basin, her mind heaving, struggling to retch reality away. Her stomach started to heave too, and she brought up a swag of sour, burning mucus, watched it slide, slow and heavy, to the plug-hole and stay on the metal rim. She wanted to flush that away. Her hand found the tap, it resisted and she began to whimper; then she remembered, with a start of terror that sent a fierce thrust of pain through her head, that the door behind her was open. She went across to turn

65

the key, which dodged her hands like a quick, mean little animal. At last she trapped it, then she had to control her other hand and bring it to help in locking the door. She leant against it then till she was steadier. 'It's all right, it's all right,' she said to herself earnestly. 'I only have to wash my face. It's all right.'

She got back to the basin and washed the dirt away with care. When she saw her face clear and unmarked in the glass, she thought, 'How easy it would have been to spare me that!' and the reflected mouth flickered with contempt, supporting her. She always despised the sober, distantly, as a soldier at the front might despise civilians; so there was a foundation already for the shelter she was building. 'How petty, how spiteful!' The face looked serene, abstracted, as she worked her conjuring miracle, separating her contempt for Phil from attendant circumstances that were not to be contemplated.

Holding fast to that mood, she could begin to face the day. Under the shower she washed her hair without remembering why, dried it very thoroughly, and combed it neatly into its accustomed shape.

As soon as she was dressed, she opened the door of the child's room and called out brightly, 'Come along, Linda. Time to get up', looking at the wall above the bed and addressing an imaginary child, an intelligent four-year-old.

Phil, who had just woken in the next room, heard her and was amazed, as every such morning, at her powers of recovery.

She gave the imaginary child time to answer before she went to the bed, where the top of Linda's head showed above the blankets. One light-grey slit of eye gleamed under its thick fold of lid, the other was hidden. As Eleanor stood beside the bed, the head disappeared entirely and a sound like the cooing of pigeons came from the wriggling heap of bedclothes. Eleanor did not accept this invitation to a game, but she moved with perfect gentleness as she uncovered the child, lifted her out of bed, took off her nightgown, and unpinned the hot, heavy, wet napkin, lifted the lid of a white enamelled bucket, and dropped it in. She took the same attitude towards dirty napkins as towards empty bottles, dealing with them efficiently without noticing what they were.

'Come on, now. Time to wash.'

The child had its changeling face fixed on hers and moved its head as she did, waiting for a game to begin. Eleanor was still feeling sick but no longer minded it. Sick was the right way to feel. She picked Linda up, took her to the bathroom, washed her and dressed her, catching her without roughness when she wriggled away, held her on her knee while she tied her shoelaces, then let her down, saying brightly, 'There you are. All set for kindergarten.'

Linda made off then to find Phil in the dining-room. He had made himself coffee and toast and was reading the paper as he ate, but put it down to shadow-box with her.

Eleanor went to the kitchen where she boiled an egg for Linda's breakfast, dreading the moment when she opened it and the rich innocent smell of it rose to sicken her. She had to face that in private and wait till she was steady again before she took it into the dining-room.

Linda was hugging Phil's knees, swaying, hissing with rapture like a little kettle.

'You're over-exciting her.'

He nodded, picked up the little girl and sat her on his knee.

'I'll feed her if you like.'

Since he didn't look at Eleanor, she thought, 'He's going to say something', and felt a moment's dread, which she stifled under cold resentment as she buttered a piece of toast, cut it into fingers, and pushed the plate across to him.

Now I must speak, he thought, as he held out a piece of toast to Linda, who bit at it like a puppy. How hard it was to speak. *But doctor, I don't like to . . . he doesn't like any talk of illness. – But that's foolish, Mrs X; you must, for your own sake. – I do mean to, doctor. I make up my mind to it and then I just can't say the words. – But your life may depend on it. . . .*

He fed Linda a spoonful of egg. She grasped for the spoon but he said, 'Not this morning, pet', and saw Eleanor looking at him warily for a second. For her sake, too. For her sake, mainly.

'Eleanor, are you willing to try a cure?'

'A cure?' She spoke in a strange, astonished tone, and stopped there, feeling that if she said, 'A cure for what?' he would have an answer.

He said it just the same. 'For alcoholism.'

From shock she uttered a brief laugh that clattered like an alarm-clock. He frowned and went on in a voice that sounded indifferent, while he fed Linda spoonfuls of egg and bites of toast: 'We found you last night in the garden, out cold. Cec had to help me bring you in. It isn't the first time. You must know that it isn't the first time.' He raised his eyes, apologetic for what he was saying. 'We just have to face it some time.'

She sat rigid and white, struck dead. He felt all the weight of the first moment that started it all. The suffering you can open your mind to when you are expecting joy . . . 'The baby's not normal, Eleanor.' And nothing was ever normal again. He had learnt to look on the sadness as disloyalty to Linda, loving her as she was. Eleanor had not, yet never showed it.

'The sooner the better, you know. There's not much money left. The practice isn't paying – it will have to go. I'll have to look for a job. If you went to Sydney now, went to see Miller . . . You have to see it as a sickness, if you are to face it.'

Eleanor was diffusing the steady radiance of an anger in which his words were consumed before they reached her brain. She collected enough breath to speak.

'What about Linda? Is there any room for her in these plans of yours?'

'I can look after Linda. Laurel would help me.'

'You have been discussing me with Laurel Prescott?'

'No,' he said in a lying mumble. He was wrong, guilty, because he couldn't go to bed with her any more. The priggishness of her sober spells put him off as much as her drunkenness. 'I took it for granted she'd help. I think she would. For God's sake, Eleanor. You can't want things to go on as they are.'

Feeling her advantage, she said, gently and steadily, 'What do you mean by that?' – daring him, taking advantage of his unwillingness to give pain.

He gasped, tried uselessly, and cried, 'Oh, think for yourself, will you?'

But of course she would not. She looked abstracted, her anger being undermined by anxiety. Where was the bottle of brandy she must have brought home? What had he done with that?

'Look, Eleanor. I don't think you're an alcoholic really. I think circumstances have been too much for you. It's not your fault; it just happened that way. But if that's right, and you could live a reasonable life without us, why don't you go? Leave us – we can manage.'

He bent to set Linda down. When he looked at Eleanor again she was staring in front of her, stupid from shock.

'You want me to leave Linda?' She shook her head, shaking the thought away. For the moment she had forgotten the bottle of brandy.

Phil got up. 'Well, you think of something then.' He added, 'Don't worry about Linda. I'll drop her at kindergarten.'

The word 'alcoholic' crawled at the edge of her mind like a poisonous insect that would not bite if she left it alone. It was some time before she murmured, 'No, that's not it.' She ventured further, 'To use that word to me –' but regretted that thought as an extravagance that abashed her, even when alone.

70

To suggest that she could leave Linda, to imply that Linda would be as well off without her . . . Knowing that everything she did was for Linda's sake – or (since the name brought no image to her mind) for the idea of motherhood, to which she had been faithful in terrible circumstances – she felt the misery of the unjustly condemned.

Yet. Something. Continual uneasiness. As if walking with the fear that her skirt was rucked up at the back and her underwear on view. They dare not laugh, but I see something in their eye.

This was something new. The old fear was of forgetting the time, destroying the shape of the day. Forgetting to call for Linda. She had done that twice. Only twice in her wretched, difficult life. Now he always called for Linda, but she still had the fear. Waking early in the night, having those hours to live through till morning – that was terrible, but it was terrible for her alone.

That night she woke and rushed to get the dinner – raw chops on the grill, Phil coming in in his pyjamas. 'What the hell are you doing? It's two in the morning.' Seeing the chops on the griller, not changing his expression. 'We've had dinner. Go to bed.'

A moment for laughter, which was absent.

He had not been astonished.

And she, realising that the light was not daylight, that she must have switched it on without knowing, was convinced that this was not the known world, that she had gone to hell without dying.

They can't catch you like that, so long as you know the time. So long as your watch is going and you can tell day from dark.

She worried about her watch as if it was her own heartbeat.

That was old, this was new.

The deep plunge into the buried sunlight, the dark underground passage, fantastic doors that opened onto daylight in unexpected places: the bank of the river, a bench in the park that was ringed with children standing motionless shining in a trance of pleasure.

Carefully she approached her own sick-bed and asked the sufferer how this had begun. Drinking outside the house – I've never done that. I'm quite against it. I never intended it.

It was the ordeal of going up to the counter, asking the knowing, grinning faces for a bottle of brandy, seeing glances exchanged. One woman had sneered and handed it over with a show of contempt.

She thought, my life is very hard.

In the lounge it was easier, the barmaid matter-of-fact, uncaring. She took a drink to nerve herself for the counter in the bottle department.

But it wasn't working out. Sometimes she had forgotten the bottle or lost it and had had to face the dreadful business twice in a day.

Thinking of that, she got up and went to the liquor cupboard. The bottle of brandy was there, open, with some gone from it. She stared at it: it was like a message in a strange language, which she puzzled over for a moment, then forgot.

Those people behind the counter were destroying her with their insolent looks. She wouldn't let them do it. She would wear a mask.

'A bottle of Saint Agnes brandy, please.' And to me you are non-existent. Non-existent. A tone of voice and an expression to make that clear.

As soon as Phil came out of the house holding Linda on his arm he began to feel lighthearted. 'Limpet,' he said to her, as she worked at expelling every particle of air that interposed between them. 'Suction cup,' he added, peeling her away from him and settling her in the carry chair fixed next to the driver's seat. While he buckled straps he told her, 'We're going to see Miss Rob-in-son.' Her face became calm and intent, as if she were concentrating on a distant chime of bells. She knew the name Robinson. 'You're a clever one, aren't you?' He left the car door open, for she would howl with terror if he closed it on her, ran without dignity to the driver's side, got in, and closed both doors. The moment when he switched on the ignition was Linda's favourite. She gave a chirp of joy as the motor started, and he answered it with a joyful smile.

He drove down the hill, still smiling. The worst of the heat was over; it was a day of bright comfortable sunshine, so calm one imagined the world was under glass – the kind of day he liked best. Lately he seemed to have become more responsive to the weather, so that it moved him often to this indecent cheerfulness. Formerly he had hardly noticed it unless it burned or drenched him.

He had no right to feel so happy. He tried to discipline himself by thinking of Eleanor, but his mind had dropped her down a drain out of sight. It was all old stuff and he was bored with it, and being bored with it was old stuff, too. He gave himself up to this random cheerfulness.

Was there a source of joy in a man that burst out when it had been dammed up too long, and drowned him?

Was it passivity? Did he lie like a pool among the rocks, reflecting blue skies, all the beauty in the world washing over him? He had never been aware till now how much beauty, wit, and kindness there was in the world.

He knew that this joy was deadly, and came over him when he should be facing reality and making plans.

'I have to think of our future.' But saying that seriously to Linda turned it into a game. 'You know, mate, if I don't get to work soon, I'll never work again. We'll be on relief.'

That was a real element in his unreal happiness: he had had a rest, after overworking for years. Convention kept him idle. Obliged to pretend that he was a busy doctor, he sat in his surgery waiting for calls and reading *War and Peace*. It had done him good.

'A job for me and a school for you. I'll definitely see about it.'

But not before he had acted in *Endgame,* sat in a garbage tin opposite Barbara Somers, and heard her say to him, 'Ah, yesterday.' That was a frivolous pleasure he promised himself before he faced the world seriously again.

When he stopped the car outside the kindergarten, Linda wailed because the dear animal had died, then stopped to look down at his hands, when he unstrapped her, with an interest that was new every day. Then she was simmering with excited laughter because Miss Robinson came out to meet them.

You're the rock pool that the sun shines on, he thought. We are a pair, you and I.

'She's happy to see you. We're a little early, I'm afraid.'

'No trouble at all, doctor.' Miss Robinson, bright-toothed and affable, bent to lift Linda with a kindness that seemed forced, but was genuine. 'She can help me put out the blocks, can't you, darling? Wave good-bye now.'

She stood moving Linda's hand up and down as Phil drove away. 'I don't know what your Daddy has to smile about, I'm sure,' she said, having mistaken irresponsibility for heroism.

CHAPTER SEVEN

Barbara's kitchen door, which caught the morning sun, opened onto a small flagged space set with large pots of red geraniums. Through the window Naomi saw Barbara's old-gold head bent over the sink, yet she dawdled, basked, and gazed at the geraniums, until Barbara looked up and called her in.

Barbara set the last of the morning-tea things to drain in the tray.

'I did my half-hour,' she said, as she pulled off her rubber gloves. 'Sitting with the old lady, I mean. And you're right, it is better. That is', she lowered her voice and her mood, 'she isn't any better but I do feel freer the rest of the time.'

'Oh, Lord.' Naomi was taken aback. 'I love to give advice but I never imagine that anyone actually takes it. I don't think I can stand the responsibility.'

'Well, I'm so desperate, I'd try anything.' She pushed a kitchen stool towards Naomi, opened the refrigerator, and took out a tomato, a hard-boiled egg, and a bowl of salad greens. 'It works, anyhow. I'm off to see my mother today and I'm leaving her her lunch.' She shelled the egg and sliced it. 'I've thought about the other thing you said, too. To make up my mind what's right, and do it. I'm trying, but it isn't easy.'

'You're darned right it isn't easy.' Naomi sat hunched on the stool.

'Just the same, that's it.' Barbara took a fearsome knife to the tomato and began to cut it into fine slices. 'Otherwise, I'm doing things to please her, or doing things to annoy her, and either way she swallows me up.' She arranged the tomato slices on a plate, adding, 'The things themselves are such trifles, you see. Though they add up to something important, as you said. It makes it easy to do the right thing once you've decided what it is. Deciding is the difficult bit.'

'That's always the difficult bit,' Naomi said gloomily. 'Sometimes doing it's hard too.' She watched Barbara arrange slices of hard-boiled egg inside a fan of tomato slices.

Barbara went back to the refrigerator to get potato salad and ham, which she added neatly to the arrangement. Then she stretched a sheet of plastic over the plate and addressed it respectfully, in a rehearsal tone, hoping to make Naomi smile, 'Shall I leave your salad in the refrigerator, Mother, or would you like me to put it on your tray?'

Naomi grinned. 'No third choice? You are developing a technique. I've got a message from Peter.' Since the message mortified her, she delivered it stonily, but with a humorous expression of face. 'He doesn't want to be Robert's clerk, thank you very much. He wants to be your cleaner.'

Barbara looked round at her with candid pleasure. Against its light her own soul stood somewhat dark and crooked.

'What a wonderful idea! When? After school? Saturday mornings?'

'After school, I imagine. He's been looking for an afternoon job for some time. But if Saturday mornings suit you better . . .'

'I don't care. We can settle that. Whatever suits him. Isn't it a wonderful idea?'

'He can climb step-ladders and wash windows, and do all the things that cleaning ladies don't do.'

'We'll start on that rotten chandelier. I'll get some cleaning stuff at Mum's. And then the banisters. Tell him to come and see me – I won't be home till about half past four. Apart from the help, it'll be fun to have his company.'

'You won't let him break his neck, will you?'

'Positively not. Don't worry. I'll hold the ladder.'

She took off her apron with a sharp movement expressive of joy. 'Things are really getting better. Does he want you to fix the money, or shall I settle that with him?'

'Settle it with him,' said Naomi, at the limit of her endurance. 'I'll leave him a note to come and see you about five. OK? I'd better go and let you get on with it.'

Barbara nodded, scowling slightly at the salad under its plastic cover.

Naomi carried her dark, crooked soul past the sunlit geraniums, thinking, 'It's all very well. It's all very well.'

Poverty was a sickening, sour odour that got into everything she ate, drank, wore, or breathed. Little pincers of anger nipped her stomach, threatening trouble for the afternoon.

There were two letters in the letterbox. One of them was a thick letter for Peter from Rick – an hour's pleasure and three days of gloom, she thought, but without the usual anguish, since she was considering the other, also from Sydney and addressed to her in a hand she must once have known. She left Peter's letter on the table and carried her own onto the balcony to read it in the sun.

Mitchell Library – oh, yes. Jessie Ford, then.

Dear Naomi,

As you are in Bangoree, I thought you would be interested in some news about Roderick Fitzallan which has just come our way here.

When Keith Lincoln died last year – you remember no doubt that he was Fitzallan's close friend, and edited the collection which was published after Fitzallan's death – his papers came to the Mitchell. Among them there were letters from Fitzallan . . .

Naomi dropped the letter on her knee, offended by its tone. She wants me to do something, she said to herself angrily. Ought to ask about my health, then. However, since the news was interesting, she picked up the letter and read on.

. . . They are not very informative, but they do make it clear that Fitzallan had spent some months at least in your town.

79

[Not my town.] They refer to the work he was doing there in terms which strongly suggest the river poems.

There can be little doubt about this. He says, 'It's an odd experience living with water running through one's sleep, like being on an unending voyage to nowhere . . . Well, yes, I suppose one is, at that. It's getting into my verse, as you see. That and other things.' A clear reference to the river poems, don't you think?

Naomi dropped the letter again and looked at the river, calm as sheet steel today, curving away from the town among the still fountain forms of the willows. She turned her head towards the bridge and the shadow of a man

Looking quietly down into the heart's worst weather,
Into the driving, the driven, the wild and hapless water.

What a moment of private and individual joy, to know Fitzallan's words and see the bridge he stood on! A discoverer's joy, to be the first to see it with that knowledge. The pleasures of travel came to visit her as she sat on her balcony. Tourists trudged through museums and the rooms of dead poets trying to rouse a faint trace of the excitement she was feeling.

With a sigh of joy she began to read again.

Maurice Ellman, who is preparing a biography of Fitzallan, would be very grateful for any help you could give him. The first letter is dated 5 August 1932 – perhaps the local paper of that year might yield some information.

There may also be people alive who remember him. It would be of great help to Maurice if you cared to undertake a little preliminary research (you are well placed for it, after all!) and, most particularly, let us know if a visit to the town is justified. He has a grant, and is working on a very limited budget.

Him and me both. Well, Jessie wasn't unfriendly, just embarrassed at what she was asking. Search the files, indeed! Look for people who knew Fitzallan. She allowed her indignation full rein with a clear conscience, since she meant to do what they asked.

She looked at the bridge again with wonder. 'I believe I never really see a thing till I've read about it.'

Stepping inside her mother's little shop on the corner of Railway and Ermyn streets, on the western side of the line, Barbara underwent a slight but visible change in character and appearance, the sookiness which used to worry her mother clinging to her like a wet dress.

'Hullo, Mum. Good morning, Mrs Morgan.'

Mrs MacFarlane looked up from the note block on which she was adding a bill, showing a small well-featured face whose prettiness had given way not so much to middle age as to shrewdness, self-confidence, and narrowness of mind.

'Oh, it's you.' She added without criticism, 'You're quite a stranger.'

She was small and dark, so unlike Barbara that the ghost of her tall, blue-eyed, ineffectual husband rose uncalled between them.

Mrs Morgan said, 'Isn't she the image of Ian, Dorothy? I think of him whenever I see her.'

'Mmm. That'll be three dollars and fourteen cents.'

'I couldn't get over before. I can't leave Robert's mother for long. She's still having trouble with her hip.'

Mrs MacFarlane counted out change.

'Can't they give her anything for it?'

'The doctor gave her some tablets but she says they don't do any good. And he said to try to keep it moving, but she can't do that. She says it's too painful.' She spoke casually, inviting no comment. Mrs MacFarlane raised her eyebrows and said nothing.

'You've got Belle Dutton staying with you?' Mrs Morgan put away her change but did not pick up her shopping basket. 'It must be forty years since I set eyes on Belle Dutton.'

'She was here looking after the old man before he died. That's when Barbara met Robert. He went in with Graves and stayed here to be with his mother.'

'She didn't go out very much. I suppose she couldn't. Did you know her when she was young, Mrs Morgan?'

'No, dear.' With a good-humoured smile for Barbara's innocence, she added, 'I knew of her. My aunt Grace was cook general at Duttons' when Belle was a girl. She used to come to our place for her day off and we used to hear all about Belle and her doings. They may say what they like, she was a beautiful girl.'

But what, Barbara wondered, did they like to say?

Her mother said, 'Handsome is as handsome does. Why don't you two take the weight off your feet?'

'Well, that comes well from you, Dorothy. There weren't many better looking than you.' Mrs Morgan took possession of the chair Barbara brought her. 'But I must say it did you no harm.' (Not much good either, thought Mrs MacFarlane, but suppressed the remark on Barbara's account.) 'And I suppose Belle was spoilt. An only child, and rich parents, and those looks, and all the boys after her. How could she help but be spoilt?' Her soft voice sighed, lulled, tucked the characters into Time's bed with traditional phrases.

'She married Jim Somers of her own free will, I suppose. She should never have let him go off to Grafton without her.' She lifted a carton of detergent onto the counter. 'Give me a hand to put these up, will you, Barbara? Give the shelf a dust before you put them in.'

'I blame her mother for that.' Since Barbara was banished to the top of the step-ladder, an excellent listening-post, she no longer seemed to be involved in the conversation, so Mrs Morgan spoke more freely. 'She never would have married Jim Somers anyhow if it hadn't been for that other terrible business.'

'Yes. Young fellow drowned himself because she wouldn't have him, didn't he? I was only a kid at the time, but I remember the funeral, and I heard some talk.'

'It wasn't right, though. It was an accident. I suppose poor Belle was no angel, but the things she took most blame for weren't her fault at all.'

A customer came in. Mrs Morgan rested, Barbara ranged packets of detergent, while Mrs MacFarlane served her, then said after she had gone, 'What did happen, then?'

'Young Jack Webster, it was. And he was keen on Belle, all right. They all were. But as for drowning himself – they were crazy about boating, in those days, out on the river every Saturday. You know Seekers Bend? Down below Walters' place, just opposite Boat Island? This Jack Webster and a couple of his friends had swum across to the island from the other bank, then Jack Webster climbed over to the east side and he must have spotted Belle. I suppose he'd seen the boat where they'd moored it at Walters' jetty. They were having a picnic. So he called out to Belle, "What are you doing?" or something. And she ran to the end of the jetty and called out to him, "Come and see." Careless, that's all she was. It seems to me a man ought to know whether or not he's tired. Well, he dived in and swam a few strokes, then he went down and never came up. That was a terrible thing.'

'But it wasn't her fault,' said Barbara.

'You know how it is when people are out of their minds with misery. They have to have somebody to take it out on. Jack Webster's mother called poor Belle a murderess. And, I tell you, Belle nearly died of it. Lay and stared at the wall till they thought they'd never get her up again. But a lot of people held it against her. I think some of them might have been waiting their chance.'

'You might hand that tinned soup down, Barbara. I'll put the cleaning powders up next to the detergent.'

'And that's when she married Jim Somers, all in a couple of months. Running away from it, you might say. And that's where old Mrs Dutton did all the damage, according to Grace. She wouldn't let Belle grow up, or do a hand's turn in the house. Out on the tennis court all day in her little white play suit – and her married and with a baby. Never washed a napkin, hardly ever got to give it a bottle.'

'That would be Lionel.'

'That's right. You would have thought he was the old woman's baby. Not that she was so old, I suppose.' With astonishment, Mrs Morgan considered a lapse of time in which old Mrs Dutton had become young. 'Jim wanted them to move out and get a home of their own, but every time he tried it the sky came down. Mrs in bed with her heart and Belle running to her father. Mrs making the bullets and Belle firing them.'

'Belle wasn't keen to go, then?'

'Belle was brought up in a house with servants, never doing a thing for herself, and I think she might have got frightened to start. Grace was sure the mother was out to break up the marriage, couldn't see Belle married to a bank clerk. Then Jim got the move to Grafton and there was a terrible to-do. Mrs took to her bed again, and it ended with Belle staying. Everybody thought that was the finish for poor Jim.'

Barbara climbed down to ground level. 'But she went to Grafton after all?'

'Oh, yes.' Mrs Morgan withdrew, brooded, nodded. 'Yes, she went.'

'Come on,' urged Mrs MacFarlane. 'Give.'

'Well, I shouldn't,' she said, forgiving herself. 'Yes, there was something. About a man. The story was, her father caught her sneaking in early one morning and packed her off. I never believed a word of it.' She stared indignantly into the past. 'Some people would say anything. The man was a no-hoper, no better than a tramp.'

Mrs MacFarlane hinted, 'But she went.'

'Oh, yes. She went. It's my belief her father put his foot down at last. Grace said that was his nature. He might seem easy-going, but when he set his mind on a thing it got done, and fast.

'Oh, there was talk all right. Whatever Belle Dutton did there was talk. And if she didn't do anything, they had to work a bit harder, making it up. But with her leaving so sudden, well, then they knew they were right, you see? And it wasn't the old man that bore the brunt. It was Mrs, and I don't think she ever forgave him. Poor Belle. When all's said and done, her looks brought her more misery than joy.'

She sighed as she picked up her basket.

'It's often the way.'

'Well, I'd better be off. You won't forget about that packet soup?'

'I'll ask the traveller when he comes.'

Conversation dwindled after Mrs Morgan left, for Barbara and her mother were not at ease together. Whenever Mrs MacFarlane looked at Barbara she thought of her younger daughter Rene, a pretty, dark-eyed, soft-feathered sparrow concealing no depths, and besides, a battler – a word into which her mother gathered a great many vague, unspoken impressions. Barbara as a girl had been lanky, sallow, and retiring. That she had done well at school only increased her mother's anxiety, which was concerned entirely with sexual success. She had looked on Barbara with love and pity; when she had discovered the pity was not needed she could not adjust her love. Besides, the flower into which Barbara had blossomed belonged elsewhere. Seeing her dressed with modest elegance for the Bankers' Ball, she had said to herself, 'On the way up.' So it had turned out. There was nothing awkward or shy about her as she waltzed about with the best in the town. But behind the counter . . . It became evident to her mother that Barbara hated the shop, which was her pride.

Why was she always rushing to help, then?

Barbara could have answered: 'Because I wanted to punish my snobbery, which I hated worse than I hated the shop.'

There was nowhere that question and its answer could meet. During ten years Barbara had begun to discern the question, but her mother had no inkling of the answer. She only knew that in Barbara there were mysteries, and so she was not comfortable with her.

Besides, Barbara had gone up in the world. People who thought themselves (and perhaps were) caused fear and resentment in Mrs MacFarlane. She looked on Robert and Barbara as a small independent country looks on a powerful neighbour. The relationship between mother and daughter was all politics and diplomacy, the mother determined to show her independence, the daughter refusing to give up her responsibilities. Her mother needed help, whether or not she admitted it, and what would people say if she neglected her? They would probably blame Robert.

A customer came in, then another, then two more. Barbara came down from the ladder where she was perched, straightening the upper shelves, and began to serve, pleased with her own efficiency which had become something of a joke.

'A smart help you've got there, Mrs Mac.'

'Oh, she's all right. Got her uses.'

All approval was a yielding of territory. Frequently Mrs MacFarlane had to admit: You have to admit they mean well, you have to admit Barbara thinks the world of Rene's children, you have to admit there's nothing high and mighty about Robert. She had given up inspecting Robert's feet for signs of clay. At first she had been against him, for he was just such a good-looking, good-tempered, easy-going man as had always attracted her, then disappointed her, turning out to be weak, self-indulgent, and ineffectual. In the end, she had begun to see that her strength drew such men, not her looks, and that made her angry; for she was drawn by their looks not by their weakness. But Robert was not a second Ian, after all. She was astonished to find him serious, responsible, and hardworking.

He took the shop seriously, knew what energy and common sense had been needed to make it a success, discussed problems of stock, changes of demand, the threat of the supermarket, with a real feeling of their importance. He helped her with her tax returns. I wouldn't know how Belle Dutton got a son like him, she thought. Almost she had to admit that she loved him.

After the customers had left, Barbara said, 'I had a letter from Rene yesterday.'

'How is she?'

'All right. Craig had bronchitis, but he's better. I brought it for you to read while you have your lunch.'

How she missed Rene! Whenever she came to their old home, she felt regret for her sister. Rene was the younger, warmer version in which she loved her mother; Rene knew her other, comic, mobile face, which had flowered in the warmth of Rene's laughter – Rene sitting on her bed, knees bent, hugging her ankles, laughing so much that her head sank on to her knees, while Barbara took off the headmaster, the science teacher, the boss . . . If her sister had been there, she could have given a real performance of her mother-in-law, and felt better.

She got lunch for her mother, minded the shop while she ate, got her own lunch, cleaned up, helped with some heavy stuff from the stock-room, and left to catch the four o'clock bus, feeling that she had maintained her position.

Her mother-in-law was in her usual chair, watching television. The plates beside her were empty. As Barbara bent to pick up the tray she looked with interest at her, trying to see Mrs Morgan's breaker of hearts in the withered, arrogant face tranquillised by the film she was watching. The golden eyes must have been beautiful before the lids sank to mould the eyeball, though now they only added power to her ill-natured expression.

'I've been hearing things about you,' she said.

The old woman turned her face towards her without any change of expression.

'Do you remember a girl named Grace, who worked for your mother? I've been talking to her niece. She was telling me what a beauty you were and how all the boys fell in love with you.'

Without comment, the old woman turned back to the film.

'You ill-mannered old toad,' said Barbara in the same sprightly tone, but under her breath, as she took the tray to the kitchen.

While she was making afternoon tea, Peter put his head in at the kitchen door.

'Good afternoon. You were advertising for a cleaner, lady?'

'Oh, yes, Pete. Come in and have a cup of tea and we'll talk about it.'

How nice it is of people to make jokes, she thought. She knew that for Peter it was a bridge over an awkward moment; but while she was under the influence of her mother-in-law's brutish silence the words 'Good afternoon' seemed to convey a blessing, and a joke was a splendid offering.

CHAPTER EIGHT

It was Cec Prescott's turn in the chair.

Naomi said to him, 'Cec, may I have a minute, before we begin?' As he nodded, she went on, 'I had a letter from Jessie Ford at the Mitchell. Rather interesting. Some papers have just come in there that show Fitzallan was here. Roderick Fitzallan. And it looks as if this is where he wrote the river poems.'

'Who is Roderick Fitzallan, Naomi?'

'You mean this very river? Oh, how marvellous.' Cathy's face shone with an enthusiasm that warmed Naomi.

'You remember, Cec: "As tense as Ariel in his tree . . ." I used to hear Sixth Class reciting it through the partition and I thought Inistree was Ariel's surname.'

Phil muttered, 'I must arise and go now, and go to Inistree', and was relieved when Naomi laughed.

'It was quite a shock when I caught up with *The Tempest* and found out.'

Cathy quoted:

> *'As tense as Ariel in his tree*
> *The sails that labour up the river*
> *Will haul along the stream for ever*
> *Their cargo of mortality.'*

She repeated, 'Imagine! This very river!'

'That's how I feel, too, Cathy.' Naomi spoke warmly, in reaction against the look of contempt on Neil's face. (Oh, my God! Fitzallan yet!) 'I was on the balcony reading this letter, and I looked at the river, then I looked at the bridge . . . I don't know what you'd call the feeling. Pure tourism, I suppose. It certainly wasn't aesthetic, but what a pleasure it was!'

'I remember,' said Cec. 'A little brown book: *Poems for Sixth Class.*'

> *'As tense as Ariel in his tree*
> *The sails that labour up the river*
> *Will haul along the stream for ever*
> *Their cargo of mortality.*
>
> *The fearless clerk, the merchant's daughter,*
> *The salesgirl and the counter jumper,*
> *Disposed about their picnic hamper . . .'*

Cathy murmured,

> *'Embarked upon the moving water . . .'*

92

Naomi added,

> *'Delighted with their Sunday spree,*
> *Do not reflect upon their lot,*
> *Their little share of time is not*
> *Corrupted by eternity.'*

They prompted each other through the rest of the poem.

> *A head is dipped to miss the spray.*
> *The light that touches hair and skin,*
> *The harmony of lip and chin*
> *Are beautiful beyond their day.*

> *The tenderness that bows a shoulder,*
> *The sudden brightness of a face –*
> *The moment will not lose its grace*
> *Although the picnickers grow older.*

> *Their laughter dancing in the air*
> *Is like the soft and shining ribbon*
> *Which sketches on the face of heaven*
> *The wind that snatched it from her hair.*

'"The Picnickers", by Roderick Fitzallan,' said Naomi in a Sixth-Class voice, and added to Cathy, 'Another Fitzallan fancier, I see.'

'I'm not quite as enthusiastic as you are,' said Brian with the modest pride of one who reads only the best, 'but I agree that it's interesting.'

Cathy looked dashed.

Do they suppose, Naomi wondered, that Fitzallan had them in mind when he was writing? One day two brilliant intellects will be born, named Brian Milson and Neil Dunn, and if I don't succeed in pleasing them my life will have been lived in vain?

'I like the one about the willows writing on the water,' she said, cooling her head in Fitzallan's verse. 'Writing the story of love, and she told him love was a house . . .'

'"A house with four walls, and they stand / Upon land",' said Cathy.

'Can't you see her?'

Cathy meditated. 'She might still be alive. She might be living in this town.'

'How is it that this didn't come up before?' asked Cec.

'The stuff wasn't published till the fifties, long after Fitzallan was dead,' said Brian. 'Except for "The Picnickers", which he must have sent to a magazine – and then, of course, it got into that collection and was taught to the young.'

Inflicted on the young, his tone said. Naomi answered it.

'I didn't understand that bit about being "corrupted by eternity" till much later. And I think it did give me something when I caught on. Learn now, understand later. There's a lot to be said for that.'

'I knew it was this river,' said Barbara aside to Naomi.

'Darling, you couldn't have known! Nobody knew . . . I suppose Keith Lincoln did, but he didn't say. It was supposed to be a secret . . . Fitzallan wanted him to burn the poems, but he didn't, of course.'

'You have just exploded a literary mystery, Barbara.'
Brian was amused.

'I can't help it.' Barbara was resolute. 'I did know.
I've always known. I used to read the poems to Robert's
grandfather before he died, and he told me. I think he knew
Fitzallan, too.'

Naomi was elated. 'What a wonderful start! I'll grill
you on the way home.' She said to the others, 'I have to
find out what I can about him for someone who's going
to write his biography. That's why I mentioned it. I thought
you might have some ideas.'

Brian suggested, 'Write to the *Chronicle*.'

'Yes, I'll do that. And search through the files.'

Neil's contempt for Bangoree outweighed his contempt
for Fitzallan. 'I don't quite see Fitzallan in the social column
of the *Chronicle*.'

'Look on the bright side. He may have made a news
item. Drunk and disorderly.' Naomi sat then like a statue
bathed in a lurid sunset light.

'Vagrancy.' Phil tossed her a word to mop her forehead
with. 'A poet would be a vagrant, by definition.'

The electric light mellowed, falling on the oak table
like sunlight on a rock as Naomi saw she was in a safe place
here. What a kind man was Phil.

'You know,' said Cec, 'that name Fitzallan means
something to me. My mother saying, "That Fitzallan – what
a monster of ingratitude!" I kept a look-out for him. I was
sure I would recognise him by the description.'

Naomi smiled appreciation. 'Wouldn't it be useful if
one could?'

'Oh, I gave up that illusion quite early. I'll ask my mother next time I go to see her. Naomi, this has been most interesting, but if we are to do any reading tonight I think we'd better get started.'

'Yes, of course.'

The conversation ended in a wing-flutter of turning pages.

Brian said, 'You must admit there's a distinction between propaganda itself, and a work that analyses and illuminates the ideas that are being propagated.'

His bright stare moved past Neil, who was looking sulkily for a chink in the armour of the sentence, to Cathy who seemed to be waking in confusion.

'What? What? Inattention?' Brian parodied himself with a sweet grin.

Phil paused in his scribbling. 'That makes a very good concluding sentence.' He finished it and dropped his pen, decisively. 'The one before, that is.'

'I was thinking about Fitzallan. Sorry. I was wondering about the girl, whether she's still alive, and who she was.'

Naomi felt mischievous, guessing, by the vague radiance in Cathy's eyes, that she was stepping into the shoes of Fitzallan's mistress.

'She might answer my letter to the paper: "Dear Mrs Faulding, I knew Rod Fitzallan, none better, and will say to his credit that I found him always the gent."'

'Oh no,' said Brian. 'Fitzallan's lady was a lady, I'm sure.'

'And she certainly won't write to the papers,' said Cec. 'She will keep her little trap shut, you'll find.'

'I think she should be proud.' Cathy was dreaming still. 'Perhaps she doesn't even know about the poems. She might be old and wretched and think her life has gone for nothing, and all the time she has these lovely poems to speak for her.'

'She's probably speaking for herself, making a great to-do about the immorality of the young.'

Brian reproved Naomi. 'You take a very dark view of humanity.'

'And humanity does damned little to correct it. I agree, it would be nice for her to know about the poems before she died, so long as nobody else did. If you sneak off to make love in a shed . . .'

'That's a summing-up for you! Thirty poems in a nutshell. Sneaking off to make love in a shed.'

'Secret meetings, he said. Our secret meetings. A girl does expect her secret meetings to stay secret.'

Cec murmured, 'How many have expected that in vain.'

'Wouldn't it be rotten luck, after all this time?'

'How dreadful it would be!' said Barbara. 'I can't imagine anything worse than having something to hide, all one's life.'

Cec raised his eyebrows in innocent wonder. 'Hasn't everybody?'

That drew different varieties of laughter, except from Barbara and Phil, who only smiled from politeness, and must therefore be true innocents. For a moment Naomi envied even Phil.

She must have shivered.

Barbara said to her, 'Are you cold?'

'A little. It's going to be cold here in the winter.'

'We must be able to arrange for some heating.' Cec changed into a local businessman, a part he wore as well as any other. 'I'll have a word with Dick Perry about it.'

The promise that this hour she so enjoyed would not die of cold was so new to Naomi that she did not smile, not knowing how to greet it.

On the way home, Cathy stopped on the bridge and looked down at the river. Neil could hear sentimental voices running in her head as certainly as he heard the steady confidential tone of the water.

'I never really listened to it before.' She added, in spite of his silence, 'You must admit it's rather interesting.'

'Oh, hell,' he moaned. 'No more Fitzallan!'

'Do you really think him so bad? I was thinking about the one, you know,

> *Investing the water's murmur*
> *With voices that die sooner and live longer.*

'How does it start?'

If Neil had known he would not have told her.

'Crap,' he said. 'Waters talking bloody drivel and smiling like girls.'

'But he knew. He was watching himself as the passion got hold of him. And a person can permeate a landscape. It's not a stupid poem, Neil. It's about giving a scene the transience of human life and the immortality of an idea. That thought keeps coming up again and again in his work, doesn't it? And he doesn't like what's happening to him. You can't call it romantic, really, though some of the poems are sentimental.'

'It's the whole set-up,' he said. 'Rubbish.'

'I suppose my reaction is childish. Tourism, Mrs Faulding called it. Just the same, I'm going to walk along the river and enjoy the thought that he walked there before me composing his poems.'

And I wish you would come with me, she thought. If one was going to fall in love, one wanted a little help. The girls at the boarding-house had their dances, their shining dresses and sentimental tunes, to cast a spell on their lovers and on themselves. She didn't ask Neil to lend himself to any of that, but the pink light had to fall from somewhere. Walking along the bank of Fitzallan's river reading his love poems together would do very well.

Neil wanted to walk along the river-bank with Cathy this moment, find a dark place, tear her clothes open, and sink his whole body, as sharp as knives, as hard as stone, deep into her. He knew no intermediate gestures, he had no words to express his desire, and he would not walk under the banner of Fitzallan. 'Crap,' he thought. 'Crud.' He hated his honesty that frustrated him.

'It's not real.'

He walked on, and Cathy followed.

'But he knew. He knew all that. That's what makes it interesting.'

The word 'interesting' maddened him. He walked as far as her boarding-house in silence and at the gate gave her a furious kiss, which alarmed her.

She thought, I don't like him, but put the thought away at once.

'That Neil Dunn!' Naomi shook her head quickly as she dusted the table, pleased with its solidity, though she had forgotten the moment when it seemed like the rock of safety. 'I suppose I mustn't backbite.' She spoke with a touch of wistfulness, acknowledging the forbidden pleasures of defamation.

Barbara, waiting for her by the door, accepted the back as bitten. 'I hope Cathy doesn't marry him.'

'Oh, she will.' Naomi put the duster back in its drawer. 'Or somebody just like him. The world is full of couples like that, flowering vines draped over craggy black rocks. Come to think of it, she's draped over Brian already.' Looking round the room, she came to Barbara's face with its startled expression, and said, 'I didn't mean any scandal. I only meant . . . she's for ever thrusting her little tendrils into clefts in the rock, looking for soil to grow in.'

Barbara said as she followed Naomi out, 'I thought that was cheek, when Brian picked on her for not listening.'

'There you are.' Naomi pulled the main door shut behind them. 'Did she tell him to drop dead? No, not she. I'm sorry, she says, with a sweet smile. Meant it, too. To do Brian justice, he thought it was cheek himself. I am always about to strike Brian off my list of the human race when he starts to laugh at himself and I'm won over. I wonder what his wife is like.'

'Judith? Oh, very nice. Sort of young for her age and always laughing. You might even say giggling.'

'Mmmm. Don't let me go past the milk-bar. I want to get some cigarettes. I suppose I tend to be jealous of Brian because your char is devoted to him. How is the charring going?'

Why couldn't she ask that more naturally, since charring is no crime?

'Oh, marvellous. You have to come and admire the hall when we've finished. Of course, we are so organised. We have a list of jobs drawn up in logical order, and he has a time sheet that I have to sign when he starts and finishes.'

The time sheet made Naomi wince. She thought, Peter doesn't like it, either.

'We really have fun. He makes me feel inferior, though. He polishes five banisters while I'm doing two, and I've been demoted to putting the polish on.' Gaiety died out of her voice. 'The old lady came in yesterday while we were working. She didn't say anything. Just stood looking at us.'

'Very gracious.'

'It was rather odd. I called out to her, "Do you notice the difference?" but she didn't say a word. That's nothing out of the way. If she doesn't feel like answering, she doesn't.'

'How did Pete react?'

'I don't think he noticed. He had his head down, polishing, and he didn't look up. But you never know . . . I thought you might say something to him, warn him not to take any notice of anything she says. I don't want him to start feeling uncomfortable. I don't want him to leave, because he's such a help and it cheers me up having him there, but if he was unhappy . . . you know, if she said

101

anything really nasty. I couldn't stop her, but at least we could warn him.'

'OK. It might be as well.'

Having been obliged to swallow a spoonful of tears in the middle of the sentence, Naomi told herself she must be ill, but the emotion that brought tears proved to be mainly aesthetic, sprung from the correspondence between her own feelings and Barbara's anxious, affectionate tone.

Barbara had slowed to a sad, heel-dragging walk. 'I shouldn't have to ask you to protect Peter. I should be able to handle it myself, but I can't. She treats me like a nobody, and that's just what I am. A nobody. That's why she can put it over me.'

'Barbara!'

From deep inside the shop they were passing, a dim light reached them over hulking mounds of vegetables. Naomi turned, studied Barbara's face, and found no indication that she was joking.

'I don't mean coming from the wrong side of the tracks or serving in Mum's shop. That used to worry me once but it doesn't any more. Robert's helped me over that. I mean in myself I'm nobody.'

They had halted in front of the shop. Naomi looked at Barbara's face giving more brightness to the dim light that fell upon it. 'You don't look like a nobody,' she said, taking care to conceal her amusement.

'Don't you dare to say anything about being good looking.' The tone, for Barbara, was fierce, and she stepped out furiously so that Naomi had to hurry after her. She slowed down to say, 'That's where it all starts, I think.'

102

'How do you mean?' Naomi had heard of the dangers of beauty and was interested to learn more about them.

'Oh –' She shook her head at the difficulty of answering. 'You hide behind it. No, that's not it . . . You think it's the only thing that matters.' Beauty was a best dress one had to be careful not to spoil, so one learnt the manners that went with it: to be modest, affable, reticent and composed, qualities not false yet not quite one's own. She remembered with dismay that she called herself 'good looking', then put dismay aside, trusting in Naomi's understanding.

'You don't behave like a regular beauty. You're always pulling funny faces and taking people off.'

'But I feel guilty about it. I used to do it when I was a sooky schoolgirl talking to my sister, and I never did it again till I met you. All the time you feel you have to be what people expect you to be.'

'We all feel that,' said Naomi.

'But you're somebody. Everybody knows who you are. When you say something, everyone thinks, "Well, that's Naomi." Like tonight, when Brian said you took a poor view of humanity. You knew what to say.'

'You're frightened to open your mouth in discussions. You have plenty to say when you're with me.'

The subject, Barbara saw, had been changed, though Naomi perhaps did not realise it. She shook her head and did not answer.

Naomi thought of mentioning her talent for acting and realised in time that it would be a mistake.

'Something is eating you tonight,' she said, thinking with disappointment that Fitzallan would have to wait.

103

'It's that play.' Barbara drew a deep breath charged with feeling. 'Being about adoption. Those plays. They always seem to be about something that's on your mind. I want to adopt a baby now. The more I think of it the more I want to, but I don't think I can because of the old lady. I couldn't be sure of standing up to her if she was hostile to it.'

They had passed the milk-bar after all without going in. When they came to the corner of River Street, Naomi said, 'Let's go over to the Bluebird and have a cup of coffee. I forgot my cigarettes, I'll get them there.'

Barbara followed Naomi across River Street and into the cafe. On their way to a booth they said, 'Good evening', nodding and smiling to Con behind his glass counter.

You could never walk your grief about a country town as you could in the city. Naomi thought of certain walks in the noise among the blank-faced crowds, indifferent, but human and present – just as much company as one needed. She was pierced by a shaft of nostalgia that left her gloomy, too susceptible to Barbara's despondency.

In the brighter light of the cafe, Barbara appeared dulled. The word nonentity was no longer absurd. Finally, Naomi could find nothing to say.

As Barbara sat frowning at the cuticle of her left thumb while she massaged it with the ball of her right, she summoned up a question. 'How does Robert get on with her?'

'She's never as bad with him as she is with me. He's always terribly polite to her, as if he didn't know her very well. That seems to work for him.'

Naomi was visited by a dark picture of human society: everybody pushing for space at the bottom of a barrel. Was that all there was? Her mind filled with horror of the darkness. There were moments when she could moo like a cow from misery.

Fitzallan, at least. In this gloom, the name shed a distant light.

Barbara smiled at the waitress as she wiped the table.

'Just coffee, thanks, Beryl. For two.'

'You on the loose tonight, Mrs Somers?'

There was no curiosity in Beryl's pale-blue eyes, no word suppressed on the lips which seemed to be about to resume a chewing movement. Beryl was speaking out of social duty.

'That's right. Living it up,' Barbara answered, but without the required gaiety.

Watching Beryl walk away, Naomi said, 'I don't know how anybody could indulge a guilty passion in this town.'

'People do, though.' Barbara reacted with automatic patriotism, suspecting that Naomi was down-grading Bangoree for its lack of opportunities for adultery. Cec Prescott's name occurred to her, though she did not mention it. The things he said! What nerve he had!

'Well, I suppose they do. They do in most places, after all. It was Fitzallan I was thinking of. Do tell me about him.'

It was time for a change of subject. Consulting memory while Beryl served the coffee, Barbara looked less depressed.

'I don't know much. It was Robert's grandfather who knew him.' She sipped coffee. 'I'm trying to think.'

105

It was strange how rooms lived and died in a house: the back room where she kept the ironing basket and the sewing-machine had been old Mr Dutton's room, smelling faintly of urine and faeces in spite of the bowl of spice-scented water steaming on the cedar chest of drawers. She saw the old man's face, cloudy-eyed, the glossy rose-pink skin jewelled with dull sores, ugly, ugly.

'He got me to read to him because he was going blind. Young people are awful, aren't they? I used to hate it.'

'You did it though, old Mrs Somers.' Naomi spoke affectionately, grateful to her for lightening her view of the world.

'I'm not so young any more, I hope. Though actually I got used to it. He was interesting to talk to. I used to forget he was old and sick. I suppose I was glad that somebody was pleased to see me. Actually, I started it to curry favour with her. It didn't work.' She had enough force now for a rueful grin.

'But what did he think of Fitzallan? Did he like him?'

'Well, the poems meant a lot to him. It was sad, really. You know the one you were talking about, the one about the willows?'

'*Languid the willows yield to the water's playing . . .*'

'That's right. That's the backwater outside Milston. Do you know it?'

Naomi shook her head, looking youthfully excited.

'I'll drive you out there on Sunday if you like. It's only about eight miles.'

'I'm having a tourist fit.' Naomi apologised for her elation.

Barbara went on, 'That's what mattered to old Mr Dutton, you see, not Fitzallan. He was blind, and those were the places he knew when he was young. He liked to talk about that. But as for liking Fitzallan . . .' She shook her head, looking puzzled. 'I don't think he did. I had the idea there'd been a quarrel Grandpa was sorry for, but I don't know where I got the idea.'

She put her twenty-cent piece on the bill and left Naomi to pay it and their social tribute at the counter.

They walked on the bridge in silence, Naomi thinking of the three in the Dutton house: Barbara and her marriage, which sometimes irked her (Robert Loves Barbara carved on every tree), Barbara and her mother-in-law . . .

A boy with his head down leant along his bicycle, the wheels muttering quietly along the opposite footpath. Then they were alone again.

'You are too sensitive to disapproval.'

Barbara laughed. 'What brought that on?'

'I was thinking about your mother-in-law and the grip she has on you.'

'Everybody is sensitive to disapproval.'

'Not as much as you. And Robert, perhaps?'

If two mild and gentle characters set out to create the climate in which they throve – well, that was love, no doubt, given the sexual attraction. Naomi often wondered about the composition of love and was astonished to think it might be so simple.

'I must ask her about Fitzallan.' Barbara's tone was resolute. Having reached the depths of defeat she was determined to climb back. 'She ought to know something about him. Now I remember – when I read the driftwood poem he cried. I can remember seeing two little tears on his cheeks and wondering if I ought to wipe them away. And he said, "How can you know? You don't know." But I didn't like to ask him what he meant by that.'

Naomi reacted sharply against the two little tears. She asked, hushed and insinuating, 'Nothing funny about Grandpa Dutton, was there?'

This idea was so entertaining to Barbara that she went away laughing down the steps to the river path.

In the sitting-room the television set had been switched off and the ceiling light switched on. Robert, who was in an armchair studying papers, looked up from them and smiled at Barbara, while the old woman turned towards her a countenance sharp and heavy with discontent.

'Did you have a nice evening?'

'Yes, nice. We didn't start the other play, we finished the Brecht and talked a bit. Do you want a cup of tea?'

'He's been waiting long enough for one,' the old woman said furiously.

'Good Lord, Mother.' Robert looked at her amazed, as if she had never made an ill-natured remark before. 'I haven't been wanting tea. And if I had I could have made it.'

'My comfort means nothing, I know that.' She tucked her mouth inwards, sealing off bitter thoughts.

'Well, what would you like? Cocoa? Ovaltine?' Barbara's amused, condescending tone deserving no answer and getting none, she went to the kitchen to get the supper.

She had been wrong, using that down-putting tone;

but what a relief it was to do the wrong thing sometimes.

When she came back with the tray, she said, 'Did you ever know a man named Fitzallan, Mother?'

The firm-set surface of the old woman's face dissolved slowly into peevish bewilderment. Holding out the cup of Ovaltine, Barbara felt as if she was offering a peanut to a crab.

'What are you asking me that for?'

Any question that did not concern her health, her comfort or her prejudices was unsettling, if not immoral.

'I think your father knew him.' Barbara gave Robert his tea. 'I thought you might have met him.'

Robert closed his folder of papers. 'Is that the poet you mean?'

'That's right. I used to read his poems to Grandpa, remember, before we were married?'

'I remember you used to read to him, but I wasn't in on that.'

'I wouldn't let you listen. I was shy.' They looked quickly at each other and away. 'Poetry, especially. Anyhow, I think Grandpa knew Fitzallan. He talked as if he did.'

'His mind was wandering.' The old woman snapped the stem of the conversation. 'After that second stroke he used to talk all sorts of nonsense.'

Barbara said to Robert, 'They were talking about him at the reading tonight. Naomi didn't know the poems were about this river. Apparently nobody knew except us. Isn't that funny? And nobody thought of asking us, so it's been a great literary mystery. Now they've got some papers in the Mitchell Library, because a friend of his just died.

Letters that show it was this river. And somebody's going to write Fitzallan's life. They've asked Naomi to help. So that's why I was asking you about Fitzallan, Mother.'

'I've never heard of him.' She had found something indecent either in Fitzallan's avocation or his mere name, so that she dismissed him with contempt. Then she conceded, 'I can't answer for your grandfather. He used to know some very peculiar people. It was a great worry to my mother.'

Robert and Barbara exchanged the solemn look of people suppressing a smile.

'Wait a minute.' Robert went to the bookshelves, stooped and found a small book. 'I thought so.' He brought it to Barbara and showed her the flyleaf, reading aloud, 'To a good friend, in gratitude, Roderick Fitzallan.'

'Oh, lovely. Naomi will be pleased. One for Cec Prescott, too. His mother said Fitzallan was a monster of ingratitude.'

'Did the Prescotts know him?' Robert looked slightly disappointed at having to share Fitzallan with the Prescotts.

'That's the only thing Cec can remember about him. He said he expected to recognise him from the description and he kept an eye out for him. He must have been a very small child.'

'That sounds like Cec.'

They had forgotten old Mrs Somers. The door closing uttered a sharp comment on their forgetfulness. They looked in astonishment at the empty chair, then at each other. Robert opened the door and called out, 'Can you manage, Mother?'

'I'm quite all right, thank you,' came faintly from the head of the stairs.

Robert came back to Barbara. It was a moment when communication was possible; after a pause, they decided against it.

'So there's Fitzallan.' The yellowing dust-jacket of the little book was still in place. From the inside back flap the face of the poet looked at them, thin, hawk-nosed, frog-mouthed, steady-eyed. There was some projection of humanity from the small time-dulled photograph: Fitzallan looked as if he wished to plead, but would not. 'I didn't realise we had this. I suppose I didn't take much notice till I heard them talking tonight.'

'Those are his early poems. They're all in the *Collected Works*. You'd have been reading out of that.'

They were both listening for a thump, a cry of distress, some sign of disaster from upstairs, Barbara with more anxiety than Robert because her thoughts were guiltier.

When she got up to take the cups to the kitchen, they did share a sigh of relief and a smile.

CHAPTER NINE

Eleanor woke feeling better than usual, almost alert. That could not be endured. Quickly, she closed her eyes again, looking for refuge in a moment of the past.

She was kneeling on bare boards, breathing in the dense floury smell of unbleached calico, the sharp dispensary smell of red colour from her felt-tipped pen. A . . . Carefully she followed the pencil line: ACTIVE NOW. Rita and Joe were kneeling near by working together on OR RADIOACTIVE LATER. The acid comforting smell of Joe's sweater, the flower scent of Rita's black silk hair. The smells were real; so were the sounds and the colours, spun out of her with pain. Only touch was missing. She tried in vain for the grainy surface of calico and the pressure of the pen barrel. It was all real, but she was a ghost.

Memories of happiness brought none. It was like looking through a cell window into that bright daylight, not escaping into it.

She hadn't been happy before demonstrations. She had been frightened. But once they had started she had been alive, loving, feeling a steady flow of love for the bodies struggling round her, not alone.

It was hard work, re-creating the past. She had to give it up at last, sitting unprotected at the breakfast table, staring at a cold, sickening piece of toast.

Phil said, 'Is that all you're going to eat? Try to finish that piece at least.'

Oh, mind your own bloody business. Consideration, concern, compunction. She could translate. Sickness, christened sickness. He never used that other word again. He didn't use the word sickness, either, but it was always there in his actions: squeezing oranges for juice, feeding Linda first and putting her out in the yard – 'She distracts you while you're eating' – vitamin tablets.

Vitamin tablets: I know what you mean. Orange juice, Pentavite, malt (pah!), egg-flips: I know what you mean.

The language of egg-flips. No defence against it.

She drank her coffee with controlled slowness.

It was the control that maddened. Of course one bottle a day was enough. It was the word 'enough' she couldn't endure. She wanted excess, abandonment. Her daily death.

Phil said, 'Have you been keeping up those vitamin tablets? You're not eating any better.'

She wanted to destroy time. Murder it.

Saturday was a bad day. What day was good?

113

Meanwhile he talked. Chatted. On and on.

'We finished the Brecht last night. I have to write the report this time. Brian Milson and water, it's going to be. I'd better get it done while I can still decipher the notes.' Thread after thread he tossed across space to fall into nowhere. Bruce's spider was a non-starter. 'We're reading *Endgame* next.' He spun out his conversation with mouthfuls of coffee and toast. 'Brian Milson wants us to put it on for Sixth Form. It's a set text this year. Of course it's a bit of a chore, learning the part,' he agreed, 'but I'd only be playing Nagg – not much in that. I could rehearse after surgery.' Surgery was as much pretence as this communication.

Oh, why wouldn't he shut up and leave her alone?

'I hope you'll come and see it.'

See what? She had to go back, pick up the pieces of his chatter and fit them together to get the answer: *Endgame.*

Endgame. I know what you mean.

'Why?' She aimed the word at him aggressively.

'I think it'll be worth seeing. Cec is very good, you know, and so is Barbara Somers.'

She saw them all having their innocent fun in the warmth of that summery name: sunlight, green grass, and blossom.

Phil stood up. 'I've got a call to make out of town. I'll take Linda.'

The wretchedness of her face moved him so that he thought he could touch her. For a long time he had been telling himself he must make physical contact with her again, but all he could ever imagine was a handshake. Fantastic. Now he put his hand over hers and pressed it.

She was quite still, tense with the effort of leaving her hand there, burning with rage. Concern, consideration, condescension, pity.

He took his hand away, startled to see how much she hated him.

News item: Bruce's spider gives up.

He thought as he walked away that he was laughing it off, but it wasn't so. The past took hold of him, memory overwhelmed him.

Under a BAN THE BOMB banner, he had fallen in love with her. Till then he had admired her in silence, but that hot day, each holding a pole of the banner, they had been jostled in the crowd and had manoeuvred to keep the relationship between them constant, two stars in a private constellation. She had grown hot and dusty, less perfect, more approachable, tired but still alight with enthusiasm. After the demonstration he had dared to make his suggestion, in a trembling voice.

Putting back a fluted lock of her hair, crisp with sweat, she had said, 'But would it spoil our relationship, do you think?'

When he saw that his words aroused no indignation, his heart had begun to beat like a fist hammering on a door.

'No, no. Improve it out of sight, I should think.' Not getting together enough breath to laugh.

What pain there was in uprooting such a moment from one's life. Though he hated her, too, from time to time; and, what is more, he had failed her. He had become worldly – and much good it had done him. The world had not shown much enthusiasm.

In the garden Linda was running up and down along the fence squealing and barking at the next-door puppy as it ran up and down the other side. He had to wait for a while, watching, till he was calm enough to pick her up.

When Eleanor had woken that day in the park, to see the ring of children round her, she had not thought at all of their faces fixed on her. She had got up and walked through the circle, which broke up with panic speed as she approached it. Those faces had come back and ringed her always, with changing expressions, moon-eyed with pity, gleeful, contemptuous, eyes always fixed on her. No way of walking through the circle any longer. The enemy.

The police had been the enemy. How amazed she had been that a man bigger and older than herself was prepared to hurt her deliberately. Later she had shown her wrist proudly, trying for nonchalance. Ann had moved it gently, testing for a fracture, while they talked in low, tired voices, listing those who had been dragged into the paddywagon: Alan, the boy from New South Wales . . . Not alone.

Memory was the only way out of the circle. She took short flights into it like a heavy bird and settled again in despair.

Now for the endless, entirely predictable day.

CHAPTER TEN

After the first reading of *Endgame* there was a silence beginning in deep respect because of Cec's reading, ending in awkwardness as the others remembered Brian's.

Naomi said, 'Well?'

Cec said, remotely, still enraptured by the part of Hamm, that he thought it would do.

All very well. Naomi hoped that meant he would help to cope with Brian.

'If you say so.' Barbara sighed resignation. 'I don't know what I'm doing, but if you're satisfied . . . I'll do what you tell me, and hope it will do.'

'I find it hard to believe that you don't know what you're doing.'

This piece of sharpness from Brian toughened Naomi, who could not bring herself before to disturb his

117

satisfaction in his performance. She took on the director's burden grudgingly.

'If we're going to do this seriously, you'll have to accept that there's a stronger contrast between Hamm and Clov. I suppose we're all agreed that they're two aspects of the same character.'

'Oh, indubitably,' Barbara said devoutly, chin on her hand and her eyes fixed on Naomi.

Naomi's smile was affection made visible. Phil wore a moon-reflection of it as he said, 'Don't worry, we'll sit safe in our garbage tins and come when we're called. And speaking of garbage tins . . .'

'That's what I want to talk about.' Brian unfolded a list, saying reprovingly to Naomi, 'We can talk about the reading in rehearsal. I think it's important to get on to the properties straight away.'

'How long is this going to take?' Phil had a look on his face of being about to add something, but he did not.

'The sooner the better, for Sixth Form. It depends how much time you're prepared to give it. Three weeks?'

'Best get into it and do it quickly.' Seeing Naomi sag, Brian said generously, 'Cathy will take as much work as possible off your hands.'

'Four or five weeks, even so.'

'OK. Now for the properties. Cathy's going to look after them. An armchair on wheels. Castors, that is. Anyone got an old armchair in the attic?'

'Yes, I have,' said Barbara. 'I'm not sure what condition it's in. I'll have a look at it.'

Cec said, 'I can do you a nice line in bamboo hallstands.'

Barbara was delighted. 'Oh, so can I. Set with little bits of mirror.'

'A row of hat-pegs and a tasteful receptacle for umbrellas.'

The desperate mood of the play had made them frivolous.

Cec went on, 'The wicker whatnot of our grandparents.'

'Well, that's a different play,' said Brian, showing respect for grandparents in the mildness of the comment. 'A step-ladder.'

'Can do,' said Cec. 'And the sheet. Put me down for the sheet.'

'Garbage tins,' said Phil. 'An acceptable substitute for garbage tins.'

'Fifth Form are working on it. We've got a big oil-drum and we're scrubbing it out and painting it.' Cathy added, to Brian, 'Bill Watson's father thinks he can get us another.'

Brian grumbled, 'They'll look out of proportion, of course.'

'Better them than us. And something inside to sit on.'

Neil murmured, 'The garbage-tin-sitters' union.'

They were off again, making silly suggestions about stools, cushions, lights, script-holders, flasks ... Naomi was sorry for Brian and annoyed with Barbara. Besides, she had brought Barbara's book and wanted time to show Fitzallan's inscription and his photograph.

'We'll follow the script and put the pair of you into sand,' she said, noting that the curse of the amateur dramatic society was on them already.

'I think that's it. Do you think we can leave the stuff here, Naomi?'

'Oh, I think so. The room's not used much.'

'How are you going to get it here?'

'Bill Watson's father's truck,' said Cathy.

'We'll have to rehearse here, to save time. Naomi can come across from the library after work.'

'We'll have to have one rehearsal on the stage, at least.'

'We'll see to that later.'

Brian and Cathy went to work, serious and strong-willed: first rehearsal, Tuesday at eight fifteen, Naomi to arrive when the library shut, Cathy to stand in for Naomi when required, to make a note of problems and look after properties.

As Brian said, 'Well, I think that's it', Naomi fished in the carry-all at her feet and brought out a plastic bag, from which she took Fitzallan's early poems.

'Do you have a moment to look at this? Cec, do you want to see your monster of ingratitude?'

Heads bent towards the open book and its inscription.

'It's Barbara's book. Robert's grandfather's, that is. He was the good friend.'

'I stand rebuked,' said Cec, who was moved at the sight of the handwriting.

Cathy asked, 'What was he grateful for?'

'We don't know.' Naomi turned to the inside flap of the back cover and they all bent, gigantic, over tiny Fitzallan. I've written about it to Jessica and asked for copies of the letters, but she hasn't had time to answer, of course. And old Mrs Somers can't help.' Or won't.

'Not handsome, really, is he?' said Barbara. 'You can see the attraction, just the same.'

120

Naomi caught the brief look of businesslike curiosity Phil gave the photograph. She thought, 'Oh, no. Not that as well, poor devil!'

Cathy said, 'It's a sensitive face, isn't it?'

Neil stared at it resentfully, thinking Cathy would be romancing about Fitzallan again on the way home. It did not change his resolution. It was now or never.

'I've never seen a copy of the early poems before.' Brian picked up the book with a gentleness that made Naomi forgive his reading of Clov. 'You've got quite a rarity there, Barbara.'

'Robert wants to give it to the library. That's why I was showing it to Naomi.'

Naomi said, 'I think it ought to go to the Mitchell.' Barbara looked dashed, since the Mitchell had no real existence for her. 'Oh, well, only a suggestion. It's your book.'

'It should stay here,' said Brian firmly.

'The Mitchell,' said Neil. 'Who'd be interested in it here?'

'But it's our business to make people interested, isn't it?' Brian said to him, bland and sweet-smiling.

'What about the school, then?' Naomi asked.

Brian's face lit as promptly as a light-bulb.

'In a display case. If we could dig out any more Fitzallan material. What would Robert think about that, Barbara?'

'He'd like that, I think. He's very keen to . . . There's the connection with his grandfather, you see.'

'Barbara knows the places he wrote about in the river poems.'

121

'Some of them. Don't look at me like that, all of you, or my memory will go altogether. It's terrible. I didn't think it mattered, you see. And I go about reading the poems and trying to remember.' Seeing her audience, even Neil, as rapt as children, she drew a breath and began, 'Robert's grandfather . . .'

'The good friend,' Naomi murmured.

'He was almost blind and I used to read to him. Especially those poems about the river because they were about places he knew and he liked to remember times when he'd been there, on picnics and so on. You know how it is with old people. I didn't take much notice. I knew it was a sort of escape for him and I was glad about that, but I didn't imagine anyone would be asking me years later what the places were.'

Brian's attitude towards Fitzallan had changed.

'Don't begin to worry about it. Relax. Whatever comes is profit. If you tighten up, nothing will come.'

Naomi thought with a deep-buried giggle. 'He'll be telling her to put her feet up and drink plenty of milk in a minute.'

'I don't see that it matters very much.' Neil looked jaded, having conquered his enthusiasm. 'It doesn't affect the poems, one way or the other.'

Brian turned and spoke aggressively.

'It doesn't matter to art but it matters to education. To culture.' He pronounced the word defiantly. 'To culture in this town. If we can show the kids that these poems belong to them in a particular way, if we can let them see the material for poetry in front of their eyes, that'll be something a few of them will keep. And that's real education, in my book.' He cared so little whether or not he was pompous that they found him impressive.

Cec, as he patted his hands together and coughed out, 'Hear, hear!' was only superficially facetious.

Naomi contributed, 'When I found out about Fitzallan, I looked at the river and I felt as if I'd never seen it before. That's culture too, in a way. I admit it's a type that's easily debased.'

'Mrs Somers, I think it's wonderful. You're a living link between us and Fitzallan.'

'Please don't call me Mrs Somers, Cathy.' Barbara spoke so sharply that Cathy's eyes opened wider.

Naomi said, 'She is the vessel of history', and Phil had a vision of chiselled gold and sapphires that sent his eyes dotty with love. Naomi saw them as he cast them discreetly down and said inwardly, 'Get out of this town. Go.' With fraternal affection she measured Phil, slight, seedy, acne-scarred, ill- starred, against Robert and begged him silently, 'Run, do not walk, to the nearest exit.'

Looking tired, Barbara said, 'You ought to talk to Robert about having the book in the school, Brian. I think he'd like that. He wants a place for it in the town. If Naomi doesn't want it for the library.'

'It's not that I don't want it. It's a matter of finding the best place for it.'

'I'll call in and have a word with him.'

Naomi thought any face lit by selfless enthusiasm must look beautiful, as Brian's did.

*

123

While she and Barbara tidied the room she was still thinking of that look on Brian's face and regretting what she had to do to him.

'That reading!' she grumbled, and added that she did not know how Brian *could*.

'He was copying Cec, wasn't he? I thought he was taking him off at first.'

'So did Cec, I think. He gave him a very odd look.'

'You'll just have to tell him,' Barbara said, easily, not knowing that people like Brian were vulnerable.

Barbara, too, was perturbed – at having snapped at Cathy. Naomi was of the consoling opinion that the matter of the remark made up for its manner. 'You were only telling her to call you Barbara, after all. A woman who knew a man who knew Fitzallan!' she added, laughing at Cathy for a weakness she knew she shared with her.

Barbara was not entirely cheered. Pushing chairs into position with abrupt movements that communicated a matter-of-fact hopelessness, she said, 'All through that play I thought it was about not having children. I was quite certain about it. Then I remembered what you and Brian said about it, and it wasn't about that at all. No wonder I'm not game to open my mouth in discussions.'

So that explained the hectic gaiety about the garbage tins, so unlike Barbara.

'So it could be.' If that was the cause of one's despair. 'You're not so far wrong. Those plays of Beckett's produce an emotional reaction – that just happens to be yours. You goof,' she added at Barbara's gasp of idiot enlightenment. 'Don't you start. I can see enough trouble ahead.'

'Not me. I'm keeping on your right side. I want you to do something for me.'

'You had better do something about that, Barbara.' Naomi checked the room with a troubled frown. 'About adopting. I've been thinking, you know, that it's one of those moments when fate sets out to insult you – you want something helpless to look after, and see what it sends you. If you did have a child of your own, it would have to put up with the old lady, wouldn't it? What do you want me to do?'

'Give a talk on Fitzallan for my Red Cross afternoon.'

'They wouldn't come.' Naomi pulled the front door shut with a decisive click.

'Oh, they have to come. No problem. People have cards or games or anything. I thought it would be a change. Besides, some quite old people come. You might pick up something about Fitzallan.'

'You don't have to sell it to me, I'll do it.' Naomi had just had an unposed glimpse of herself, which gave her a shock. Saying, 'They wouldn't come' in that closed, complacent voice. A contrast with Brian. She didn't care to be inferior to Brian. In fact, I'm going to drag you in. Will you read some of the poems?'

'Oh, yes.' Seeing the quick startled turn of Naomi's head she said, 'I'm not afraid of the Red Cross. Only of the drama group.'

'Colour slides. What Brian said, you know, about bringing it home to people that it's their own river. That's the point, isn't it? If we had colour slides of the places, if you can identify enough of the scenic ones . . .'

'Oh, yes. I think I can. Four or five, at least.'

125

'That ought to do. We'd show the slide while you read the poem.' Hastily she reassured the ghost of Fitzallan: 'We wouldn't try to illustrate any abstractions. Most of the scenic ones are pretty lighthearted.'

'We'll have to move fast, to get colour slides back in time.'

'How long have we got? It'll have to be a Wednesday, of course.'

They were still making their plans when they reached the river and paused on the bridge.

'Oh, look.' Barbara's tone was happy. 'Young love.'

Thirty yards upstream, the light of a street lamp dwindled down the gentle slope of the town-side bank defining two figures on the path: Neil walking ahead with an arm outstretched behind him to hold Cathy's hand.

'I know where they're going. They're going to Lovers' Rock.'

The two had vanished now into the darkness that belonged to them.

'Funny.' Naomi spoke with respect. 'One doesn't approve of him yet one approves of that. You know, a bit of happiness of the common sort might make a different person out of him.' She laughed at herself. 'Like the Frog Prince.'

In the silence, as they looked after the lovers, the persistent undertone of the river was audible. Naomi thought about Phil Truebody and wondered whether a hopeless love was better than nothing at all. The river insisted quietly that to live, love, live was better. Not much better, yet better.

A river taught to speak.

126

Naomi yawned. 'All very well for them. I'm tired. Let's go home.'

Walking across the bridge, they went on planning their lecture.

'Sunday then, if it's fine,' said Barbara at the top of the steps.

'What about the old lady?'

'Robert will be there. And she's getting about now so much better. She cleaned out Grandpa's desk one day last week. Even took the papers to the incinerator herself – I could hardly believe it.'

'Barbara!' Naomi cried out in anguish as Fitzallan manuscripts tensed, sallowed, cringed, and burst into flame before her inward eye. 'You shouldn't have let her do that. You should never burn old papers without looking through them.'

'Oh, Robert had, ages ago. They were nothing but a lot of old bills and things. I don't know why we hadn't thrown them out before. I suppose Grandpa hadn't been dead long enough, and then we forgot.'

'Don't ever do it again, will you?'

Barbara started down the steps. 'All right. I promise. If it makes you happy.' She started down the steps, calling, 'See you Sunday!' the word 'Sunday' hanging on the darkness like the promise of sunlight.

As the glimmer of the narrow path disappeared into the darkness of the patch of bush, Neil changed his grip on Cathy's hand. It had been loose, formal, with the suggestion of a joke; now he held her fingers firmly in his, waited till she came close behind him, and stiffened his arm to guide her on the uneven ground. The hazards of this sort of thing: he should have brought a torch; but that would have looked like premeditation. Premeditation ... he supposed you could call it that, but what a word for these particular ideas!

Cathy liked the new style of hand-clasp much better. Full of proper, acceptable meaning, the strong fingers holding and guiding her on the dark path where her feet felt for stones and bushes brushed against her. He held a tall bush back from her face. This was right. He wasn't a graceful wooer, but if the essential was there ... She had so much respect for love, so much joy in receiving it, she could hardly control her breathing and only hoped she would know the right thing to say, not gush or say anything silly. He was so critical, so sensitive to values ...

They had come out onto an area of grass and rock with a few trees, not enough to block the faint light that seemed to come from the water, though its surface was dark.

'Want to sit down for a bit?' They had reached a flat rock which he examined by match-light. 'Fitzallan might have sat on this very rock.'

'You're laughing at me,' she said, too winningly.

Annoyed with himself for mentioning Fitzallan, he waited for the quotation he had brought on himself, but none came. Cathy sat down without speaking on the edge of the rock and he sat beside her.

The silence as it extended disconcerted her. Neil picked up her hand, at last, and examined it minutely by touch, stroking her fingernails and pushing back cuticle in a way

128

that seemed to her idle and meaningless; then he put his arm round her and pulled her close to him.

Still silence.

'How lovely the river is,' she said.

'Um.'

He pulled her face round to him and kissed her. Her position on the rock was not comfortable and he was kissing her too hard. He was pulling her over in a great heavy huddle of flesh inclining towards the surface of the rock. She struggled to stay upright. His hand slid between her thighs. Fighting for balance, she could not . . . She clenched a fist and pushed it as hard as she could against his jaw. Now communication was established. He let her go and she dealt his face a great swinging slap that was too weak for her feelings.

They had both got to their feet and were staring at each other, two dim, wild faces in the dark.

'You,' she whispered, 'you . . .'

'You vulgar bitch,' he said, rubbing his face.

Seeing her so distraught, hearing her frantic breathing, brought the word rape into his mind. The dangers . . . how a man could get caught . . . indecent assault . . .

Angry and horrified, he turned and went along the dark stony path, swearing when he stumbled, glad of the excuse for swearing, hoping when a tree root tripped him that it would throw the silly bitch and break her neck, stopping before he reached open ground to steady his body and his breathing.

Cathy sat on the rock and waited to start crying. At first she was too ashamed, not for the incident, but for her expectations, which had proved foolish. Then she began to indulge in thin, bitter weeping, but it was not the sort of tear-burst that relieved the feelings. Finally, in a mood of furious self-pity, she filled the patch of bush she had to cross alone in the dark with poisonous spiders crouched on branches, ready to spring into her hair or attack her clutching hand, with snakes moving like one long muscle across her path, to be trodden on, with tree roots like knife-blades and behind them unknown forms of life lurking . . . When she grew tired of that, she found the creatures far more easily created than destroyed. When common sense had done its best and failed, she had to fall back on anger at her own stupidity to drive her along the path to the open ground.

CHAPTER ELEVEN

Peter dragged the step-ladder into position under the chandelier and climbed up to straddle the top step, looking, in his long apron, with a scarf knotted over his abundant, shining, waving hair, like a great strong-boned, hobble-dehoy housemaid born to drudge and die unloved. Barbara stood at the foot of the ladder, handing up a bowl of hot water and a sponge.

'We should have done the brasswork first,' he said, frowning.

'I don't think so. Wash off the worst of it and we'll rinse it again after you've polished the brass.'

Peter squeezed out the dripping sponge over a cut-glass flower and let the runnel of grey foaming water run into the bowl.

'This is a pretty fabulous thing really, isn't it?'

'Robert's great-grandfather brought that from Italy.'

How good, if one could say, your great-great-grandfather . . .

'This is a fabulous house, in fact.' He looked down at her with an expression untainted by admiration. 'What are you doing down there?'

'Holding the ladder.' She apologised: 'I promised your mother.'

'Oh, for Christ's sake!' His curse was the louder for not being entirely heartfelt.

Barbara looked scared, put her finger to her lips and turned her face towards the open doorway to the sitting-room.

'Sorry, sorry,' he muttered. 'Don't blame me then if you get dirty water in your hair.' He washed a flower directly above her, threatening her with drips. 'On your own head be it.'

'Don't, Pete! Now watch it, do!'

When the old woman showed herself, the hall became a stage set in preparation: newspapers spread on the royal-blue, pink-flowered carpet, the splendid staircase glowing, ready for the play, Peter on his ladder a stage hand, the doorway in which she was standing the entrance to the wings – so dramatic was her stance and so frightened but resolute her expression.

'I don't like this sort of thing in my house.' The line was delivered with timidity supported by self-righteousness.

Silence followed. Barbara looked at her as if she had said something interesting that required thought, Peter simply looked, being startled out of the present moment. With a vague memory of the sort of talk that pleased grandparents, he said at last, 'Where's your house?'

132

Obviously he had not pleased old Mrs Somers. She glared at him, uttered a loud caw of rage, turned and hobbled away – a real hobble of defeated old age, not the sad limp that announced her sufferings from the disputed hip.

Peter groaned and muttered, 'Oh, hell, what did I say? I didn't mean to upset her. I couldn't think of anything to say.'

Since Barbara didn't answer, he looked down and was appalled to see her head bent into shielding hands. Then she looked up and he saw that she was laughing.

'Nothing. It's all right.' She laughed longer, flushing away the old woman's extraordinary remark. 'It's quite all right.' She murmured, 'She thinks this is her house, you see. Just as well to remind her that it isn't, but I can't seem to do it. So you did very well.'

Peter went on washing the cut-glass flowers clustered on their branches of brass.

'She can't think that, Barbara,' he said kindly. 'It isn't sensible.'

'She manages.'

He worked in silence, while tedious wire fences grew across the clear plain of the future. Should one marry an orphan? But Barbara of course should have married Robert. What would Naomi be like when she was old? He saw clearly, then, that Naomi was old already, though not much older than Barbara, who was hardly middle-aged; so he stopped thinking and began to work with such concentration that the chandelier was washed with twenty minutes to spare.

'I could start on the brass.'

133

Barbara had turned on the lights. He sat admiring his piece of the Snow Queen's palace.

'No, that's enough for today. Come and help me get the armchair out of the attic. For *Endgame*. Hamm's armchair. Robert's grandfather had one that I think will do. You stow the ladder while I clear up and we'll go and look.'

Untying the scarf and shaking loose his curls, Peter became handsome. The thing the old woman had said rose to her mind's surface and now she recognised it, an insult so outrageous that it could not even annoy her.

The leather armchair was not far out in the ocean of lumber, but submerged under old records, books, and albums.

'So long as it has all its castors.' Barbara climbed across a trunk to investigate, peered and said, 'Yes. It'll do. Now how do we get it out? Here –' she picked up a pile of albums and handed them back to him, 'stack these by the door, will you? I'll have to look through those for your mother.'

Her voice was dulled by awkwardness. Suppose Peter woke up to what the old woman had meant?

But Peter had no inkling of his glorious promotion, being overwhelmed by the attic. He looked round it amazed. What sort of life shed such complicated lumber?

He found room for the albums under an antique sewing-machine and began to clear a path for the armchair.

As they were carrying it slowly down the staircase to the hall, Barbara's awkwardness was turning into steady anger against her mother-in-law at the thought of innocence insulted.

'That is my father's chair!'

It was a moment before they looked up, first at each other, then cautiously at the old woman standing at the foot of the stairs with her arm extended towards them, like a prophetess about to curse them.

'Take it back! Take it back! Put it back at once!'

Peter was elsewhere and would come back when he got instructions from Barbara. Seeing him stand like a footman in an English comedy, she thought she might snigger. As it was, her voice, being tremulous, sounded gay.

'We're not going to do it any harm. We're only borrowing it for a play.'

'Heaven knows who, sitting in my father's chair. Take it back at once, do you hear me?'

'It's a very good play,' Barbara said, not knowing what she meant by that. It was a moment when anything one said was absurd. She was about to say the Prescotts were a very old family, but her sense of the ridiculous began to function just in time. 'I've promised it. I can't take it back. We really aren't going to do it any harm.'

They carried the chair two steps farther, the old woman screaming at its approach as if it threatened her safety. 'Do you hear me? Take it back. Take it back!'

Right or wrong? Barbara no longer felt like laughing. These split-second decisions were wearing her down.

She straightened up and said, soberly, 'I think you are wrong. It's something very important. We're doing it for the school. This is just the sort of thing Grandpa would have liked. He would have wanted to help. I know he would. Look how keen he was on that poet Fitzallan. He used to talk to me about him and get me to read him his poems. He loved everything like that . . .'

Barbara stopped because the old woman had turned and was going, looking diminished. Right did prevail, then, but defending it was tiring.

'Whew!' said Peter softly. 'Is she off her head?'

Barbara shrugged. 'Don't let her worry you, will you? I suppose she's taken a dislike to you, now. She might be a bit nasty. Don't mind her.'

'I'll bear up,' said Peter, yet he was frightened and didn't know why. They shouldn't put up with her, he thought, refusing to admit there was no alternative.

It was time to start dinner when Peter left. While Barbara was working in the kitchen she heard the front door open and welcomed Robert with enthusiasm, though she would not see him yet. He spent the time before dinner making conversation with his mother over sherry.

Barbara turned down the heat under the saucepans and went to join them for ten minutes before she served the dinner.

Robert was standing by the fireplace, smiling politely at his mother, who was saying in a sobbing, confidential tone, 'I've known a lot of people with eyes that colour and they've always been terrible liars.'

Now, Robert, you know what she's like. Unmasked. Caught.

Robert's smile did not change.

Barbara stopped at the door, thinking, that isn't Robert. It's somebody else. She felt as if a solid, comfortable brick house had sunk into the ground and left no trace.

Robert saw her then and his smile came to life. He poured a glass of sherry from the decanter on the mantelpiece and brought it to her as she came in.

Perhaps they hadn't been talking about her. But then, the look on the old woman, addled, defiant, settling now into complacency, since Robert had said nothing.

Barbara began to feel angry. Her anger, which expressed itself during dinner in exquisite table-manners and brief, courteous replies, ran to nothing on the smooth shore of Robert's innocence, and was replaced by her earlier bewilderment, which was more depressing.

They all watched television until bedtime. I mustn't let it pass in silence, she thought. I'll wait till we get upstairs.

On the way upstairs, Robert, walking behind her, took her by the waist and kissed her between the shoulder-blades, a customary signal. The tingling, tightening, and shuddering that answered it Barbara had always taken to be signs of true love; she was startled that they all occurred, though love was in abeyance. Her body went galloping off to the stable like an eager horse and took no account of her finer feelings.

It would have been the time to speak to him after they had made love and were lying peacefully side by side. She would not spoil the moment – and, after all, what was she to say? It was nothing, or it was too much. Was your mother calling me a liar? The worst of insults. She was a liar, of course, here and there. Who wasn't? Is that what made it such an insult?

She fell asleep and woke to daylight and an infantile wail that struck her ear just as she was adjusting the burden of childlessness to which she woke every morning.

'Robert! Robert!'

Robert hadn't assumed his day-time burdens yet. He said, 'Oh, bugger', in an uncharacteristic tone, got up scowling, put on his dressing-gown, and went gloomily across to his mother's room.

I'll adopt a child, she thought. Naomi's right. I'll talk to Robert about it when he comes back. She lay smiling, creating the parcel of soft flesh and delicate bone that sometimes her arms seemed to conjure out of the air. It could be real. She would belong to it, though it didn't belong to her.

When Robert came back he wandered slowly about in the room as if he was looking for a place to put something down, paused in front of the dressing-table, looked at himself and looked away, frowned, sighed, and said, 'Did you have a bit of trouble with Mother yesterday?'

Show me the day when I don't have trouble with Mother.

'Nothing special.' At least, there was the odd scene . . . I don't like this sort of thing . . .

'Oh, the chair!' she said with relief. 'Grandpa's chair. We were getting it out of the attic – they want to borrow it for the play. She saw us bringing it down the stairs and she did carry on about it. I'd forgotten.'

She saw Robert wince at that and was glad he had got the message that trouble with Mother was a commonplace. It was too early in the day for saintliness.

'Do you have to use it, if it upsets her? Can't you get another one from somewhere?'

She didn't think this time, 'That isn't Robert', though he looked so unlike himself, inglorious, stooped, unbeautiful.

'Was she talking about me last night? People with eyes that colour being terrible liars, was that me?'

She had held onto it too long now. It came out reeking of the resentment it had been steeping in.

The point of amazement in Robert's eyes was like a door opening on light in the far distance. He had not known till now that he could be thought responsible for anything at all that happened within his mother's sphere of influence.

'I never take any notice of what Mother says.'

He had felt that door opening, but it was a nasty cold draught it let in, not light.

'You shouldn't have let her say that, just the same.'

'Oh, you know Mother,' he said vaguely, and the door closed again. Nevertheless, he wore a sad and helpless look. 'She didn't say anything about the chair, actually. She says she wants to go back to Grafton.'

Barbara got out of bed and bent her head over the business of pulling back the sheets.

He burst out, 'The thing is, she says you are hostile to her, darling.'

Barbara continued to make the bed, neatly, in silence.

'I suppose, if it was just the chair, it would be easy enough to get another one, wouldn't it?'

A clear, strange voice came from Barbara's mouth. 'You must tell her that she can't go back to Grafton. If I tell her, she won't believe it. It has to be you.'

'Oh, darling.' He looked completely dejected. 'She's old.' He came and put his lips, begging, against Barbara's cheek. 'I know she's difficult, but . . .' Save my dignity, hide my weakness from me.

139

'I don't suppose it matters about the chair. But I've promised it and it would look silly. Besides, she's probably forgotten about it by now. Someone's calling for it this afternoon and if she doesn't mention it again I'll let them take it, shall I? If she says any more about it. I'll tell them they can't have it.'

'Yes, that's the best way.' They were both trying to make out that everything was settled. Robert made an effort towards communication. 'She'll settle down, love.'

'I wish she could bring herself to have more of a life of her own. She was born here. Her friends can't all be dead. She doesn't seem to want to see anybody.'

'Maybe she will, now that she's getting about more.'

Robert knew better than Barbara what his mother's idea of a life of her own was. She was living it at this moment, to the full.

It was time for his shower. He escaped to the bathroom, concealing relief.

Old Mrs Somers said no more about the chair. All day, she said nothing at all. Brian arrived with one of his pupils after school and loaded the chair onto a station wagon. As she watched them go, Barbara thought, out of what had now become habit, though no easier on that account, 'Right or wrong?' That brought the real cause of her anger to the surface: all this tedious, laborious study of virtue – decide on the right thing and then do it, Naomi had said, and she could hardly have known how much she was asking – all this had been undertaken not for her own survival but simply to be, to remain, good enough for Robert. To be good enough for Robert had been her aim since she had first seen him at the Bankers' Ball, before he had spoken a word to her. She did not have words for her grievance now, but saw clearly that she was asked to practise virtue on his behalf as well as her own, which she had not foreseen. Virtue for its own sake, or for the sake of her own survival, as Naomi had seen it, was meaningless to her. She was alone, and felt the empty spaces of panic close to her feet.

After all, he had married her though his mother didn't want him to. He must have stood up to her then.

That seemed a very respectable attitude, to give way in small things and stand firm when it mattered. The trouble was that after this morning she could no longer imagine Robert standing up to his mother about anything. Yet he had; she must hold onto that. He had stood up to her – when it mattered.

Wondering whether her mother-in-law had resented the removal of the chair, she looked attentively at her when she brought her afternoon tea. She met a look that said nothing but was brighter and steadier than usual, and now remembered having seen the look before, that day. It was fixed on her and she sensed that it remained fixed on her when she walked away. There was hardly anything to be said about it – it could not be called a glare; one could even mistake it for a remote, dreaming look brightened by a secret thought. Still Barbara hoped, uneasily, that she wouldn't keep it up.

CHAPTER TWELVE

Finding himself alone in the staff room with Cathy, Neil turned his back and studied the playground duty roster that was taped to the wall.

'Neil,' she said in a thread of voice to the nape of his neck, 'I don't think we ought to go on like this. We ought to talk things over. I mean, there's no point in being enemies. It's destructive.' She paused, but his silence seemed to draw words from her. 'I suppose we have different attitudes and I don't suppose we can reconcile them, but I think we ought to try. We'd get something out of discussing our differences, some knowledge of ourselves, maybe.'

He didn't answer, and she couldn't stop. Her voice went on, thinned by strain, saying words spun out in a week of obsessive thinking. She wished someone would come in and interrupt her.

'I know I over-reacted and I'm sorry.'

He uttered a sarcastic huff and puff which showed at least that he was listening. Well, the slap was excessive, but the punch on the jaw, being self-defence, was justified. Supported by that thought, she said more steadily, 'It isn't a matter of morals. I'm not against sexual relationships. I just don't put them first, that's all. I'm a person and I'm entitled to my priorities.' Her voice had returned to its thin monotone, creating an insensitive, self-righteous character out of the air she drew into her lungs.

'Well,' – she began to extricate herself by pretending he had answered – 'I still think we ought to talk it over.'

He turned suddenly and gave her a sweet, joyful smile.

'All right. What about tomorrow night?'

'Yes, that would be fine.'

She sounded doubtful, being bewildered by the smile, which seemed excessive. Yet why should he not be pleased? She had apologised, made the approach.

He said gaily, 'OK. See you then. Round about half past seven.'

He went out, leaving the memory of that smile, so unexpected that though she said to herself again, 'Of course he must be pleased, why not?' she found herself repeating that 'Why not?' too often.

She was still thinking it when Brian called her to inspect the garbage tins contrived out of oil-drums.

'What do you think of them? They're too big, aren't they?'

'They look authentic. The proportion's right; that's the main thing.'

143

She gave them such a worried look that he grew bored with his own earnestness.

'Oh, hell. I suppose they'll do. We'll see how they go at rehearsals.'

Cathy thought, a relationship is often stronger for overcoming difficulties at the beginning; and she was reassured, having dimmed with words the excessive brightness of Neil's smile.

The garbage tins, which were too big already, seemed enormous to Brian after they laughed at him. He had to begin the play with a laugh, which he uttered confidently, hearing it clearly in his mind and feeling close to the mild, dogged Clov. At once the garbage tins rang with real laughter. He looked at them sharply and was disconcerted by the blankness of their appearance. Then the lids lifted, one after the other, and the heads of Phil and Barbara appeared.

'I'm sorry,' said Barbara. 'It was funny, not being able to see. It just sounded funny.'

'We are the product of our environment,' said Phil, looking mournful.

Diminished by the scale of the bins and dwindling further from shame, which they tried to cover with droll exaggeration, they looked like two examples of a stylish species of garbage-haunting grub.

Cathy allowed herself to giggle.

After a moment long enough to suppress a smile in, Cec emerged from under the sheet draped over his chair. 'Very difficult, starting cold with a laugh. A laugh is never easy.'

Brian looked silly with astonishment for a moment, then recovered himself.

'There should be a sheet over those bins, too.'

Cathy had meant to change the subject, but, her voice sounding severe, Phil and Barbara hung their heads and disappeared in synchronised motion, a couple of accomplished clowns.

While Cec and Cathy laughed at them gently, Brian stared warily at the bins. Now he was supposed to lift each lid in turn and laugh as he did it.

'I'd leave the laugh this time,' said Cec. 'Just do the actions.'

That was the remark, with the friendly encouraging tone it was made in, that put into Brian's head . . . glimpsed, like a little green man from outer space and dismissed likewise as too improbable for acceptance . . . the notion that he could not act.

Naomi came in after half an hour and introduced the strange idea again.

'Brian,' she called, 'a bit more contrast with Hamm, I think. More resigned, less dramatic.'

But that's what I am doing, he thought, and tried again.

'They have to be opposites, don't they? Or the play loses meaning.'

He was indignant, feeling that the meaning of the play was his special province. Everything he did was wrong, it seemed.

'Tone it down a bit, Brian! Not like that, Brian!'

At last he despaired and began to deliver his lines in a sullen, toneless way that was meant to be a comment on Naomi's nagging.

'Oh, that's it! Exactly right!'

Driving Cathy back to her boarding-house, Brian waited for her to say something about the aggressiveness of Naomi's directing, but she did not. He thought of complaining, decided that would be undignified, and grumbled, 'I hope that pair are going to take the play seriously.'

'Phil and Barbara? I'm sure they will. I think they'll be marvellous. I didn't realise, you know, how visually funny the play is. I'd got carried away by the sadness of it. It shows you the value of a performance, doesn't it?'

Just the same, I hope they don't do too much clowning. It would destroy the balance.'

'Oh, they won't. Naomi will watch it.'

Her blind trust in Naomi jarred him. He let her out in front of the boarding-house and drove home feeling he had swallowed a small stone which wouldn't go down.

Cathy walked along the veranda past Marlene, who was sitting with a boy on the sofa just beyond the light that fell from the sitting-room window.

'No kisses at the gate tonight?'

Sheltered in the curve of the boy's body she spoke out of a cave of warmth and security, searching Cathy out and finding her sitting pierced with misery on a rock beside the river.

'No, no luck tonight.'

Marlene laughed, but not, Cathy thought, at her joke. No wonder they didn't like her. She didn't speak their language, and when she tried they were quick to detect the artificiality of the imitation.

Naomi said to Barbara, as they walked home together, 'Oh, dear. It was a mistake. I've enjoyed that drama group so much, and I knew that as soon as we tried anything serious it would be done for.'

'You are a pessimist, Naomi. How can it be done for? It will just go on for longer, because we're not doing the readings while we rehearse.'

In the face of this unexpected sharpness, Naomi kept to herself her opinion that Brian would leave as soon as *Endgame* was over. To her the end of the drama group would be such a calamity that she was glad to shelve the idea.

'The atmosphere changes. Speaking of which, is it very bad in the garbage tin?'

'Not too bad.' Barbara was shocked by her immediate longing to be back there. She had a freakish idea that she was safe there from the steady golden gaze of her mother-in-law. What tricks the mind did play! She was glad nobody could see into hers.

'I suppose it will be different when Phil Truebody goes.' By her tone she conveyed that the difference would mean little to her. 'Cec was saying he's looking for a job in the city.'

'He's getting wittier. He must get wittier as his life gets worse. Though she doesn't seem to be breaking out much, lately.'

'It's the little girl. He's got to make up his mind to put her in a home, I think. That must upset him.'

147

Now Barbara's tone was as sad as Naomi's. Neither of them mentioned his failure as a doctor, for they both felt the disgrace of that misfortune.

For a while their minds followed parallel tracks in sporadic conversation.

'Robert would join if you had a discussion group. He'd like that. But I really couldn't. I'd listen in and get the supper.'

'I wish Jessica would send those photostats. Oh, I had an answer.' Naomi brightened. 'I forgot to tell you. From a Brother Joseph who taught with Fitzallan at the College. I'm going to see him tomorrow. He's staying with Father Mahon at the presbytery. I was beginning to think I wouldn't find a trace.'

'Something always does turn up, you see.'

'I wish you'd change your mind about discussion groups, just the same. The plays are going to run out some time.'

Barbara shook her head and said nothing, closing her lips tight against the idea of intellectual discussion.

CHAPTER THIRTEEN

On Wednesday evenings Mrs Martin was out, which made the atmosphere of the boarding-house more relaxed, but, on the other hand, it made Bonnie and Marlene worse. As she came a little late to the dining-room door, Cathy heard their laughter, which stopped as she came in. They looked quickly at each other, then at their plates, and began to eat neatly and demurely. Before they had finished their curried lamb with rice, Gladys brought in a tray of dessert. She dumped it on the sideboard, exchanged Fred Allen's empty plate for a dish of jelly and blancmange, and went to stand over Bonnie, effusing hostility as she watched her eat.

There were undercurrents, that was clear. Nothing to do with Cathy. That sudden silence when one came in . . . one always imagined . . . but nonsense, it was simply coincidence. Still, she was depressed, feeling that it was dreary and damaging to live on this level.

Marlene raised her head and looked with somnambulist arrogance at Gladys, then said to Bonnie, 'What are you going to wear?'

'Oh, nothing special.' Bonnie shrugged minimally. 'We're only going to the pictures.'

'What's on?'

'Haven't a clue.'

They talked slowly, making a game of keeping Gladys waiting. When their eyes met it was clear in spite of their sober manners that they were riding a secret roundabout of glee.

'I'd wear the pink floral if I was you. You always look nice in that.'

Chewing a mouthful of curried lamb and considering the pink floral, Bonnie laid down her fork. Gladys snatched her plate away. Bonnie looked angrily after the unfinished curry, then with disgust at the jelly and blancmange Gladys put in its place. With an odd little smirk (Who cares? I know what I know.) she began to eat again.

Cathy said to herself, I have to get out of here. One should remember one was a plant, flourishing in some conditions, wilting in others. A vegetable, people said with contempt, and how wrong they were to be contemptuous. Everyone was part vegetable and that was the most sensitive part.

How to find the conditions in which one flourished? That was the problem.

Mr Allen dropped his spoon and fork into his dish with a clang, a signal to Gladys to pour his tea. She poured it and brought it, unoffended. He did not know what an insult that was; he did not know that he had become mineral.

One might come to that.

Gladys handed out cups of tea, collected dirty dishes, and went back to the kitchen.

Cathy looked at her watch. The girls looked at each other and grinned. Why? She drank her tea quickly, glad to get away from the table and back to her room.

There was a tap on the glass panel of one of the double doors leading to the veranda. Expecting Neil, she went to open it and found Gladys, who hustled her inside and said in a low, indignant voice, 'Do you know who that Bonnie is going out with tonight? Your boyfriend, that's who.'

Cathy smiled at her with amusement.

'Oh, no, he can't be. He's coming to see me.'

Gladys sat on the bed, heavily. 'Well, the mean little bastard! What did you do to him? Got across him somehow.'

Cathy sat beside her and began, slowly, to prepare to listen.

'You got to believe me. He's got a date with her. You should hear her crow. Enough to make you sick. What time's he supposed to be coming to see you?'

'Half past seven.' Cathy answered unwillingly, feeling she was endorsing nonsense.

'That figures. She was telling the other one she's got to be ready at twenty to eight. Give you ten minutes of his valuable time and then watch your face when he's off to the pictures with madam. You must have got under his skin, all right. You get out, love.'

'But Gladys . . .'

'You just get out. Don't be here. Go on, leave him a note, get a bit of paper.'

'Oh, no. I couldn't do that.'

Gladys had found a writing-pad in Cathy's brief-case and was looking for a pen. Cathy gave in to this determination and took one out of her hand-bag, still arguing, 'I can't go away, really. I mean, I made the appointment. It looks silly, running away.'

'Oh, you!' Gladys looked at her without respect. 'They'd kill you. They'd finish you off between them. Come on, hurry up.'

Cathy wrote, 'Neil, called away, back soon. Hope you can wait, Cathy.' She handed the note to Gladys, who thrust the edge of the paper between the looking-glass and its frame, then stood back and read it.

'That'll do. Now get out.' She gave Cathy her bag, looked at her, then at the note, left her in the custody of the note and departed, pausing at the door to say, 'You're well rid of that one. Good riddance to bad rubbish, say I.'

Cathy got up, slow and unwilling, feeling she was lending herself to a very sordid view of society. One thing Gladys would never be able to understand: people who took the theatre of the absurd seriously and read Mallarmé in the original didn't waste their time on plots to make others look silly. But there was that smile.

She went along the veranda, down the steps to the path, and out into the street, turning away from the long, low hill that led past Naomi Faulding's place to the river and the bridge. She might meet Neil there. One thing Gladys did understand, very well: she would never stand up to the embarrassing moment. She could see herself, with eyes in pain and a silly smirk fixed on her mouth, an object of ridicule. How mortifying that Gladys could see her so, too!

She wandered, it seemed for a long time, but not for long enough, for as she came back along a side street Neil and Bonnie walked over the crossing, Bonnie's hair glittering, the pink floral glowing under the corner street lamp, both of them wearing a gentle and reserved expression, keepers of the mystery.

Cathy turned and walked away unseen, drinking the long, sour drink of mortification, which puckered her mouth and burnt her stomach.

At a corner she stopped and thought, 'This is rubbish.'

Somewhere, recently, and in strange circumstances, she had heard the voice of love. She could not remember where; she had not recognised it then, but now she knew why it had made her ashamed. She didn't even like Neil. And right up till this evening she had been planning to marry a man she didn't like. Talking herself into it.

Back in her room she rummaged about in her life as if it was a cupboard, examining, setting in order, throwing away: out with false feelings, see what is really there and what can be done with it. It took nerve, seeing what was in the cupboard: loneliness, fear of the future, a depressing romantic history. First Tom, aimed at her daunting, intellectual family, which thrust freedom and equality upon her. (I'll give you something you can't approve of.) False feeling again. No wonder he had left her. The nervousness about sex came from Tom, and explained Grant. No, she had truly loved Grant, remembered with anguish the cosy city life, films, plays, and concerts, the closeness of conversation . . . It explained the length of the affair, their slowness in realising – his wanting to disguise himself, not admitting his own nature, her wanting just what he gave really, but wanting to call it something else. The isolation had begun when Grant had left her for Michael. It had seemed so shameful to lose him to a man. She had dropped friends and avoided familiar places, and the move to the country, which had seemed like a new beginning, had made the isolation permanent.

Timidity, otherwise known as cowardice, was at the bottom of it all. What a coward she was, sitting shivering on a rock, not daring to walk through the bush in the dark, cringing at the table, playing the old-maid schoolteacher to the cues those two fed her!

She had walked through the bush in the dark: courage can be found. Courage is a habit. Cowardice can be cured. She had thought her timidity appealing until she saw the reflection of it in Gladys's charitable, contemptuous eye. Sweet little Cathy. False feeling again.

It had been a long evening's house-cleaning. She went to bed tired, but with her resolution made: she would not yearn to be out of the boarding-house, but would use it as a training ground for social courage. Bonnie and Marlene would do very well to practise on. She must repeat to herself that Bonnie and Marlene did not matter at all. In her life they were expendable.

At breakfast Marlene said to Bonnie, confidentially, 'How was last night?'

'Oh, all right. Very nice, really. The film wasn't much.'

'Something must have been all right. You were in late enough.'

'Oh, well – we had supper after and went for a walk. You know.' Casual and coy.

Your turn, Cathy. Come on, speak up.

It was hopeless. Nothing had changed except the tone she used to herself.

'He's very nice, really. I thought he might be a bit of a stick, being a schoolteacher, you know.'

Mrs Martin neighed over her bacon and eggs.

'Was that Neil you were out with, Bonnie?' Cathy asked in a thin, trembling voice.

What a performance: two out of ten for elocution. Expendable. 'I thought I saw you walking down the street together.'

Bonnie and Marlene looked at her in silent amazement.

'What if it was?' Bonnie asked, prepared for battle.

'Only that, if you're friends with Neil, I'd like you to do me a favour. We had a quarrel, you see, and he won't speak to me. I think I did the wrong thing and I've said I'm sorry, but he won't listen. Put in a word, will you?' She found she was staring at the bottom of the salt-shaker. She had picked it up, stoppered it with her finger, turned it over, without noticing what she was doing. She put it down, quickly. 'It's very awkward, when we work together. A bit childish, too, I think.'

She managed to smile steadily at Bonnie, who looked as if she had been offered too great a variety of dishes and had some fear of poison.

'It's nothing to do with me. I must say I find him very easy to get on with, myself.'

'Oh, yes. I'm sure he'll get over it in time. It's just a bit awkward at the moment.'

Aware of density in the silence as she rolled her napkin and put it into its ring, she looked up and was startled at the degree of resentment in the faces of the three women. It might be that people needed their victims and would not give them up easily.

It would be nice to know how one got to be a victim in the first place. They knew, somehow. Like cows, knowing one is afraid. If she had a manner . . . she thought with envy of the inborn elegance of Barbara Somers, who could clown and make faces and still inspire respect. No woman would ever dare to bully *her*.

CHAPTER FOURTEEN

Advancing into unknown territory, Naomi rang at the presbytery door. It was opened at once by a slight, white-haired, light-eyed man in a long black coat, who gave her a self-possessed smile and said, 'Mrs Faulding?'

Naomi was holding out his letter like an invitation card. 'Brother Joseph? You wrote me a letter.'

'About Roderick Fitzallan. Please come in.'

She walked into a carpeted hall – just like an ordinary house, really: occasional table with bowl of flowers and a few letters ready for posting, one religious picture, the boy Christ with grey-bearded men around him, listening in wonder.

They arrived in a sitting-room: high-polished floor and table, white walls, Indian rugs, more flowers, leather armchairs, a television set, which caused her first surprise, then amusement at her surprise.

'Do sit down.' He settled in the opposite armchair and looked at her with interest. His face would have been pixie-like but for its composed intelligent air.

'It is only by chance that I saw your letter in the *Chronicle*. I happen to be on a visit to Father Mahon. But I taught with Rod Fitzallan many years ago at the College, when we were both young men. What would you like to know about him?'

'Anything, really. You're the first person I've met who actually knew him. Maurice Ellman ... have you heard of him?'

Brother Joseph shook his head.

'He writes, literary criticism mainly, and he lectures. He did a study on Henry Handel Richardson that's rather well known. He wants to write a biography of Fitzallan.'

'Dear me.'

'Yes, if one knew at the time who was going to be famous it would be easier, I know. Anything you can remember about him, the sort of person he was.'

Borrowing, with a sophisticated air, from an alien idiom, he murmured, 'Just that little thing.'

'Yes.' Naomi was jolted. 'Well, if you knew him as well as that, I suppose you could write the book yourself. And it would be a very good one.' She said more carefully, 'If there is anything you could contribute to Maurice Ellman's knowledge of Fitzallan –'

Though you certainly didn't like him, she added silently.

'We taught together at the College here. It wasn't usual, a layman, and, at that time, not a Catholic. But the senior

158

classics master fell ill suddenly, a replacement was needed at once, and he was recommended. He wasn't there long. Brother Anselm became ill at the beginning of the year and Roderick replaced him for two terms, I think – not a whole year, in any case.'

'You remember him well.' It wasn't a question.

'Oh, yes. Two young men among older men.'

'Did he become a Catholic?' Brother Joseph looked somewhat shocked at the question. She reminded him, 'You said, not a Catholic at that time.'

'Oh, so I did. There was some question of his being received into the Church. He was taking instruction, I remember. But he left us rather abruptly, and I don't know the outcome of that.'

'But that's so important, for his work, you know. As an influence.' The look in his eye, though mild, caused her embarrassment. At last she said, 'I admit it's a specialist view.'

His smile forgave her.

'You were friends?'

'Our work threw us together, and we were the same age. Both finding out how difficult it is to love God in one's pupils. I don't suppose Roderick saw it in that light, but our difficulties were the same.' He reflected, decided, and said in a tone of resignation, 'Yes, we were close. And we talked about faith. He was a very unhappy young man when he arrived, in deep spiritual trouble, unable to find a meaning in life, unable to write . . . One is very careful not to proselytise, of course, particularly in those circumstances.'

'Why?' Naomi would have thought it was just the moment.

He would have thought the objections obvious. 'A young man of his type, exposed without any preparatory education to the monastic life, already disgusted with the world . . .' He shook his head.

'Brother Joseph, do you mind if I take some notes?'

'Will they be used in evidence against me?'

His smile was impressive. A pure smile, whatever she meant by that. It asked nothing.

She got out her notebook and her ballpoint, wrote, 'Arrived depressed, thought life meaningless, interest in religion', then looked with inquiry at Brother Joseph.

'The monastic life can seem to offer a refuge from the world.' The smile answered her thought. 'It does not.' Then it's had a lot of misleading publicity, she thought. 'There might be the danger of a false vocation, you see, not merely conversion. I remember the director warned me, though I was aware of the dangers, of course, already, and he was kept away as much as possible from the routine of the religious life. The director was very much aware of his reponsibilities. And, after all, the danger was to me. I was the one who got into difficulties. Don't form any false impressions, please,' he said, with a transient grin, having allowed her just enough time to form one. She must admit it hadn't taken her long. 'Though I sometimes suspected Roderick of an improper interest in Saint Augustine, I doubt that it went as far as sinning in thought.'

She said to herself, he's having me on. But there was a trace of human affection in his voice that brought a touching picture of the two young men talking, and made her feel fond of him.

160

'Mine was an intellectual difficulty.' He thought again. 'There was one truly religious element in Roderick's character. He was troubled by a sense of sin. There were things in his past, I believe, that distressed him deeply – or traits of character he saw in himself that he hated. He was most interested in the concept of grace and the concept of absolution.' Naomi wrote 'sense of sin' in her notebook and reflected that if that was religious she had it too. 'Well, he asked questions and he borrowed books. Of course I congratulated myself that I was bringing his soul to God.'

'But weren't you?'

'It isn't for the instrument to congratulate itself, even if I had been. As it happens, it was the other way about. He was the instrument that tested me.' Naomi closed her notebook. He looked at her with momentary friendship because of that. 'It's not unusual for a young religious to have a crisis of faith, of course. The idea the world promotes, that the religious life is an evasion, a flight from the world, can trouble young people very much. That was not my problem. When Roderick told me of his conversion, with such an absolute lack of humility . . .' His eyes looked with astonishment into memory, seeing some expression of fatuous self-approval. (Here I come, God. Me, Fitzallan.) She folded a smile inwards. 'And saying that he was writing again. As a reason, one gathered. As if one could make bargains with God, as men used to do with the devil.'

Have they given that up? She wouldn't have thought it.

'And thinking God had done rather well out of it,' she ventured. Too daring? No. He smiled.

161

'I see you understand what I'm trying to say. Yes, I looked at that arrogance and I was appalled.' He shook his head. 'Troubled.'

'But you weren't to blame for that.'

'Oh, no. It would have been an equal arrogance to think so. Of course not. But I had come close to him, found so many points in common in our thinking . . . worldly conversation . . . I used to think that meant getting stock-market tips from millionaires.' He talked about himself without any residuum of relish, as if he were somebody else. 'And from thinking his faith corrupt I began to examine my own. It led to quite a crisis. Faith to me . . .' He was silent. He was not going to talk about that. Like one's love life. Amazing that he talked to her about it at all. But then she was hardly there for him at all, and it was a long time ago. 'Eventually I was persuaded to accept the gifts of God in a humbler spirit, and the crisis passed. But Fitzallan, you see . . . there is always some trouble in my mind about him.'

'It's very complicated, isn't it?'

'Infinitely.'

It wasn't all one-sided. She could see him getting Fitzallan in, even if he didn't mean to. He gave one the feeling of being excluded that one got from talking to lovers.

'You know,' she said, 'he was committed already. Just as committed I should think as one is to the religious life.'

'There is one God,' he said factually, then bridged distance with a smile.

'Well, thank you very much.' Naomi got up quickly. 'It's been very interesting. Valuable, too, I'm sure. Maurice Ellman will appreciate it. May I give him your address?'

He saw her out, and she went with relief and some envy, beginning to compose a letter: 'Dear Jessica, I've made my first vicarious contact with Fitzallan. I've just been talking to a small (neat?) urbane (suave?) monk with a great gaunt soul and I'm in the mood for sin. Well, that's what I think till I remember what sins are available – shop-lifting pantyhose from Foster's department store, for instance . . . and the glamour goes. There are sins of pride I never heard of before and have been committing all my life, but they won't do. I must be hardened to that lot. Seriously . . .' Seriously what? She had been close to Fitzallan but had to admit she had liked him better at a distance. Romanticising. 'Fitzallan seems to have been filled with the innocent conceit of genius.'

The bus arriving, she stopped her monologue for fear it showed in her face.

At home she found a thick manila envelope from Jessica in the letterbox. 'Fitzallan day today,' she rejoiced, feeling the beneficial effects of a brief trip abroad.

A thin wad of slippery odoriferous photostats, a boyish uncertain handwriting, a note from Jessica:

Dear Naomi,

Sorry to take so long. I had to go through the lot, but this is all that bears on the stay in Bangoree, I think. No clue to the girl, I'm afraid. If she's still alive, she'd be interesting to hear from. I hope the local gossip turns up something,

Many thanks,
Jessica

163

Now:

Dear Keith,

So the last refuge turned out to be no refuge at all, and here I am, driven out from my chill and musty Eden – no, not driven. Let us be just. Driven by my own nature, no doubt. Well, I left, all at a moment's notice and without the week's sad little paypacket – the luxuries the destitute afford themselves! The weather right on cue sent flaming swords across the sky, to make up for the lack of them elsewhere – the heavens thundered, then opened, I, on my way to town, the most utterly drowned of rats. As usual, Fate sends you mad, then makes you look a damned fool. I was conspicuous, with my shoddy suitcase pulping in the rain, coatless, umbrellaless – but an umbrella can only add to the ridicule of any situation, even a rainstorm – Enough to make the bystander laugh or weep, according to his nature. I came to the river. The sight of so much water, the thought that there was another mile or more to be slogged before I reached the railway station, and the persuasive sucking of my shoes, led me to adopt the water as my element – no, I didn't jump in, as you see, but sat on the bridge, on the top step of an odd little flight of steps leading down to a path along the river.

Naomi, who was enchanted by any letter, no matter how dull, that was not addressed to herself, was hypnotised by Fitzallan's; but at this she surfaced, with a stupid impulse to run to stand at the spot.

164

I let the rain pour over me, and felt a perverse pleasure in it. This sight, of a wet man submitting to rain, had the kind of logic the common man finds curious. I was hailed by one of the species, who climbed the steps then and invited me, simply, to come in out of the rain. A lordly invitation this turned out to be. Maecenas is enchanted at having fished a poet out of the rain – no alas! I was not recognised. My fame has not spread so far. Needing something to give me countenance, you understand, and counteract my wet, bedraggled appearance, I dragged my little book out of my pocket. Nothing could have worked a stronger charm.

I am installed now in a room over the family boat-house – not quite what we offer the most distinguished guests. The faint rotten smell that rises from below speaks sadly of the world's corruption and the clunk of the water adds its note of melancholy, which suits my mood fairly well.

As for the family of Maecenas – I am only too clearly Father's protégé and a cause for resentment. He, quite cock-a-hoop at intervening between poetry and pneumonia, haunts me rather, in the hope, I suppose, that I am gestating a masterpiece to which he will stand godfather. He is somewhat comic in his innocent enthusiasm, an odd sort of good fairy, tall and lean, with a cuneiform face, skin stretched over bone, faintly intrusive teeth and two blue marbles rolling in delight at his own adventurousness.

I sing for my supper, or listen rather, providing responses to literary chat of an unsophisticated nature.

Any prospect of rescuing me from my perch over the running water will receive my earnest consideration, believe me. Otherwise here I stay, unwilling – yes, I feel so defeated – to face the bleak unyielding town. Mail reaches me c/– Dutton, 62 John Street, Bangoree.

No surprise, that. Naomi had been hoping poor Maecenas was not Robert's grandfather, but in vain. A faint rotten smell rising from the letter, too, and the worst of it not the contempt for Maecenas but the picture of Fitzallan sitting in the rain, contemptuous of self. The weakness in the wall, through which death enters.

'You're not like that at all.' Angrily she addressed the photograph on the jacket of the book lying beside her. A good quality stare, meant to last, those eyes looking so intently at the camera seeking any pair of eyes that came their way. Her own, for example.

She was annoyed with him for putting her in an embarrassing position with Robert and Barbara, and also . . . she had been looking for someone to admire. Emotional undernourishment turned her into a perpetual scavenger.

She began the next letter:

14.ix.1932

Dear Keith,

Thanks for the kind offer, but I've settled down for the moment. Freedom – one breathes it in. If one has only a brief spell of it between one rotten tyrannous little job and the next, at least one remembers its existence, and that's something. The whole of my duty is to play a game

166

of chess after dinner with Maecenas. He plays very well and is revealing himself as a person of interest.

There are disagreeables, of course. It's all in the teeth of Maecenas's consort, who makes me feel her disapproval. Being set on downgrading me socially, she refused to send the servant across with my dinner. The alternative was to present myself at the kitchen door. From a little chippy, gleeful at the opportunity to throw a stone: 'Mrs Dutton says you're to come and fetch your own tray in future because us servants have got our work to do.'

We parasites have our pride. I found the old fellow in his study and said I was leaving. He dealt with that, sent for the girl – you can't tell whether the light in his eyes is good humour or anger. Money is his armour. Of course he tipped the girl, but not in front of me. Understanding the pride of parasites, he followed her out. I like that.

He's not so simple as he appeared at first. Cheerful and innocent, but it's a hardened innocence, an obstinate cheerfulness, and all based on a pleasing self-interest. He likes his game of chess in the evenings, and he means to have it.

There's a bit of guerilla warfare from the other side, but what the hell? Society has turned the writer into a parasite. I want time to think, and I want to be by myself for a while, so here I stay, for the moment.

Thanks for the effort with the book.

Yours,

Rod

The rest of the photostats were of undated notes.

Dear K,

New Age can have this if they want it. No chance of getting any money out of them, I suppose?

> I thought not.
> More later.
> Rod

Dear K,

Could you send me some books? Anything you've read and liked lately. Mr D's library displays too much simple faith in the human intellect.

Sorry I'm taciturn. I've started to work. It's an odd experience living with water running through one's sleep, like being on an unending voyage to nowhere . . . Well, yes, I suppose one is, at that. It's getting into my verse, as you see. That and other things.

> Yours,
> Rod

Dear K,

Sorry I didn't answer your last-but-one letter. Yes, you're right. I am hammering out a fairly sizeable thing. It's making me tense and irritable. Solitude is eroding, too. People kindly taking me up. I can hardly stand it.

> Bear with me.
> Rod

Dear K,

Thanks for the clippings. Not bad I think. Anyhow it's something to be reviewed at all. There's been a great roar of silence everywhere else, so thanks for your efforts.

Enclosed, a thing or two, perhaps a little better than I've done before. If E.M. asks and you think they're worth it, show them to him, will you? Perhaps even if he doesn't ask.

I am uncommunicative, as you say. Sorry. I can't help it. Can you imagine what it might be like to walk into a world of one's own creation? I can't reduce it to the terms of talk, at least not in letters. I'll tell you all about it some day.

Rod

Naomi would have liked to go directly to Barbara and ask to see the room over the boathouse, but she resolved, for the sake of her reputation, to conceal her juvenile enthusiasm.

When Peter came home at four o'clock the photostats were still on the table. Naomi looked up from her book, but casually, omitting for once to take his emotional temperature with her first glance. He found that a relief.

'No charring today?'

'Barbara's out at some do. I could have started on the ironwork on the balcony, but I thought I'd come home. As it's Wednesday. You're looking bright, Mum.'

'I've had an interesting day.' She got up to make the tea and nodded towards the table. 'Fitzallan's letters came. And this morning I went to see Brother Joseph – that was interesting, too, in a way.'

Though he was not very interested in Fitzallan, Peter went, from politeness, to look through the photostats, causing Naomi some regret. She didn't mind his indifference but didn't want him to handle the photostats indifferently.

There was something of the sadness of death in them as they tumbled in uncaring hands.

'He lived at Barbara's, in the room above the boatshed.'

'Is that right? Not a very nice character, is he? All this bitchy stuff about the old man.'

'Oh, I know. And all those pretty poems.' Naomi connected the phrases with a sigh.

'Who was this old man? Robert's grandfather?'

'That's right. And it was Robert's grandmother who was so nasty about dinner. And the old lady is their daughter. She must have heard of him, surely, even if it was only complaints from her mother. I'll have a go at her this evening. Old people's memories are so exasperating – when you know there's something there that you want, and it seems so important to you that you can't believe they've forgotten.' She frowned. 'I suppose I can't complain, seeing what my own is like.'

She was astonished when Peter said, 'Stop that, Mum. Stop sniping at yourself.'

'Do I do that?'

'You never stop. You're not that much worse than everyone else.'

Since she thought herself better than most people and had no doubt that Peter knew it, Naomi laughed.

'*Touché*.' She translated into his idiom: 'I'll pay that one.' Peter grinned, warmed by pride.

'Is it all right if I go and stay with Rick for the holidays?'

'Sure.' But her face tightened.

'I've got the money.' His tone was amused, reassuring. 'Most of it, anyhow.'

'I can manage a few dollars.' Did she talk so much about money?

'Great.'

He got a history textbook out of his brief-case, opened it, and withdrew from social life.

Naomi walked through the Somers house and paused at the door of the living-room to enjoy a comic scene. Robert and Barbara, side by side in armchairs, were peacefully repeating a melancholy, eccentric dialogue out of *Endgame,* Robert reading from the script while Barbara, leaning back with her eyes closed, tested her memory of the lines. They were unaware of the old woman, who had put down her copy of the *Women's Weekly,* laid her reading glasses on it, and was staring at them with disbelieving anger but was kept from interrupting by a feeling also plain on her face – that the enemy was unknown and unknowable.

Naomi allowed herself a moment to savour the old woman's frustration, then tapped sharply at the door-jamb and came in.

'Sorry to break it up. We could use you, Robert.'

'I'd enjoy it, too.' Robert got up and pushed the armchair towards Naomi. 'I haven't done any serious reading in years.'

At the words 'serious reading' the old woman uttered a long metrical hiss of disgust, to which Robert paid the tribute of silent attention without looking in her direction. He smiled then at the papers Naomi was carrying. 'You've brought Fitzallan's letters.'

'So I have.' She handed them over. 'I don't know what you'll think of them. Of him. He lived here. In this house. Well, in the room over the boatshed.'

Robert and Barbara greeted this with cries of joyful astonishment. Even the old woman lost her bad-tempered expression, and looked strangely meek and stupid without it.

'Give! Give!' Barbara took the letters. Robert came to sit on the arm of her chair and read over her shoulder.

As from outer darkness, Naomi looked into the shared, lighted room of love.

'He doesn't come through as a very noble character, I'm afraid. You might think . . . Oh, never mind. Read it for yourselves.'

They read with murmured annotations. 'Yes, I see what you mean . . . Oh, dear me, poor Grandpa . . . But you can understand . . . Nobody likes taking charity, and Fitzallan . . . Robert, where's the key of that room, do you remember?'

Robert explained to Naomi. 'We've kept it locked for years.' His eyebrows caricatured condemnation. 'People were using it for immoral purposes.'

'Spoil-sport.'

The old woman registered disapproval of the word, but uncertainly, as if anger was a wrap she had dropped and was groping for. Perhaps she knew of no other way of communicating.

'He's rather bitchy about your grandmother,' said Barbara, 'but I can't help seeing her point of view.'

'You'll be interested in this, Mother. Would you like me to read it to you?'

'I'm quite capable of reading for myself, thank you.'
She put on her reading glasses but returned instead to the
Women's Weekly. Robert took the letter to her, laying it
on the open page with a pleasant smile, as if she had asked
for it nicely. 'There you are, then.'

That would drive Naomi mad, to be for ever snap-
ping at people who never snapped back. In fact, Robert
seemed to be translating what his mother said into another
language before he took notice of it. But Naomi was not
going to begin pitying her. It was a rare enough pleasure,
meeting someone one could dislike with a clear conscience.

'Could it be in one of the drawers of Grandpa's desk?
The key?' Robert reminded Barbara, who looked abstracted.

The old woman had begun to read the letter, after all.
She looked up from it and said, 'It's not there. If it was,
I should have found it.'

'Do you remember him, Mother?' Robert tried to
sound careless.

'This is 1932. I was in Grafton then. Your brother
Lionel was a baby.'

Surprise kept Robert quite still for a moment. 'I thought
Lionel was born here.'

'I must be expected to know where my own children
were born.'

'Of course.' Robert looked puzzled still.

Barbara got up and began to search in the drawers
of the sideboard. The words 'a hardened innocence, an
obstinate cheerfulness' had conjured the old face with its
thickened eyes, its shell of rosy brittle skin, and herself
saying, half-sobbing with anger and sadness, 'I'll still

173

come and see you, even if I don't marry Robert.' Talking to him for relief, as if he were a doll or a baby. She had not doubted his understanding but thought him so remote from the matter of her marriage that she could talk to him like that. Then she had been astonished when the doll spoke. 'Why shouldn't you marry Robert? Do you want to?' So she had told him the story forgotten till now: postponements, disappointments and now this last difficulty: Mrs Somers's doctor was referring her to a heart specialist and they must put off the wedding till the decision was known. 'If we're putting it off at this late date, Robert, we might as well give it up altogether.' But she knew she should have delivered her ultimatum over something less serious than his mother's health, for she had seen Robert look with desolate eyes into a future without her. Faces: the old man nodding with the peaceful, decisive look Fitzallan's words had preserved, Robert looking wretched and helpless. It was the old man who had fixed it, after all. She had only wanted to believe that it was Robert.

She pushed the drawer shut. 'It's not here. Mother, don't you remember anything about him at all? Even if you weren't here, you must have got letters from your mother. She would have said something about him, surely.'

She sounded fretful, as if Fitzallan had been mislaid like the key of his room.

The old woman had put the letters aside and returned to the *Women's Weekly*. She looked up from it grudgingly.

'Well, she might have. It wouldn't have meant much to me. He used to pick up some very funny people.' Talking, she grew angry and became herself again. 'It was a great worry to my mother, apart from the inconvenience of getting meals for all the hangers-on he used to bring in. She used to say it would be his fault if we were all murdered in our beds. If he did bring this fellow in, it wouldn't be the first or the last. I couldn't be expected to remember.'

Having disposed of impertinence, she began to read again. They looked at her, disappointed, wishing they could tap at her mind till they found the concealed spring that opened memory's door.

'What's in the room?' Naomi asked.

'Nothing much. It's just furnished, that's all. The houseman used to sleep there.'

'Do you want to bring it in to the lecture, that he lived here?'

'I don't know. What do you think?'

'I'd wait to see if anyone was really interested, I think.'

'Oh, the lecture . . . Mrs Braddon wants us to put it off for a week. She wants to have it when the regional director is here – the eleventh. Is that all right with you?'

'I don't mind. It'll give more leeway with the colour slides. That's school holidays, isn't it?'

'There's only the headmaster's wife – she's no loss, really. And Judith Milson. She won't care.'

Anticlimax had made them listless.

'What about a drink?' Robert got up. 'Whisky and soda, Naomi? What about you, Mother?'

'I won't have a *drink,* thank you, Robert. Just a little Barcardi and coke.'

Naomi had been thinking that Robert and Barbara should have persisted longer with the old woman, but

175

hearing this said with righteous serenity, she absolved them and accepted her own sinful alcoholic drink with resignation.

'The key will turn up.' Robert's tone was apologetic. 'And if it doesn't, we'll get Bob Liggett in to open the door.'

A sharp rustle of annoyance from the *Women's Weekly* made them leave the subject of Fitzallan for the evening.

CHAPTER FIFTEEN

In the lounge-room Mrs Martin and Bonnie sat facing each other across a card table. Bonnie was splendid in her evening make-up and a new dress printed in tawny colours, yet she looked childlike, wearing the respectful and attentive air of a little girl receiving her Sunday-school prize. Mrs Martin, her usual look of ferocious good-humour subdued by respect for mystery and her own intuition, was reading Bonnie's fortune in the cards she was dealing.

'A journey,' she murmured, laying a card beside the queen of diamonds. She frowned at the next one. 'A disappointment. I see a disappointment.' She put the card down regretfully.

'Any romance?' Marlene, sprawled on the settee, looked up from the magazine in which she was rummaging impatiently.

177

'Oh, it'll be along.' Grinning, Mrs Martin looked ferocious again. 'He'll turn up, never fear.'

Bonnie smiled downwards, Marlene looked sidelong at Cathy, who met the look openly with a threadbare smile. Like Bonnie, she was ready to go out, and sat nursing her hand-bag and the script of *Endgame*. She had chosen to wait for Brian in the lounge, being determined to face the moment when Neil came to call for Bonnie.

'And here he is!' Triumphant, Mrs Martin uncovered the jack of clubs. 'Here's your lover. Tall, dark, and handsome. Medium dark with grey eyes, that is.'

Bonnie looked demure. 'That'll do nicely.'

'Ah! There are difficulties between.' Mrs Martin nodded knowingly at the queen of clubs. 'There is a jealous woman close to both of you.'

Marlene giggled sharply. Cathy came boldly to look at the cards. 'It can't be me. I'm a heart; medium dark with grey eyes. That must be Marlene. Are you jealous of Bonnie, Marlene?'

Marlene popped indignation like a goldfish.

Mrs Martin said, 'She's got no cause', with an ill-natured emphasis. She was angry at having betrayed the cards, and to no purpose, since Cathy was so smart.

'Maybe she'd like to be a diamond.' That would be envy, not jealousy, she told herself conscientiously, but if she aimed too high she would get nothing out at all. 'Would you like to be a blue-eyed blonde, Marlene?' Words came easier than manner, stolidity and sham innocence being the best she could manage.

Marlene muttered savagely, 'Bloody cheek!'

178

'I thought we were joking. I beg your pardon.' The gate clanked and dragged. Neil or Brian? Heaven send Brian. 'I must say, Bonnie, I'm jealous of your dress. It looks lovely on you.'

Her! The three women looked the message at one another.

Bonnie said to Mrs Martin, 'It's not the colours I usually go for, but a certain person was very keen. We saw it in Foster's window. What do you think?'

'Very nice.' She gathered the cards together as the steps approached.

Neil came in, smiled round him, raised his eyebrows at Cathy, endorsed Bonnie's dress.

'My, you look really something.'

Genuine love shone from his eyes. She was his cream and gold, fresh and sweet, transcendental loaf of bread, though she tended to slide out of his grasp as bread should not.

'Well, if you're happy, I suppose that's the main thing.'

As Bonnie got up with the grace of the secure, Neil looked past her to Cathy.

'Going out?'

She held up the script, sheltering her pinched expression. 'To rehearsal. I'm waiting for Brian to pick me up.'

'What a way to spend an evening!' He smiled at Bonnie, offering her his contempt for Cathy, who was too shocked by what he had said to notice the smile.

'The play is going very well,' she said faintly.

'Oh, that is good.' He spoke kindly and managed to shine like the desired object which he was not.

179

The atmosphere, which had been tense, became bleak after they had left. Marlene wriggled with boredom, put down her magazine, and said, 'Are you going to read my cards?'

Mrs Martin shook her head, jerked it angrily towards Cathy, neatened the pack with a sharp tap on the table, and set it down.

Clearly, they were waiting for Cathy to go, but if she walked out now to wait for Brian on the veranda, the tears she was holding brimming in her eyes would begin to roll. She held up her head and without stirring departed from the scene.

Last Sunday, with a book of Fitzallan's poems and biscuits and cheese for her lunch in a shoulder bag, she had set out to walk upstream along the river, hoping to walk in Fitzallan's footsteps. Just outside the town she had come to a spot where the river widened and ran calm between shelves of dark rock under low striated cliffs: Fitzallan's dark striated document. A charming moment and altogether her own. She had opened the book and read, ceremoniously, sitting on one of the flat rocks near water level:

'We, keeping lovers' time, suppose
Our moment will endure for ever,
Are condescending to the rose
And careless of the sliding river . . .'

She transported herself to that place and concentrated on re-creating the scene. The tears dwindled, neglected.

180

Often she thought, 'If only I had somebody!' Since others did not see into her mind, she did not have to add, 'Not necessarily a lover', but sometimes she did add that. Now it occurred to her that on the rock by the river she had not been quite alone: there was Fitzallan. Thin stuff for a lifetime, but it would do as an antidote to this malice, which was just as impersonal as a writer's love for his reader.

When Brian sounded his car horn outside she got up and said a firm and cheerful good-bye which she noted as her first real social achievement and was happy, though the abrupt howl of the horn reminded her that rehearsals were not the fun the readings used to be.

Brian was gloomy, as she had foreseen. He leant across her to close the door with a grunt of salutation. Brian did not scatter the small change of love as he passed. Humour was his grace, but dread of the rehearsal had knocked the humour out of him.

He was the class fool. The hopeless or too hopeful faces of defeated children presented themselves: Jackie Johns, Maureen Thomas, Derek Fenner. He had no cause to feel guilty towards them, having a sober and responsible love for them as strong as his proud delight in his own children. Some unspoken feeling warned him that to see himself as one of them would destroy that love, which was the best of him. He never should have got himself into this. He thought of past readings with which he had been satisfied – mistakenly, that was clear. Had they read his satisfaction in his face?

Nothing but bloody wounded ego, he snarled at himself. What if he had something real to worry about? His mind sheered away from disaster to Judith or the children. Suppose you were hurt in a car crash, paralysed? He felt somewhat paralysed already.

How much better it would be if he could find the tone they wanted straight away. He never could. At the beginning of each rehearsal his self-confidence returned and misled him. The right tone had to be struck out of his humiliation.

He complained to Cathy, 'I'm sick of this play. I don't think it holds up.'

'Oh, Brian! I see more and more in it, all the time. You're just tired. End of term blues.'

'Maybe I've got too close to it. It was a mistake to take a part. It interferes with the overall view. And the overall view interferes with the part, I suppose,' he added, with a strange laugh.

What had made him do that? Drawing attention.

'That's an interesting idea.' Cathy's tone was unsuspecting. What a wife she would make for someone! Brian grinned to himself, shamefaced, more knowing than she. 'You don't think it's better for actors to have a general insight into the play? Mind you, I think that's how it is with Phil and Barbara. I'm sure they're just having great fun, popping up and down in their garbage tins. They've forgotten what the play is about, if they ever knew. Barbara says she doesn't, anyhow. And they come over so well, don't they?'

Now he found her innocence excessive.

'Oh, they're full of verve,' he said, and fell silent.

*

182

As Cec drove down the western hill, he said, 'About the school holidays. How are you going to manage when the kindergarten shuts?'

'I haven't focused on that yet.' Focusing on it now, Phil sounded harried.

'Beth and her husband are coming to stay with us, you know. Do you think Linda might be able to play with Phoebe? She's two and a half.'

'You are all very kind.' He spoke in a strained tone he felt to be an insult to the Prescotts, who shared his troubles so willingly. His emotions were in disorder. Sometimes he could talk to Cec about Eleanor without even the discreet embarrassment that expressed itself in jokes; sometimes, as at this moment, he felt such intimate, enveloping disgust that he could have been wearing a second-hand skin.

'Would Eleanor take it badly?'

'It wouldn't matter if she did. The policy is recognition, just now. Mine, that is. Not hers.'

Cec drew and exhaled a sympathetic breath. 'How are things going?'

'Now that's a question. I'm wondering that myself. On the surface things seem to be better. She's paying a lot of attention to the house and I suppose that's a good sign.' But was it? Punishing floors and skirting-boards, trying to polish brass away. 'And she isn't breaking out, though I suppose she must be drinking. Only I have a feeling that things are really getting worse. I don't know why.'

'Keep it in mind, then, that Laurel could take Linda.'

'I'll take her with me as much as I can. Eleanor mustn't be left with her all day, that's certain. I always did think

183

it was too much for her, but she wouldn't admit it. She was trying to be superhuman. Poor Eleanor.' Speaking of her as if she were dead, he brought the conversation to an end.

When they stopped outside the School of Arts, Barbara Somers was standing beside the Somers car on the other side of the road, teaching the street lamps to shine tenderly. She turned away from Robert at the wheel and started towards them. She never wears blue, he thought, looking, impassive rather than casual, at her white shirt and olive-drab pants. In blue she would be prettier but more commonplace. He felt a wretched, keen excitement, a paper wall away from unimaginable happiness.

His own fault. He had worked at it without knowing what he was letting himself in for, carrying the thought of her about like a plaything in his pocket. My gilt and sapphire worry beads, he said fondly to himself. The words flooded him with unreasonable delight. Now his plaything had sprung full size, was flesh and breath, and had destroyed his peace.

He tightened control of his face and his voice. There were pleasures still, but they depended on Barbara's innocence. When she strained forward from her garbage tin, trying to kiss . . . The whole joy of that was in her not knowing, feeling no constraint. Lucky he had his own garbage tin to hide in.

'Good,' she said to them. 'I'm not the last.'

She came to walk beside him down the corridor past the open door of the library where Naomi was still at work.

Her easy ways with him were marvellous. He felt as if a wild antelope had come to eat out of his hand.

He had it badly.

Brian was standing at the end of the room where they had cleared space for a stage, scowling at the garbage tins, while Cathy studied her script at the table.

'Brian, Cathy,' Barbara said gaily, 'has Naomi told you? She got copies of the Fitzallan letters. And he lived at our house. That is, in the room above the boatshed.'

'Oh, how marvellous!' said Cathy stiffly. Could she really be jealous of Barbara because Fitzallan had lived in the room above her boatshed, before she was born? So it seemed.

'I am annoyed,' said Cec, settling into Hamm's armchair. 'I thought the Prescotts were in the running. We have an attic. I was hoping that it was poet-haunted. Though I must say I was giving up, as my mother couldn't remember anything about him. I wish they had taken him in. I would have felt more cultured.'

Barbara said, astonished, 'I do feel more cultured. I don't know why.'

Brian had stopped scowling. 'What's the room like? Has it been changed since Fitzallan's time?'

'Anticlimax. We can't find the key. The room's been locked for years. Oh, we'll find it. Or get Bob Liggett in to open it.'

She opened her script.

Cec said, 'Brian, will you run through the section with the toy dog before Naomi comes?'

'Do you want me to prompt, Cec?' Cathy looked for the place.

'I'm afraid so. I'm not very sure of it.'

Brian, having grown sensitive, suspected that Cec exaggerated the difficulty he had in learning the part to balance his own troubles with acting. He could not feel grateful.

Naomi came in during the second run through, sat down beside Cathy, and called out, 'Brian . . .' in a strained tone.

'We're only running through for my lines,' said Cec.

It was true. He was being protected. Realising that gave him his worst moment yet.

Naomi had spent a bad night walking barefoot over the stones of the past. For two hours before the library opened, she had searched the files of the *Chronicle* without finding any trace of Fitzallan. She had tired herself further by composing a letter to Jessica in the style of the *Chronicle*'s 'Notes about Town': 'The well-known poet Roderick Fitzallan was not among the many friends assembled to do justice to a handsome repast in honour of the sixtieth birthday of one of our best-known and most popular citizens – he was not responsible for any of the sounds of merriment emanating from the Oddfellows' Hall on the occasion of the twentieth anniversary of the founding of the local branch of the society . . .'

Having begun the letter for amusement and being overtaken half-way by exhaustion, she had driven herself to finish it, thinking as she forced out the lighthearted words, 'One has to make an effort, after all.' An effort, she supposed, to remain herself. Now the print of the script drifted in front of her and she wished she had never got involved with the play.

Phil and Barbara climbed into their garbage tins and settled the lids above them. Cec spread a handkerchief over his face and left the stage to Brian.

Naomi was not going to do battle with Brian tonight. She listened in silence till she began to fear they found her silence odd.

When Barbara and Phil leant towards each other from their garbage tins and talked of Lake Como, she said, 'You make it all sound radiantly worth while, I must say.'

'Oh, it was, it was,' said Phil, dream-voiced.

The silence that followed informed him slowly that some real longing in his voice, truth thrusting through his frivolous tone, had pierced the social surface. Barbara's bodiless head appearing above the rim of the garbage tin wore a mild astonished look. Turning away from her, he saw Naomi staring disagreeably at her script and wished he could sink out of sight. He was sordid, and would become more so, would spend the rest of his life chasing women who reminded him of Barbara, growing older and seedier, a restless wooer turning at last into a shabby old pest. The moment brought him close to Eleanor. The immoderate Truebodys.

Barbara asked, 'Are we overdoing it, Naomi?' Her tone comforted him though he could not read it.

'I don't think so.' Naomi sounded dejected. Her displeasure was for herself and the mischief she had done without meaning it – though she could not even be sure of that. She was not hostile to Phil. Was she hostile to love? 'After all, it's a clown's part. It has to be exaggerated a bit.' The broken-hearted clown. How the emotional clichés did turn up. 'I think you can skip the tailor story, Phil. You're all right on that.'

'Everybody is all right, except me.' Cec without urbanity was a stranger. 'It's the length of this part. I cannot rehearse and study too.' He recovered his equilibrium. 'I request a study break.'

Naomi dropped her script and looked about her. 'What about it, then? Shall we call it off till after the holidays?'

Yes! Yes! Sighing, yawning, stretching, they released themselves from the bondage of the play. Phil and Barbara stood up, he scrambled out and went to help her, Cec tossed his script and caught it, Brian began to smile.

'You won't put off the play, though?' Phil asked.

'No. We'll be right for the second week of term. As Cec says, the rest of you are all right, and he doesn't need any directing.'

'Shall we move the things up to school, then, and start getting the stage ready? That would give me an extra week. I could do with it.' Cathy said to Brian, 'I could get hold of a few Fourth Formers to help.'

'Good idea.'

Phil explained to Naomi, 'I've promised to take over for Grosvenor while he goes on holidays.'

Barbara had leant on his arm and grasped his hand. Now she had let it go and that must be that, for ever.

'What a relief,' Naomi said to Barbara as they walked home. 'We'd have been at each other's throats in a couple of days. And when I think what fun the readings used to be! I hate amateur dramatics.'

And myself. She winced.

'I thought I'd hate it, but I've really enjoyed it. Everyone's been a bit frayed the last couple of weeks, but mostly it's been fun.'

'How are things at home? How's the old lady?'

At Barbara's soft whinny of misery she asked herself whether her question came from true sympathy or from a desire to cause suffering even to Barbara. She thought she must be possessed by a devil.

'Terrible. The old lady . . . Naomi, I know it sounds like nothing, but she stares at me all the time. She doesn't talk, she just stares.'

'Oh, you poor girl! How dreadful!'

Barbara sighed. 'Oh, what a relief! That you think it's dreadful. I thought it might be nothing, something I ought to laugh off. But I might have known you would understand. It doesn't seem so bad, now that somebody else knows. It's like being h-haunted by a b-bloody owl.' She paused and reined in her voice. 'You know, I took your advice.'

'Don't hold that against me, love!'

'No, no. It worked. It was good. I tried so hard always to think what was right and to do it, and it worked. She stopped sneering, and complaining when I went out, and I think she's forgotten all about the hip. Only, she hates me. And she shows it.'

She drooped as she walked, wishing for the shelter of her garbage tin, where no harm could reach her.

'Would there be any point in telling her to cut it out?'

'I don't think so. She doesn't think she has to answer you if she doesn't feel like it.'

189

'She doesn't recognise any social obligations. I've noticed that.' Naomi added, 'I take it this doesn't happen in front of Robert.'

'No.' She spoke desperately. 'I wish that he knew. I don't want him to do anything about it. There isn't anything he could do. I just wish that he knew. The other day, while I was dusting the sitting-room and she was looking at me, I found I was humming a mad little tune – not a tune at all, really.'

'You don't think you could tell Robert?'

Barbara being silent, she looked, to see her shaking her head.

'No wonder Ivy made that trunk call.'

Shaking her head, Barbara had shaken despair away. 'Well, don't let's think about it. What about our lecture? Now that rehearsals are off, we can get down to that.'

'Work.' Naomi uttered a sighing laugh. 'Oh, I'm not complaining. Just thinking that it's the one thing that never fails you.'

Did she mean that love had failed Barbara? Did Barbara understand it so?

'When the poker machine isn't paying,' she said.

That could be an answer.

CHAPTER SIXTEEN

Peter followed Rick up the stairs to the first floor of the old house, to a landing where light and the sound of voices, a little removed, spilled out through a half-open door. They crossed a small empty hallway and went into a crowded room, the source of the noise, ringing with voices and hazy with cigarette smoke that veiled the naked stare of the electric light. At once Peter felt at home there, and uneasy because of the feeling. It seemed the furniture knew something discreditable about him and would speak up any minute. Rick began to make his way among the groups of talkers, holding his flagon of wine high out of their way and visible to a short stout man to whom he waved and who raised a hand in answer. Peter followed, carrying biscuits and cheese. On the other side of the room they reached an open kitchen area. Rick put the flagon on the table, opened a cupboard and found a plate for the food, looked for clean glasses, gave up and washed two used ones from among those on the sink.

Peter stood waiting, investigating the feeling of familiarity, which was growing stronger. The people in the room were dressed as he was: cotton tee-shirts stretched tight across a shelving landscape of pectoral muscles or neat enticing hillocks of breast, jeans that looked (echo of Naomi) as if they had been beaten with stones at the river's edge by primitive washerwomen. The memory of Naomi's voice made him homesick.

It didn't help at all that he was wearing the same clothes. For a long time now he had looked on jeans and tee-shirts as the enemy uniform and wore them like a spy in the ranks, expecting discovery at any moment.

Rick filled their glasses from an open flagon and they moved back into the crowd, looking discreetly for Veronica. That was a sequel to last night's talk, which had gone on until three in the morning, about school, loneliness, and sex. Rick had said, reasonably, 'That school's too small. A small school had advantages and disadvantages. In a big place, we wouldn't have been friends, being in different forms, and then, you can't talk to the teachers the way we used to talk to Brian. I missed that, I can tell you. Christ! that English teacher I had was a bore.' They came back from a discussion of teachers to the topic of Peter's unwanted virginity. 'You'd be mad anyhow to tie yourself up with a Bangoree girl.'

That was a new angle. Peter pictured Fran Dennison, whose charm, which he had taken to be of a modest and subtle kind that was visible only to perceptive observers like

192

himself, had proved to be obvious to everyone, including Stephen Grant. That had settled that.

'Mad to tie yourself up at all.' No prospect of falling into that madness. 'Get to Sydney first.'

Peter had spoken only about his depression at not having a girl, not about his fear of never getting one; but Rick had sensed it and had said, 'Experience is the cure', without saying what it was the cure for.

Now they had arrived at the fringe of a group, where a girl was sitting alone on the carpet in front of the bookshelves.

Rick said, 'Hullo, Veronica.'

She looked up, shifting her weight from one small buttock to the other because of the hardness of the floor, and said, 'Hi!' without smiling. Eyes too close together. Dark hair, a great fall of curls as fine as spills reaching half-way down her beautiful white neck.

'Crowded tonight,' Rick said firmly.

At this she picked up her glass and wriggled sideways to make room. Rick nudged Peter, who sat down beside her, while he remained standing, waiting for the moment to move away and leave them together.

Were they being too obvious? Peter was worried again by the undefined familiarity of the room, which offered a threat to mature and sophisticated conduct.

The girl paid them no attention. She was listening to the conversation which was ruled from the central armchair by a tall, thin man sprawling, head back, one leg stretched out, the other swung over the arm of the chair. A pretty, smooth-haired girl sat on a cushion and used the other arm

193

as a back-rest. He stroked her neck while he talked, mainly with a short-haired, square-faced girl in a long Indian dress sitting cross-legged on a cushion almost at his feet.

'Kerrie is becoming a professional victim,' he said, yawning the idea of sympathy away. 'I have a notion that if she did get out of this lot and move on to an entirely different set of people you'd find her getting right back into the same situation, supporting a drunk, working twelve hours a day, looking after somebody else's children.' He sipped his wine and added, 'Delinquent children.'

The girl in the Indian dress met this with a deeply incised frown. 'But why? Why?'

'Don't ask me to explain. I merely observe. Perhaps she likes to be the object of pity.'

Disappointment added to the weight of Peter's feelings. He looked around him: everyone in the group wore the lively, cosy expression of people talking about somebody else, except for the two speakers; and the slight exaggeration in the man's detachment and in the girl's concern suggested that they were deliberately avoiding that expression.

This was not what he had expected.

'It's a damned expensive pleasure, then.' The girl sounded angry.

'Of course it is. The neurotic satisfactions are the most expensive of them all, aren't they?'

'But how can she move on and leave a four-year-old child? It isn't old enough to be a delinquent, anyhow. Though I must say it's working at it.'

'Oh, they're all delinquents. All four-year-olds.' He shuddered.

194

Secretively, Peter studied Veronica, in order to have a compliment ready to offer. The best thing about her was the shallow secant of underbreast her tee-shirt clung to, but it was too early to mention that. The faults in her face, the close setting of her eyes and the long, pointed chin, were more striking than its charms, which were present but were difficult to isolate. The eyes were a nice colour – the colour of beer; better not mention them at all. The eyebrows were like the wings of a little eagle swooping down to kill – was that too fanciful? He began to panic, feeling that he had been given five minutes to prepare for an important oral exam.

'You know, Evan's got something there. There are people who get the short end of the stick so often you begin to suspect them of grabbing for it.'

'Come into my neurosis, as the fly said to the spider. You think neurosis is a pairing device.'

'Oh, more than that. Look at Mickey's terrible family. Like an insect colony with a corporate soul.'

Indian dress said, 'What about the other half? The bastard? Is he neurotic, too?'

Evan shook his head, with a tremor of silent laughter. 'No, no. That's perfectly healthy behaviour. Exploiting the profitable situation.'

A glade of denim-covered thighs stood between them and the speakers.

'Long live neurosis, then,' said Veronica.

Feeling that the examiner had unfairly changed the topic at the last moment, Peter groped for an answer.

'That's what my mother says.'

Disastrous. It was that bloody refrigerator standing naked over there behind the armchair, next to another bookshelf, like a solid white ghost that knew all about him. My mother says ... Damn and blast Naomi for having something to say about everything.

Veronica appeared to be simply interested. 'Does she? What's her angle?'

'She says it's an advance on original sin, one way or the other.' He tried for the elegant detachment that Evan practised. 'Not that she's a Christian. She doesn't believe in anything so far as I know, except original sin.'

This conversation was going in the wrong direction.

'Those curls,' he said. 'How do you make them?'

'Round my finger, with a tail-comb. It's either that or the world's champion natural Afro. I'm tidy by nature.'

He wanted to say that he liked them, but Veronica had withdrawn her attention. She tilted back her head to look at the faces above her till the group moved on and Evan was revealed, saying, 'Of course, if the bastard and the victim do seek each other out, we'd have to admit that Tom got his signals mixed the first time.'

'That's for sure,' said Indian dress, grinning. 'Bastard met bastard there.'

'Are you a friend of Rick Lodge?' asked Veronica.

'We went to school together.' Neat. A year onto his age, without a lie. He decided to plunge, do or die, on the eyebrows. 'Do you know, your eyebrows are like the wings of a little eagle, just getting ready to swoop.'

Veronica became abstracted again, looked about her, found nothing to hold her attention, looked back at Peter

196

and said, 'Have you heard anything about me?' She watched him with a serious attention against which he found no defence. 'Like that I'm a pushover?'

The skin of his face took fire. She stared into her glass of wine, hesitating, then said without looking at him, 'I'll tell you.'

Peter sat immersed in humiliation, feeling an owlish look settle on his face as the blush faded.

'I was out one night with this character and one thing led to another and he called me a frigid prick-teaser. He'd been getting on my nerves pretty much before that, so I lost my cool and I said to him, "Oh, no I'm not. I go to bed with almost anyone." With a sneer. Satire, you see. I didn't mean a word of it. Well, I meant the message, all right, but not the fact.

'Then all of a sudden, my social life brightened up considerably. The phone rang like it never had before, and I wasn't complaining. Until it dawned on me that I was being type-cast, and I began to think that my friend had been spreading the word. And the thing about that was that I was turning into the very thing he'd called me. It started me thinking about communication in general, because I was the one who'd said it, wasn't I? And I wasn't actually talking to him when I said it. More at him and about him.'

Peter mumbled, 'But couldn't you . . . wasn't there anyone you liked enough . . .?'

'But, you see, the approach was wrong.' She looked at him now. 'The fact being that I'm a . . .' she shielded her mouth with her hand as her lips formed the word 'virgin'.

'Type-cast and miscast. Not at all what you want when you're expecting a pushover.'

That was the truth, all right.

'What gets me is that the opposite news never got out. It makes you think.' Thinking, she wore a cold, settled expression that repelled him. 'Pardon my frankness.' She drank a mouthful of wine. 'I've embarked on a policy of communication. Communication before copulation.' Seeing him wince at the clinical word, she added primly, 'Before in the sense of preference, not of precedence.'

'I don't see that they have to be alternatives.' He hoped he had made up for the wince.

'Ah. It's not as easy as that.' She looked at him directly. 'If I've made a mistake, then I look a great fool.' She meant that kindly. It wasn't she who looked the fool. 'It's a risk we communicators have to take.'

'You didn't make a mistake,' he answered, glum and awkward, but steady.

She smiled at him. Her smile was beautiful.

'Well, thanks for telling me. Maybe I'd better wear a badge. Virgin's Club.'

'But you wouldn't want to be a life member.' He supported himself with a gulp of the wine, which he didn't like.

'That's how things are heading,' she said sadly. 'Unless I go back and throw myself at the feet of rotter number one. Might cause him some remorse. I doubt it. That character wouldn't know remorse if it bit him.'

'That's what remorse does do. Bites.'

By the tightening of irritation on Veronica's face he saw that she knew that and had chosen the word deliberately. She smoothed her expression quickly.

'What do you do? Tell me about yourself, as they say.'

'I'm just down spending the holidays with Rick. I don't live in Sydney. I was born here, but we moved to the country years ago. This is the first time I've been back.'

Another group walked past, causing them to cower against the bookshelves. It was private enough, with conversation clamouring above them, but uncomfortably cramped.

Veronica stood up. 'I want to get out of here. Want to come touristing? Sydney by night. Come and look at the Opera House.'

No wonder she had a bad reputation. She was careless enough of it. He got up too.

'OK. Suits me.'

He looked round for Rick and saw him in a group round the short stout man he had greeted when he came in.

'That's Ken Willis, is it? The one holding forth.'

'That's right. You don't know him?'

'He's Rick's English tutor. I'd better let Rick know we're going.' And let him think . . . he saw again the cold and settled look with which Veronica had said that the opposite news didn't get out, and shame materialised disagreeably in his stomach. He felt compelled to undertake the duties of friendship towards her.

In Rick's group they were talking about censorship.

'It's no use saying you have to draw the line somewhere. That's just what you don't do.'

'But can't you distinguish . . .? I mean, pornography isn't communication, isn't information . . .'

'Oh, come on! Not information! Of course you reject, but you don't reject for other people.'

'Not even . . .'

Peter managed to catch Rick's eye and to indicate Veronica and the door. Rick nodded, expressionless, and they left.

Swinging onto a bus Veronica looked good: slim and easy-moving. It was a relief to him to be out of that room, where he had felt solitary in a crowd. He had made a mistake trying to do two things at once, looking for a girl and a revelation. And what sort of revelation had he been hoping for? That guff about censorship you could hear anywhere. The ones who were really working their minds were talking about somebody else's business.

Riding uptown Veronica was quiet. She dug in the pocket of her jeans for her fare without a look in his direction – that was a relief, a small problem solved. She swung off the bus ahead of him, charming him again with her movement.

'I love it,' she said, looking up at the Opera House. 'You simply can't call it a building. They'll have to coin a word. Come on, enthuse. I want somebody to be enthusiastic about something.' She turned, observed Peter's expression, and relaxed. 'Good. You're doing fine. Come and walk along the broadwalk. That's my favourite thing. The bubble lights like street lamps. As if the water was a street and the ferry was the apotheosis of the bus.' In his mind

200

he saw her wandering solitary, living a lonely life. She led him away to the other side of the pile. At Man-o'-War steps she sat down on the stone edge, dangling her legs, dropped her head forward, curls falling away from her white neck, and began to cry quietly and steadily. Peter, who had been thinking her behaviour odd, now found it coherent. He sat down beside her, put his arm round her, and pulled her close to him for comfort. The air was chilly enough to make the warmth of her body surprising. No romantic excitement. No, that wasn't true. But the romantic excitement was in the dark water and the steps of bread-coloured stone leading down into it, elegantly into nothingness, and Veronica's dark curls falling away like water from her white neck. He thought, I am travelling. I am seeing the world.

Veronica found a tissue in her pocket, smoothed it out, dried her eyes, sniffed and wiped her nose.

'Rage,' she said. 'Helpless fury. Anyhow, thanks for a straight answer.'

Peter thought, accurately, that if he hadn't looked so young and simple she wouldn't have asked him the question.

'My own fault, really. My tongue is hung too close to my brain, or something. He might even have believed what I said.'

'I suppose he would if he had any choice. Rather than believe what you really meant, that he was the last on earth.'

'Mmm.' She looked at him and he saw he had gained ground with her by saying that. 'That's right. Some people have more choice than others about that. I get disagreeable messages loud and clear, myself.'

'I get a few.' She was like a doll's-house with the front off and the interior clearly on view. One might get tired of that, quickly. 'But there may be others that I'm missing.'

'If you never get any, it's time to worry. But then, you wouldn't worry, would you? Wouldn't be the worrying type.' She talked languidly, staring into the water. 'I know one thing, I'm not ready. I don't care if I'm the oldest virgin in Sydney, I'm still not ready. My parents got divorced. It's two years ago, but I'm not over it yet. I wouldn't have reacted the way I did to a civil question except for the divorce. I have to re-educate myself about men. Friends and fellow humans.'

'My parents are divorced, too. I can't remember my father.'

Only a sensation of being carried high and safe, close to a warm, joking voice.

'Gosh! How does that feel?'

'I don't know. Feeling you've missed out on something, I suppose. That's a thing I was thinking of doing while I was in Sydney, going to see my father. But I don't know.'

'Oh, but you must. Of course. There it is, communication. How much of it is just missing? Just not there where it ought to be.'

It was Peter's turn to stare at the black water with the coloured lights spilling oily into it.

'Have you built on it, much? I mean, one would be bound to. Make a dream figure of him. I would have, I know.' She was flustered by his silence. 'Perhaps you wouldn't.'

202

His silence came from wonder that any other human being could guess at the series of heroes, explorers, scholar princes, who had moved in slow procession through his day-dreams. Guess at and accept.

'No, it's not that. Nothing like that,' he said, sounding amused and scandalised. 'But he's never tried to see me, so I don't know.'

'But you can't know why, either. Perhaps your mother . . .'

'Oh, Mum wouldn't stop him. Never. She gave me his address.'

'Well, I think you have to find out. It's better to know.' She added, firm and sombre, 'It's always better to know.' This discovery she had inscribed somewhere. 'Gee, this stone's getting hard. Let's move.'

As they walked, she said, 'My mother told me to leave home so that she wouldn't become dependent on me. And I did.'

'That was pretty terrific of her, I think.'

'Yes, so it was. I don't think she meant it. My mother likes to sound good. I think she wanted me to talk her down. But I didn't. I took her at her word,' she said in a sad, sing-song voice.

People in evening clothes were coming out on to the broadwalk. The play was over. Veronica walked among them, thin and straight in her jeans, her tee-shirt and her thonged sandals, her elegantly dressed head challenging the theatre-goers she did not seem to notice.

'Do you want to go back to Evan's? It's getting pretty late, I suppose.'

'No, I don't care.'

'Come and have coffee at my place. Some of the girls will be up.'

'I have to get back to Rick's place in Glebe.'

'I live in Glebe, too. So does everybody, just about. We'll get you home safe, never fear,' she added, with a humorous protectiveness that had, he feared, a serious basis.

In the bus, he thought how the evening had disappointed his expectations, and was aware of relief rather than disappointment. He had been struck by the phrase Veronica had used: friends and fellow humans. This approach to sex he had had in mind – what was it? An initiation ceremony, a kind of ordeal? There wasn't any thought of friendship or fellowship in it, that was certain.

At least, sitting next to Veronica, he was not alone. That was something. He had no romantic feelings about her, except for a tenderness for that moment of tears, dark water, pale stone, and warm flesh. He thought her odd, over-articulate, bossy, ugly except when she was moving. She was the first girl, though, he had ever thought of talking to straightforwardly, without seeing every remark as a move in a game. That was something. Nothing to get delirious about, but not negligible.

A short fair-haired girl in a dressing-gown was standing at the open refrigerator. She turned a pale, neat, puffy face towards Peter and Veronica and moaned, 'Don't talk to me. Don't say a word. I'm off. Don't stop me.'

'Have a cup of coffee. It'll help you to keep going.' Veronica said to Peter, 'Sarah has a term exam tomorrow.'

204

'I can't afford the time. I'm sorry,' she said to Peter, 'but I have to swot.'

'This is Peter. We were at Evan's and they kept tramping on us, so we left.' Veronica filled the jug and switched it on. 'I'll bring you a cup when it's made.'

'Oh, I don't trust myself,' Sarah moaned, centre stage, and sat down to wait for the coffee, showing how right she was.

'Where's Cheryl?'

'Frank came round after all and she went out with him.'

'After all that!' Veronica grimaced at folly.

'Louise is in, though. Shall I go and get her?'

'Yes, do. A lot of work she's going to do,' she grumbled to Peter. 'And then we have to live through her miseries while she waits for her results. And if she fails . . .' Looking anxious, she got mugs from a shelf, peered into them, scowled, rinsed them under the tap, scowled at the tea-towel and found a clean one in a drawer. 'There's damn all to eat. We should have lifted some of that load of stuff at Evan's, if we had had our wits about us.'

The girl who came back with Sarah was tall and thin. Her body under a long loose cotton dress appeared more pliant than Veronica's. Her hair was dark, her skin was white, and both had a gloss that intensified the good humour of her expression to the point of gaiety. Her dark-rimmed spectacles flashed. She smiled sufficiently, showing small, white, glistening teeth.

The idea of falling in love, as an alternative approach to sex, suggested itself to Peter. Not necessarily with Louise or Veronica. Certainly not with Veronica. No, nothing was

205

certain. The risk, of course . . . exposing oneself to rejection. He could face that. No life if he didn't.

What had the urgency been that had sent him looking for an easy mark, a pushover? That was stupid.

He ate toast, drank coffee, and listened to talk about exams. Finally he trusted them with the truth – that he hadn't done the HSC yet. Nobody snickered at the news that he was still at school, and the sophistication of that impressed him.

'That's the most traumatic of the lot,' Louise said. 'After that, nothing scares you quite so much again.'

He thought he caught in her tone and on her face a tinge of disappointment that he was younger than she, but that was nothing like a snicker. Far from it.

Sarah said, 'Speak for yourself', in a tone of real misery.

At that, Louise and Veronica pounced, lifted her by the elbows, marched her through the door, and closed it after her, both of them looking elegant and epicene. It was at that moment that the phrase 'friends and fellow humans' came alive for him, warmed him and involved him. He didn't know why, but he knew he could never look at girls again as mysterious and beautiful animals to be captured.

He came in without putting on the light, but Rick was awake and switched on his reading lamp.

'Well?'

Peter sat down on the end of the bed, his own being an air mattress on the floor.

'I went to Veronica's place for supper. Have you been in long?'

'No, not long. How was it?'

'Interesting in a way. It was an experience, but not the one I was looking for. We went for a walk and had a look at the Opera House.'

'Christ!' Rick looked a prayer at the ceiling.

'No. It was all right. She's an interesting girl.' He began to pull off his clothes and drop them on the floor. 'That direct approach, I don't think it's for me. I think you miss too much. If it happened to come your way, well, all right. But I don't want to go looking for it.' As he put on his pyjamas, he added, head down, thinking of Louise, 'I think I'll idle along for a while.'

'Fair enough.'

'Shall I put out the light?'

'OK.'

In the darkness, he said, 'There's a nice girl living at Veronica's place.'

'What is it? A commune?'

'Just a small house. Only girls, I think. This girl is sapling type, you know.' He knew it was a foolish luxury to talk about her, yet he went on, 'Something about her and you just can't say what it is.' All light and dark and no colour.

'Dark or fair?'

'Dark.' He admitted it unwillingly, knowing Rick's taste.

'Is she unattached?'

'So far as I know.' Well, good-bye, Louise. He could bear it. He consoled himself by thinking of the abundance and the variety of the female sex.

'What did you think of Evan and his crowd?'

'Oh, I don't know. There were some smart remarks, but what did it all boil down to? Chewing somebody's character to pieces. She ought to leave him and why didn't she? I was a bit disappointed.'

'Mmm. Evan gets some very bitchy moods, but he's brilliant when he's in form.'

'Like last week and next week.' Peter's tone was hollow with pessimism. 'Look, about Veronica . . . She told me about that. The reputation, I mean. She says it's all a lie. It came from a smart crack she made, she said. A fellow got nasty when she knocked him back and called her a prick-teaser and she told him she went to bed with almost anyone, meaning he was the absolute last. She thinks he must have told it around. Seriously.'

'It's a bit hard to believe.'

'It could have been a polite knock-back, I suppose.' The words had come out steadily and the world seemed still to be turning at the same pace. 'But she was pretty convincing. She pinned me down about the reputation, and you could see she was upset.'

'You didn't tell her I told you, did you?'

'She didn't ask me. In fact she was blaming herself. For saying it. She reckons she's hostile to men because her parents got divorced and she's not going to try till she's started seeing them differently.'

'She really said all that?'

'Oh, she talks. That's what she's on about, communication. She's a weird one, but she's interesting. I tell you what . . .'

'Mmm.'

208

'I'm getting to understand Mum a bit better. I mean, in Bangoree she's a bit of an oddball, I have to admit.'

'Don't knock Naomi. I think she's terrific.'

'I'm not knocking her. It's just that, you have to admit, in Bangoree she doesn't exactly fade into the landscape, does she?'

'She wouldn't fade into the landscape anywhere.'

'I can see though . . . You sort of can see where she comes from, and what she was like when she was young.'

'I wouldn't say she'd changed much. You ought to have my parents – I wouldn't mind swopping.'

'That's all very well. I wouldn't mind having the sort of parents I could shrug off with a clear conscience. The trouble with her is that I'm all she's got.'

'Does she say so?'

'No, of course not. But it makes it all the worse when you wake up. And she sort of sweats on me, you know. If I'm miserable, she's miserable. It's a bit of a load to carry. And then, when I think of coming down here and leaving her, I just wish she'd be a bit more selfish, so that I could go and leave her with a clear conscience.'

'She'll never get to be selfish if you stay around.'

'No, I suppose you're right. Oh, she's got friends. I don't know. Sometimes I think I'm having myself on. That really I don't want to come down.' He confessed, 'I'm scared of the city. Don't think I'm a nut. I get this sort of dream sometimes that I'm in the city and it's empty. I keep going from one room to another and I get exhausted, but I can't stop going from room to room and they're all empty. It's damned silly but it gets on my nerves a bit.'

'It can get lonely, I tell you. I'm cheesed off, living here alone. I'm only keeping the flat on hoping you can come in with me next year, but if you can't I'll look for a place in a house.'

'I thought from your letters you were having a marvellous time.'

'Ah. I did for a while, I suppose. Sort of a flash in the pan, that was. I'll tell you all about it one day. What do you think about moving in?'

Peter muttered, 'Money, money, money, money, money.'

'Get a Teachers' College Scholarship. You can live on that.'

'I'm not keen. I'd rather work part time than tie myself up. Be a cleaner. I got a job cleaning at the Somerses'.' He laughed. 'Poor Nao. She nearly flipped.'

'She wouldn't be so conventional.'

'Oh, wouldn't she! Very socially insecure, she is. Too broadminded to complain, but she felt it.' His voice slowed as he struggled against sleep. 'Anyhow, I don't mind cleaning, so I might get onto that contract cleaning stuff.'

'I'll hang onto the flat till I know what you're doing. Good night.'

'Good night.' He yawned, contented. Rick had not replaced him. Girls were fellow humans. And in the city there were inhabited rooms.

CHAPTER SEVENTEEN

Eleanor held fast to her anger. It reminded her of old times, though then she had had things to be angry about with a clear, shining conscience: Vietnam, nuclear tests, pollution, the treatment of Aborigines – and she had had people to share her feeling. She had supposed Phil to be one of them till they had come to Bangoree.

At first she had been angrier still, seeing the Aborigines come to town on Saturdays, in bright clothes, with shrill voices, laughing, quarrelling, despairing, invisible and inaudible, it seemed, to everyone but Eleanor herself. When evening came, some of the women sat on the steps of the Commercial Bank at the corner of River and John streets, talking softly among themselves, falling silent and gazing steadily as she passed. She had smiled once at a young woman who was suckling her baby there, and discovered with dread that she, too, was invisible to them.

Coming home in a rage from a Red Cross meeting she had said to Phil, breathing harshly, 'Jumble sales. Disaster funds. Help for earthquake victims. They don't see the disaster that's all around them. I can't stand it. I have to say something.'

He had answered, 'Wait till I've got a practice, for God's sake', feeling like a victim himself, and guilty as well.

Anger gave her courage, but not enough to act alone. After that, she had played the part of the doctor's wife, as she supposed Bangoree to see it, with a remoteness that alienated the women she met. Then Linda was born and anger became irrelevant. There were no unfortunates on earth to be defended any longer.

Now she found she could be angry without cause, and the feeling supported her. She set her hostility to work against everything around her except Linda: against the housework, which she did furiously, full of borrowed energy; against the brandy bottle, which she used, watched and dominated; against the contemptuous sellers of liquor, whose contempt she outdid with a careless glance; against Phil, radiating a silent enmity that kept him at a distance.

As fuel for anger she had Laurel Prescott and her daughter Beth, who came in the mornings to ask if Linda could come to play with Phoebe. They took it in turns, Laurel with a strained and timid smile on her gentle, fine-boned face, her daughter lustrous with health and youth and reeking of conspiracy.

'Would you like us to take Linda for a while?' In case you get too drunk to look after her.

212

With gracious astonishment, she would consider the offer.

'Why, thank you very much. How kind of you! Perhaps for a little while this afternoon.'

She used them, just the same, if Phil didn't take Linda with him after lunch. Wheeling the child in her stroller, she would ring at their front door and, still with the air of bestowing a favour, say to whoever answered, 'Would you mind taking Linda for a while?'

Then she would set out for the hotel, so enclosed in her cell of anger that she hardly noticed the relief of being without Linda. The constant ball-tossing, doll-dangling, rattle-shaking, and prattling that went with looking after Linda she had learnt to perform mechanically, using the brandy to keep it at a distance from her mind. At the Railway Hotel, the nearest – she no longer concerned herself with appearances – she looked the attendant in the bottle department scornfully in the eye and asked for a bottle of brandy. She did not drink outside the house any longer. By the time she got home she was shaking, suffering badly, had trouble in pouring a short drink and getting it past her chattering teeth. The steadying, tranquillising fire. In a little while she pulled herself together enough to go and fetch Linda.

Then an hour of freedom for drinking, till Phil got home.

One morning she woke up and found that the feeling had grown and possessed her. She felt like an archangel, translucent, glowing with joy and power. When Beth came to

213

the door Linda was fed, washed, and dressed and she was ready to go out herself, though she did not know yet what her plans were.

'I'd be so glad if you would take her for me this morning,' she said to Beth with a genuine whole-hearted smile, and was jarred that it was not returned.

'Of course. Will you come with me, Linda?' Beth offered Linda the smile she had denied to Eleanor, in a manner that seemed disagreeably pointed; but she smiled again, feeling invulnerable, handed over the bag of napkins, and watched them both out of sight.

She took the bus to the Royal Hotel, where the lounge was most comfortable. There she settled herself in an armchair and ordered a brandy and dry. The expression of the waitress, who must see something comic in her manner, trailed a dirty rag across the unshadowed brightness of her mood, but was forgotten at once.

Half-way through the second drink, she thought, 'A day off.' That was it. A day off. She leant against the cushioned back of the chair and relaxed deeply.

The third drink crowded her solitude with lively memories, which gave way to glorious insight. She began to know the enemy, all around her, unrecognised till now. She had not dared to recognise them because she was alone against them. One must be faithful, even though alone. Alone. The word had a sad, proud ring.

Time passed. She did not know how much. Her glass was empty again but the waitress did not come. She stood idle at the bar window and though Eleanor caught her eye she did not move. Another of them.

She stood up with dignity, went down the stairs at a stately pace, went into the Ladies', where she passed a splendid stream of urine, consulted her face, approved of it, combed her hair, and went out full of noble, blind emotion into the street.

The policeman was walking slowly down John Street from the Station. Around him the streets were empty, for her friends had gone. They had ceased to fight, but she would be faithful. The peaceful street heaved with a great melancholy sob as she saw the victor strolling smug and relaxed. Only she was left to bear witness. She would not fail. It was a moment of deep meaning.

Dismayed, Jack Fairley watched her approach, then tried to make sense of what she was saying.

'It isn't over. Whatever you think, it isn't over.'

'Mrs Truebody,' he pleaded, 'take it easy. Don't get worked up. Just take it easy.'

Wasn't that their cry, all over the world? While children were burnt with napalm and the innocent starved in a poisoned landscape?

She shouted, 'Never. I'll never take it easy. Do you hear?'

More words came than she needed, spilling out, offering evidence, leaping from incident to incident, galloping away at last beyond the reach of her mind.

Jack looked about him with furtive horror.

'Mrs Truebody, quiet down a bit. Please.'

She staggered a short dancing step. He put out his hand to steady her and she swung her hand-bag against his chest, then sagged against him following its short heavy flight.

'I think you'd better come and have a sit-down and a nice cup of tea.'

Thanking Christ they were so close to the Station, he seized her by the elbow, hung her bag on her forearm, and guided her along, moving slowly, feeling with the nape of his neck that the whole bloody town was watching him. Have to phone that poor devil doctor. The sergeant would. She was struggling, not enough to get away – didn't even want to get away. Just putting on an act. And abusing the police. 'Pig,' she said to him in a happy voice. 'Tool. Tool of the oppressor.' Not following her reasoning, he took the abuse to be earthier than it was.

'Pull yourself together, Mrs Truebody.' He spoke the name emphatically, like a message.

At last they were in the Station. The sergeant came out from the inner room and looked at them, appalled.

'Mrs Truebody needs to sit down for a bit. Needs a cup of tea.'

They sat her down on the wooden bench and propped her against the wall. She sagged at once into the horizontal and lay, mouth open, eyes shut, legs bent and sprawling, and began to snore quietly, her open mouth still preserving traces of a smile.

'Not my fault. She went for me. She's got some bee in her bonnet about the police.'

'Who hasn't?' The sergeant spoke with absent-minded bitterness while he stared at Eleanor.

'She was hitting me. Hit me with her handbag. And calling me for everything. I had to get her out of sight.'

The sergeant's stare was contemptuous. 'That poor devil!' He went on looking, feeding his disgust and his pity for Phil. She can't stay here. Anyone might come in.'

Their eyes agreed that there was nothing for it but the lock-up. They hauled her, shoes dragging, hands trailing, out of sight of the public, dropped her on the tough, narrow mattress, and let the door clang on her, with satisfaction.

Jack said, wincing, 'What about ringing the doctor?' The sergeant shook his head.

'Not yet. She might come out of it. They say that's how it takes her, she passes out easy and comes to in a couple of hours. Not like a real alky at all.'

'Maybe she isn't an alky. Maybe she's just a drunk.' Now that Jack had shed his burden he felt the need to be cheerful. 'They reckon it's better to be a drunk than an alky because you don't have to go to those meetings.'

He felt dejected, since the sergeant didn't laugh but said gloomily, 'If she comes to and can get home under her own steam, he needn't hear about it at all. Not from us.'

'It's going to give her a bit of a start when she wakes up and finds out where she is.'

'Do her good.'

The sergeant sounded vindictive, not hopeful.

She woke up and saw bars on the low window. 'They got Eleanor.' She heard her name spoken with respectful love by voices far away. 'Eleanor was arrested. They took Eleanor.' The voices moved farther and farther away, into the past, while she slid with panic into the present.

217

She sat up carefully and fixed her gaze on the wall facing her. It was like a dirty, scrawled, age-yellowed page. Panic reared in the distance now like a tidal wave far off. There was a routine for such moments: shut down on all thinking, move with care from object to object. Handbag. On the floor beside her. She opened it: wallet, cheque-book, comb, coin purse. All right, all right, all right.

The time. She looked at her watch. Ten past three. That was all right, wasn't it? No, it wasn't, but she didn't know why. She closed her bag.

At last she had to look at the door. No use trying it. It was a locked door. A door of that nature.

Her concentration failed her. She uttered a loud, high wail and began to tremble, while tears poured down her face.

Footsteps came and the door opened. The Sergeant looked calmly at her face in disarray.

'Do you want me to call you a taxi, Mrs Truebody?' he asked with scalding deference.

Having no voice, she shook her head. She was getting her face under control. The man's contempt was somewhere in the same world as the tidal wave, visible but elsewhere. He stood back and left the doorway free for her. In the face of that contempt, it was no use caring what sort of exit she made. She took her bag, forced herself to her feet, and went.

She walked across to the park, sat down on a bench and slowly and steadily wrote a cheque for eighty dollars. She left the name of the payee blank. She knew now why she had been dismayed at the time: the bank was shut. She stared at the blank line as if she was making up her mind, but she knew what she had to do. She folded the cheque and put it into the side pocket of her bag.

This was harder than buying brandy. She walked down to River Street, suffering in the sunlight, and stopped outside Prescott's Pharmacy. Then she took one deep breath for courage and went in.

Cec was serving a customer. She shook her head at the girl assistant and waited till he was free. Then, fetching a winning smile from far in the past, she said, casual and cheerful, 'Cec, I've missed the bank. Can you change a cheque for me?'

He didn't smile back. That enraged her. People observed no decencies, felt they could walk naked in front of her. He looked seriously at the cheque as if it was a prescription and said tonelessly, 'Of course.'

She had to wipe her hands dry before she could write his name.

Now she had the money and everything else was easy. Another exit: she took a leaf out of their book, and went without saying thank you or good-bye.

At Woolworth's she bought a toothbrush, toothpaste, a pair of thongs, a cotton nightgown, and a fancy paper carry-all to put them in. Then she set off on the long walk to the station.

Sweat covered her like a sheath of thin silk, and she began to feel giddy. At the Railway Hotel she stopped to buy a bottle of brandy and was amused because the girl sold it to her without any sort of comment, sniff, sneer, or secret glance. She had trained them at last, but it was

219

too late. Then she went, dogged and careful, across the street and up the ramp to the station. She sat down in the waiting-room, keeping her eyes fixed on the daylight of the doorway.

Now she was here, she wondered if she had come with the idea of throwing herself under the train. No, because of the paper bag. That was just something in a book.

There were no other passengers yet. She heard a station worker calling to a friend across the line, a cheerful, meaningless crow call.

There was something she had forgotten.

She heard the rattling slide of the ticket window opening but she didn't get up. There was time. For the moment she was tired of looking at eyes.

The thought of something forgotten nagged at her until she had to look in the paper bag and make sure of the bottle of brandy, though she knew it was there and was angry at herself for looking. Outside she heard voices, other passengers arriving, like birds bringing the promise of land to a castaway. She went out then onto the platform, where she saw a middle-aged man and two girls excited and chattering at the journey's promise.

She bought her ticket. 'A single to Sydney, please', pushing the notes across without looking up. Whatever it was she had forgotten, it was too late to worry now. That was almost a cheerful thought.

Her tongue was thick with thirst. She looked at the station bubbler, but the thought of the tepid, gently dribbling water made her feel ill.

A woman arrived, elegant, hatted and gloved, carrying a hatbox. Her husband walked beside her carrying a large case. Eleanor knew them though she could not remember their name. Oh Christ, they must see her in a minute. He set down the suitcase beside his wife and kissed her. She said, 'Don't wait. I can manage.' She waved at him as he left, then looked round the platform.

Here it comes. The woman's glance rested on her, recognised her, did not acknowledge her presence. She was being cut dead.

Oh, the relief. How good to have ceased to exist, to have nothing left to lose.

Then at last the train came.

With a spiteful grin, which seemed to have alighted on her face like a large insect, she pushed past the woman who had cut her, to take possession of an empty compartment. Sitting in a corner seat with her paper bag beside her, she stared out the window at the opposite platform, as if she could by concentration set it sliding past. She was sharply aware of many separate miseries, and besides headache, thirst, tremors and nausea, she felt a sort of physical horror that possessed her like an emotion. Yet her tense excitement had some likeness to joy.

There was a small, cheerful commotion at the door. The two girls were looking for a seat. She turned on them a deliberate lunatic expression which sent them scurrying, gasping, away.

The train began to come to life spasmodically, sending steel arrows through her head, then it vibrated steadily,

221

gathered force, and moved. Once they had left the station, she was filled with a serene joy that quieted her bodily sufferings. The rhythm of the train took the place of thought, while she gazed peacefully at faded paddocks, cows, houses and windmills, gently flattered by the mild afternoon light. That state lasted until she discovered its name, freedom. Then she remembered – it was such a violent mental process that she groaned with pain – what burden she had set down: Linda.

The wave of panic crashed down then and she floundered under it, icy cold. She did not remember at all what she had done with Linda. Was she alone in the house, wandering from room to room looking for the eternal playmate, her giggle changing to a whimper which would change to a scream? How long ago? If she screamed, someone would come. Surely, if she kept on screaming for long, Laurel Prescott would come.

She remembered then the young woman at the door that morning. She had taken Linda to play with her child.

That should have been a relief, but it was no longer possible to feel relief. She began to shout, 'Linda, Linda, Linda', with loud groans between the bouts of shouting. She couldn't stop. Trying to hold her jaws closed with one hand she pushed the door to with the other and struggled with the blinds while her cries forced their way out of her mouth like little living monsters.

Once she had closed the blinds she lay face down on the seat muffling the shouted name against the sharp-smelling plastic. It was a word, not a name. It did not recall a face to her mind.

At last she began to weep because of that, because it was not a name but a word. She went on weeping then, lying limp on the seat in the darkening compartment, shaking with the beat of the train and weeping for her own destruction.

CHAPTER EIGHTEEN

'*We have a confidence that mocks*
The dark striated document,
The sullen statement of the rocks
Declaring us impermanent,'

read Barbara.

Meanwhile the ladies of the Red Cross looked uneasily or with discreet indignation at a colour slide of the rocks that bordered the river opposite the golf course. So close to home! Naomi cast a glance at the screen to make sure it did not show a marihuana plantation or a nude bathing beach.

On the other hand, there was Mrs Foote, the visiting area director, leaning forward, rapt in a moment of self-forgetfulness which might be the very thing the others feared. And Laurel Prescott, with her habitual look of

melancholy melting in repose. Mrs Latter, whose appearance at the lecture had seized Naomi's intestine like a giant
fist, sat at the back of the room looking well fed in mind and
body, showing no emotion. A mixed reception.

When the slide of the island appeared, the ladies had
composed their faces, having grown accustomed to the idea
that one was nowhere safe from poetry.

The willows of the backwater were greeted with smiles
of approval. Sweetly pretty, and besides, in another town.
Naomi desisted from the sharp thoughts with which she was
keeping up her courage, and listened to Barbara reading:

> 'Languid the willows yield to the water's playing,
> Splaying
> Fingers that move in the silent language of meeting,
> Fleeting
> Arabesques, tangle of runes that the water effaces,
> Replaces,
> The line evanescent, the pattern for ever recurrent,
> "The current
> Is writing the story of love," I observed with a sigh.
> In reply
> You assured me that love is a house with four walls,
> and they stand
> Upon land.'

Her turn now. She began the story of Fitzallan's life with
the information that the year he had spent here was one in
his total of twenty-eight, and thought the statement had
some effect. At one moment such deep attention composed

225

the audience that she thought she had worked a miracle. 'Fitzallan's fantasy became a reality,' she had said. 'The girl who in his imagination had walked along the river with him now entered his life and became his lover.' Great wings of silence had folded over the audience. She was elated till she realised they were wondering who the girl had been.

She forgot them, talking about the love poems, in which the river was no longer visible but could be heard and felt as the drive of passion or the movement of time.

'It's a moot point whether one can die of love, but we must at least say if the end of this affair didn't actually kill Fitzallan it was the end of happiness and of achievement for him. Who the girl was who played this part in his life and in his work we don't know, and we need not care. All we know is that the love object proved to be indeed an object – against which he was shattered. His last poem, which Barbara is going to read for you in a moment, is scenic again and resembles superficially the lighthearted poems he wrote before the dream figure became a reality, and entered his life – for his misfortune – but this time the superficiality expresses despair. He died a few years later from tuberculosis, and one of his last letters was to his friend Keith Lincoln, asking him to burn the river poems. But his friend took the view that a man who sincerely wants his work destroyed does it himself, and at last, after many doubts, he published them.'

While Barbara was reading, 'This driftwood once . . .' Naomi looked at the audience. My God, was old Mrs Somers dead? She sat there blank-eyed, shrunken, sag-mouthed.

Barbara read:

'*It jigs along the river, pirouettes,*
Bright as a watersnake and smooth as stone,
Spinning so merrily that one forgets
The life it celebrates is not its own.

It is a fragment that the stream will throw
To whiten like a bone upon the shore
Unknowingly. Since the forgotten blow
Dealt the last mercy, it will feel no more.'

Old Mrs Somers was stirring. She turned her head towards her neighbour, old Mrs Ferris. Had the mention of death shocked her so that it showed in her face? Naomi thought of old age with sudden dread.

Clapping now, a vote of thanks from Mrs Braddon. The audience rose and headed for the dining-room and the reassurance of lamingtons.

Mrs Foote lingered. 'But who,' she asked, 'was the benefactor? Who took him in, do they know?'

It was Barbara's line and Naomi left it to her.

'He lived here. My husband's grandfather took him in. My mother-in-law's father.' She nodded towards the easy chairs where the old women were still sitting. 'He lived in the room over the boatshed behind the house.'

'I told you, Belle,' said Mrs Ferris. 'I knew we knew him. A dark, thin young man with quite a nasty way to him. Very clever, I'm sure. It must be the one. He coached my brothers in Latin, and they used to call him old Fitz.'

227

'That must have been after I went to Grafton.' She spoke as if she had been arguing this point for hours and could stand no more, yet the other persisted.

'We went on a picnic one day. I was sure you were there. I thought you had quite a quarrel with him. Dear me, I'm afraid none of us liked him much. He had such a sarcastic manner. And our parents made us invite him for fear he felt out of things, but we thought he looked down on us. I suppose he did.'

Mrs Somers had now composed her face to an obstinate serenity. 'You must be mixing me up with somebody else. I don't remember him at all.'

Mrs Ferris was disappointed. You have your memories, they said, but it wasn't true. All you had was a glimpse now and then when a door stood ajar, you didn't know why – a word might open it, or an old china vase, there were no rules for that – and you looked through a chink into an old summer for a moment, then the door shut again. For once it had swung wide on a blue day, with armfuls of white cloud and the water twinkling, and Belle's beauty, which no longer caused her pain, being no more to her than the bright daylight that shone on it. Belle was looking calmly at the angry-looking young man as he said, 'I wouldn't have you on my mantelpiece. You might cast a spell just for the hell of it.'

She said, resigned, 'I must have made a mistake.'

Seeing a question on Mrs Foote's face, Naomi asked, 'Did the key turn up? The key to the room?'

'Oh, yes. Just when we had given up. We were going to get Bob Liggett in to open it when Mother found the key.

It was in Grandpa's desk, after all, right at the back of a drawer.'

Mrs Foote assumed a muted social smile as Mrs Braddon fetched her away to the dining-room.

'I'm afraid to go in.' Naomi was almost serious. 'Mrs Latter will sail up and say to me, "Mrs Faulding, do you think some of that verse was quite suitable for a gathering of the Red Cross?"'

Barbara had sat down again. 'I'm not going in until someone else has taken charge of the teapot. We've done our bit. Who is Mrs Latter?'

'A large queenly woman who thinks I'm obsessed with sex. She blames me for all the dirty bits she finds in library books. Fat and straight-backed, with a pretty little head.'

Society was a curious affair. It was clear, as Barbara searched her memory for Mrs Latter, that Naomi had nothing to fear from her in the Somers dining-room. Barbara echoed the thought. 'I wouldn't worry.' Barbara herself, so lacking in confidence at the drama group, was much bolder on her own ground.

In the dining-room Mrs Latter sat alone, eating a lamington with tiny bites, looking dignified but deposed.

Laurel Prescott came up to them. 'Barbara dear, I must go. I shouldn't have come, but I couldn't bear to miss the lecture and I'm so glad I didn't. I've left Linda with Beth and I don't like to be away too long.'

'But where's Eleanor?' They asked the question together, in voices raised by astonishment.

'I thought you knew.' Laurel had lowered hers. 'Eleanor's gone. She's left them.'

'And we know why,' said a humorist near by. 'She got run in, she did. She 'it Jack Fairley over the 'ead wif 'er 'and-bag.'

'Oh, never!'

'It's true, all right. The girl from Vic's office was ordering the lunches in the milk-bar and she saw them.'

'Best thing for him in the long run, I think.'

Laurel addressed the wall in a voice that trembled. 'I don't think we've ever realised what she has had to bear. I've had Linda for less than a week, and with Beth to help me, and Phil taking her whenever he can, I'm exhausted. I know I never realised quite what it was like. If I'd been put in that position, I don't know how I would have turned out.'

Naomi said, 'I don't think I could put up with a mongol child. And I don't think I'd be capable of refusing to, either.'

The humorist cried out, 'I don't really think it's funny. I just don't know how else to take it.'

We think too much, they agreed, of troubles far away, and not enough of those close to hand; yet Eleanor Truebody was not an easy person to help. Barbara asked how Phil meant to cope.

'For the moment, I'm helping. His mother is coming for a fortnight while he takes over for Dr Grosvenor, and she'll be able to help him pack up and settle everything. He has a job to go to in Sydney. Of course the poor little thing has to go to an institution. He can't see it yet, but he'll have to come round to it.'

With a shake of the head which said as clearly as Naomi's cry, 'Oh, poor Phil!' Laurel left them.

*

230

'What a lovely woman Laurel Prescott is!'

This was spoken in a tone of pitying regret that placed Laurel among the world's unfortunates. It seemed to astonish nobody but Naomi.

'Well, I think the Truebodys' troubles are going to bring the Prescotts together again. That's my opinion. What they say, you know, about the ill wind.'

Mrs Braddon, looking proud and puzzled, had brought Mrs Foote back to them.

'Barbara dear, Mrs Foote wants to see that room where the poet you were talking about used to live. Can I take over for you here while you show it to her?'

Barbara said she was delighted, but summoned Naomi with a quick peremptory glance, not knowing to what degree of culture she might be exposed without warning.

They left the others feeding contentedly off cheese-cake and Cec Prescott's love affair, and walked through the chilly, summer-forsaken back garden to the jetty.

'No wonder he got TB.' Barbara, as she climbed the wooden steps above the cold river, was suffering from the anxieties of the hostess, though forty years too late. 'But it isn't bad inside.'

Inside there was the ghost of Fitzallan, more clearly perceptible than they had foreseen. An iron bed, a table and a chair of writing height, and thumb-tacked to the wall two colour plates cut from a magazine. Naomi opened her mouth to say that surely only Fitzallan would have chosen a detail from Botticelli's *Primavera* and *The Bar at the Folies Bergére,* but she found she could not speak. On a shelf above the table there were a few books: Gepp and Haigh's

Latin Dictionary, Hodder and Stoughton, *Exercises in Latin Grammar*, and a little book with an indecipherable name which must have been left out in an ink storm.

'Are they his books, do you suppose?' Mrs Foote, too, sounded subdued.

Barbara answered, 'Oh, I think so. I don't see that they could have belonged to anyone else.'

Naomi opened the dictionary, and found R. Fitzallan written in a childish hand on the flyleaf. She showed it to the others in silence.

Mrs Foote sat down on the naked mattress and patted it with a look of tender amazement. She must sense in the room as the other two did the emanation of solitude, boredom, and intensity of passion, more compelling for the contrast with the scene they had left behind them in the dining-room.

Below them the water nagged quietly at the piles and the boards of the boatshed. 'The unremitting fretting of the bickering water / Captures the senses finally like a passion, / Takes eye and breath and skin, and gives no quarter / To blood or marrow either. It can fashion / Thoughts into stone-shapes wrought on by the river . . .' Naomi had the words in her mind before she had isolated the sound that had prompted them. Now, soft as it was, she was hypnotised by it.

Mrs Foote said, 'I wouldn't give you twopence for bones in catacombs, but to sit here and listen to the same sound he heard . . .'

They did not answer. She had daunted them with her reference to Europe.

232

'Dear me,' she said, 'I was expecting to be bored. Oh, my God, I am sorry.'

'That's all right.' Barbara smiled. 'The poker machine paid. Naomi says that life is a poker machine that pays out just enough to keep you playing.'

'Oh, it paid. Three aces.' Mrs Foote's smile ebbed. 'It didn't pay for Fitzallan, did it? Poor young man. I wonder if he really did die of love? I wonder if one could.'

There was silence while they all consulted memory. Naomi said, 'With complications, maybe.'

'There are always complications.' Mrs Foote stood up.

'He might have had the disease already, and I don't suppose he always got enough to eat. Things were pretty bad in those days.'

'It makes me feel so sad.' Sadness seemed to have attacked Barbara like a sickness. It was unreasonable for the death of a poet forty years ago. The look on her face set them moving towards the door.

'One thing . . .' Mrs Foote resumed her public personality and set them at a little distance with her praise. 'It's good to see you young intellectuals giving to the town, instead of standing aside and feeling superior.'

They were silenced again, but later, drinking sherry in the kitchen after the others had gone, they recalled the remark.

'She called me an intellectual,' said Barbara with wonder.

Naomi outdid her in amazement.

'She called me young.'

They looked at each other and laughed, though they were both thinking of the Truebodys. They were too tired to admit such sadness to their conversation.

233

Once he had passed the shopping centre and turned a corner into a darker suburban street, Peter began to ask of the close-set houses, the corner shop, and the street lamps, a memory they withheld. It gave them a wasteland look that chilled him.

A corny frame of mind: sad light of street lamps, drawn curtains lit from within, the passer-by in the cold evening air. One of life's more worn clichés.

Here was number seventeen, which stirred no memory either, even when he stood on the doormat studying the front door with its inserts of coloured glass that glowed faintly from a light deep inside.

He twisted the doorbell. After a moment the glass brightened and he heard footsteps approaching slowly. When his father opened the door and looked out, doubtfully, Peter saw such gentleness and simplicity in his broad, pale face that he held out his hand to him spontaneously, saying, 'Dad? It's Peter', in a joyful voice, as if he was bringing a rich present.

The news brought little change to his father's face. What appeared showed him at once that the signs of gentleness and simplicity were part of its geography, not of its history. The hair had receded from either side of his firm, suet-coloured forehead, leaving a comic woolly patch that stirred affection; his eyes were dark, soft, and long-fringed; nothing disturbed the tender curve of his mouth above the fat-padded chin. The indifference with which he looked at Peter was shocking.

Peter had dropped his hand to his side and stood observing, too astonished for embarrassment. Slowly an emotion formed, cloud-like. Reluctance. Reluctance to be called upon. Then uneasiness. It took definite form in ill-temper.

'Well, I suppose you'd better come in.'

Speaking, he tried to put a gloss of humour over it, but the ill-temper showed through.

Peter followed him down the long, narrow hall into a kitchen where a plate with gravy marks and a meat bone, a used knife and fork, a milk bottle, a sugar basin, spoon encrusted with hardened sugar, a cup and saucer stained with tea, stood on a tablecloth of quite remarkable dirtiness.

Dirty and cold, that kitchen.

Mum, how could you ever?

'Well, sit down.'

The man had found himself now, had definitely retreated and come to rest in the familiar territory of an old grievance. He wore a confident dourness of expression.

Peter sat. 'I came down to stay with a friend, and I thought I'd come and see you.'

His father nodded, bowing to fate. He sat silent.

Peter wanted to leave him to it, but he found to his dismay that he began to work for him, with the instinct that makes one take up the cripple's burden.

'I'm finishing school this year. I hope I'll be coming down next year to go to university.'

Now you can ask me what I'm going to be.

That didn't occur to his father. A different thought shadowed his face.

'I haven't made up my mind yet which faculty I want. I'd like a profession, I suppose. I'd like to do Arts, but it doesn't lead anywhere.'

While he talked, he read the sulky anxiety in his father's face. Does he really think I want to come and live here?

That stopped him. He made no more efforts. Sitting passive, he felt himself with quiet satisfaction drawing curtains, lowering blinds, retreating, wrapping himself in a shroud of pride, burying himself deep. He knew that his presence caused awkwardness and he was glad of it. He was becoming the image of the man across the table.

After all, he couldn't keep it up. It wasn't even genuine.

He was trying to force his father to speak to him and it wasn't going to work. Incredible as it seemed, his father was prepared to sit in silence, resentful no doubt that Peter wouldn't accept the social burden and leave him his privilege of unresponsiveness. He began to cast uneasy looks in Peter's direction, then to turn his face to the door which led into the backyard, as if relief might come that way.

236

There was a knock at the door. It opened immediately after and a small, plump woman came in.

'Hullo,' she said. 'We've got a visitor. Who's this, then?'

Go on, say it. Use the word.

He didn't. He waited for Peter to speak, then said unwillingly, 'Peter.'

'You mean your boy? Your boy, Peter? Well, no wonder you're struck dumb,' she said bravely. 'What a surprise, eh? And you've come to see your Dad. Isn't that nice?' The word 'nice' was directed, with either severity or desperation, towards Dad, whose obvious gloom caused a slight falling-off of cheerfulness.

Dressed for an outing in her good dark silk and a fur stole, she was like a soft toy made with much care and little skill, her neat features blurred with fat, her thin hair dyed black and waved, her eyebrows drawn neatly in black to match, the nails of her pudgy, crackled hands shaped and polished.

'You won't be wanting to come down to the pub, then,' she said firmly to Dad.

Released from his mean mood, Peter said, 'Don't worry about me. I just dropped in. I'm on my way to a friend's place.'

'Stand up and let's have a look at you. My word, I see the likeness. Can't you see yourself in him, Terry?' Mouth-to-mouth resuscitation. She must be getting desperate. 'You're a big boy, aren't you? The long hair suits you. Some it does and some it doesn't. You've got the features for it.'

Peter had turned slowly under her gaze. Now he bowed, acknowledging the compliment.

237

'Well, I suppose you've got your mother's ways' – that was a remarkable piece of boldness, for which he was grateful – 'but you sure have your father's looks. My name's Nellie – Mrs Thorpe.' She added, nodding indulgently towards his father. 'He'd never think to tell you in a million years.'

She was a glossy little hen, warming a china egg.

'And you haven't washed up yet, either. Why don't you go and get ready and Peter can keep me company while I clear up?'

She opened a drawer and got out a clean tea-towel, which she tied round her waist for an apron. Her position in the household was clear and she made no attempt to hide it. Peter, who had liked her for knowing what his father ought to feel, liked her still more for that.

The man, sitting there with a faint stupid smile on his face, waited until it was clear he was going of his own free will and not at Nellie's request, then got to his feet. Peter hated his lumbering walk, his forward stoop, and the wide rump draped in baggy trousers.

'He's a very shy man, your father,' she murmured. 'I suppose you never let him know you were coming?'

'No, I didn't.' He had meant it to be a joyful surprise.

'Ah. It will have taken him unawares. He never likes that. But he's pleased just the same, never you fear.' She was scraping cold fat from the grill pan with quick strokes of a plastic spatula that did not falter at the lie. 'He doesn't like to show his feelings.'

Doesn't like being put in a position where he ought to be showing feelings he hasn't got. Peter felt sick, then, knowing that Naomi must once have formed exactly that same thought. He pictured himself walking down a dark gravelled lane past back gates and garbage tins and knowing his mother had walked that way before him – a vision that was meaningless but nasty.

Nell knew how he was feeling, all right.

'Why don't you come down to the pub and have a beer with us?' she said, beginning to stack plates on the drying rack.

He fetched the tea-towel from its hook and came to dry the plates, so that he could refuse without offending her.

'I'd better be getting along, I think.'

'He's just shy, you know. If he got used to you . . .'

Fat chance of that.

She saw the anger in his face and refused to yield to it entirely.

'Wait for us, then, and we'll walk a bit of the way together.'

In front of the loud, lighted pub, Nell took his hand and said, 'Well, now you know where we are.'

From his father's face, so blank yet so legible, it was evident that he had reflected and decided that he was entitled to display the cold reserve with which he nodded good-bye.

Good-bye it was, too.

Peter bent to kiss her little marshmallow cheek. It was some kind of demonstration. As he walked away she called after him, 'Come again. Do', allowing herself to sound urgent because she knew that he wouldn't.

An empty drink can glinted on the pavement. He kicked it and it rolled into the gutter, so slowly that he realised he wasn't angry.

What did Nell and his mother see in that great, pale, self-satisfied lump of suet? His silence?

Mystery, he thought. Note to avoid mystery as a sexual attraction. 'My tables – meet it is I set it down . . .'

The histrionic tone of that shocked him sober. He had taken a sharp dislike to *Hamlet* when they had studied the play in Fifth Form – not to the play but to the character – our suffering hero, Brian had called him, with more affection than respect.

Whatever his feelings were, he could not take them onto a bus. In a dim laneway he paused and let each eye discharge its millilitre of tears. He shook and sniffed them away and walked on with a casual air that was almost jaunty.

Since Rick was out, he called on Veronica on the way home. 'A quarter of an hour,' she said, and led him to the kitchen where there were books and papers spread on the table. 'I've got an essay to do. Everyone's out and the light's better in here.'

'I only called to see if you'd help me buy a present for my mother, on Thursday night.' He felt bruised, wondering if there was a welcome anywhere.

'We might as well have a cup of coffee. Yes, I could do that. The essay's due Thursday. That'll be fine.' She looked at him with attention. 'Did you go to see your father?'

Had she guessed by his face? He smoothed it with care.

'Yes, I went.'

With the electric jug in her hand, she stood at the sink, looking and waiting.

'The fatted calf was not killed,' he said, in a tone more discreetly histrionic this time. He had rehearsed it on the way.

She said, reflective, 'There's a lot of crap talked about parents loving children. Sometimes they don't and then they feel guilty because they think they ought. Which prevents them from being decently friendly.'

No doubt she meant to be sympathetic, but when she was observing life she appeared to be peacefully occupied, like a good cook tasting a sauce. It was maddening if one happened to be an ingredient. He was annoyed too that, like Nellie, she made excuses for his father. Why did they overlook the simple fact that he was a self-centred bastard? He waited sulkily for his coffee and as he accepted it said, 'I can't imagine what my mother saw in him.'

Veronica bit her lip and grinned.

'Sorry,' she said to his offended look. 'It's the cliché. I don't blame you for using it, because there are positively no other words for it. But just think, it's been handed down for generations, and the use that it's seen!' She shook her head slightly, curls quivering in a tactful substitute for laughter. 'He was probably pretty good looking, you know. After all, you are.' She offered this amazing information flatly and carelessly.

'Oh, go on.' He had almost choked over a mouthful of coffee. 'Who says so?'

'Louise, for one.' She wasn't looking at his face. That was lucky. Her thoughts were elsewhere, and were sad.

241

'It's frightening, though, how that gets people in. The physical attraction. And people will always marry for it.'

'Better than marrying for your neuroses, the way they were saying at Evan's.'

'That's right. At least it's an even chance. Oh, marriage!' She looked depressed, and he remembered that she had troubles of her own, but he could not share them. Her words were drifting past him, he was trying not to smile.

'I'll be off and let you get on with your essay. What time Thursday, then?'

In the darkness outside he let his great silly grin of pleasure blossom and wore it half-way home.

CHAPTER TWENTY

A chilly wind blew across the platform at Bangoree. Nothing changed here except the weather. Emerging from different compartments, Cathy and Peter looked along the row of Ticket Office, Waiting Room, Ladies, Luggage, Gents, with the same thought and were both conscious of change in themselves.

Cathy called, 'Can I give you a lift, Pete? I'm getting a taxi.' Now she was Miss Bates, English teacher, again, and Peter, saying, 'Thanks, Miss Bates', and picking up her large suitcase, put on his old self, so that they were both aware how much of themselves belonged in the eyes of others.

Passing by, Neil paused beside them.

'Did you have a nice holiday?'

'Splendid, thanks.' That was not altogether true. Still, she smiled cheerfully.

Her new russet slack-suit became her very well; she was wearing, besides, the shining cosmetic of indifference. Though he had not meant to go out tonight, he said, 'Tell Bonnie I'll be round after dinner, will you?'

'Will do.' She nodded, smiling an untouched smile. He thought, 'She has met someone.' The thought enraged him.

The taxi ride passed pleasantly, after all. To Cathy, though Peter was immature, he was not a Sixth-Former, but Naomi's son. She talked about the play and said, as he got out, 'Tell your mother Tuesday night at the school. As soon as she can make it after half past eight. We'll arrange for somebody to pick her up at the library. OK?'

When he got to the door Naomi ran to him, beaming under her built-in scowl like a joyful Scotch terrier, and hugged him, saying with less wit than usual, 'You're home.' He let the idiocy pass, comforted by the greeting, though not remembering why he needed comfort.

He had brought her a pewter pendant on a long chain. She unwrapped it and stared at it silently.

'Well,' he said defensively, 'a girl helped me pick it. Don't you like it?'

'Oh, I like it.'

'Mum, you should see how your face lit up when I said "girl". Like a procuress. You ought to watch that. I told her what you were like and that's what she thought would suit you.'

Naomi put the pendant on, wondering what he had said about her.

'What is she like?'

244

'Veronica? It's not like that, anyhow. She's all right. Not good looking, really, but sort of attractive. She says she's sexually retarded because her parents got a divorce and she got hostile to men, so she wants to learn to be friends . . . she's pretty bright, I think. Mum,' he bellowed suddenly, 'Mum, how could you have done it?'

'Oh, you went then.' She looked daunted.

'Yes, I went.' He breathed deeply and said with disgust, 'What a nothing!'

'Oh, he would have been something. At our expense, he would have been.' She frowned with anguish, looking ferocious. 'He wasn't pleased to see you?'

He answered bitterly, 'I'm not absolutely certain he did see me. I didn't catch him looking.'

'What a desert he must live in!' She shook her head in horror.

'He was frightened I was going to ask if I could come and live with him. Likely!'

'He must have cared, more than he made out. He must have been interested in you.' She shook her head again, rejecting the idea of such indifference.

'You sound just like his girlfriend. That's what she tried to make out. He was interested in me all right, as a threat.'

'You mean as a threat to his indifference. Yes, I see that. But at least you could threaten it, so there must be some feeling there.'

'Oh, what crap! You mean he's got a vague idea of how fathers are supposed to feel, and people are going to pick on him for not feeling the same. Which isn't fair. It's just a great big grievance, that's all.'

'Oh, my dear.' How had he seen all that? It was true, but how could he know it?

'You just can't bring yourself to admit that he doesn't care about me at all, because it's not respectable. That isn't like you, really.'

'I suppose you're right.'

'How did your Fitzallan talk go?'

'What you'd expect. Some of them liked it, some were like fishes out of water. Eleanor Truebody's left Phil. That was the news at afternoon tea.'

'Good riddance, I'd say.'

'That was the general verdict.'

'It was like being dumped in the Antarctic, that's what it was like. The kind of cold you could never imagine.'

'He was crazy about you when you were a baby. Used to carry you about and cuddle you and talk to you for hours on end. As if he was a child and you were a Teddy bear.'

'I kind of remember that.' He withdrew with the thought into silence.

'Maurice Ellman's coming up for a few days. I got a letter from him on Friday, he wants me to book him in to a hotel. We've found someone who knew Fitzallan; the talk did that much at least. An old lady named Ferris. I'll get him to go and see her.'

'Mum, why did you leave him actually?'

'Because of you,' she said faintly. The memory of her husband running at Peter (playful, trusting, three years old), running at him swinging a heavy leather belt, was

246

clear in her mind but incommunicable; disgusting (worse than seeing a strange man with his fly open) yet comic in the way shameful things are comic. If she tried to speak of it she would laugh and never stop, go mad laughing. 'You thought he was joking. He played with you all the time, and then this new note crept in. I didn't realise it myself at first. It was when he'd been drinking, I think, but he never showed that much. There just wasn't any warning. He got this bee in his bonnet about obedience; you would have thought he was training a sheepdog. You were at the No stage, saying No to everything. It was the treachery,' she cried. 'I couldn't bear for you to meet the treachery. I just picked you up and ran.' She rested like a winded runner. 'Look, it must have been the first time he ever had power over anyone. And then you started to be a person, and he couldn't stand that, I think.'

He had listened in a settled silence which he did not seem inclined to break. She got up and began to get the dinner ready, saying as she peeled the potatoes, 'Those genes and chromosomes have been in use for generations. Don't worry about that.'

He said too firmly, 'That sort of thing doesn't worry me. You make your own life.'

During dinner, she said, 'It was terribly hard on you, losing him.' How much of that did he remember? She could not ask. 'I tried to go back. I went to see him.' The killing moment. What a comfort that Peter knew what it was like without being told.

He nodded. 'I can imagine.'

Later she added, 'But you kept the illusion, you see.'

His bleak expression informed her that illusion was not much. Then he cheered up, deliberately. 'Ah, well, look what a splendid specimen I turned out to be.'

That was intended to end the conversation, but it started up of itself, again and again.

'But if he has a girlfriend . . . He must show some feeling.'

'She plays both halves of the dialogue. Funny.' The memory of Nell made him smile, and the smile brought a cheerful thought: worrying about a refrigerator in the sitting-room – a person could be living inside a refrigerator! 'Oh, forget it, Mum. I went and I saw him and I'm not sorry, but that's the end of it.'

'We went into Fitzallan's room. Get Barbara to show it to you. It was quite . . . it has a sort of atmosphere.'

'Yes, I'd like that. Where did you go when you ran out?'

'To Nanna's. Oh, that was ghastly.'

'Nanna was a bit of a cold fish, too, wasn't she?' He was thoughtful.

The remark was searching. Naomi considered her answer while she poured the coffee. 'That's right, I suppose. You're drawn to what's familiar. It seems safer, somehow, even if it doesn't make you happy. Happiness seems just too venturesome. Not for you. So you repeat the pattern.'

'Well, I don't have anything to worry about in that direction.'

That did end the conversation, for Naomi would not speak. She did not want to obscure her memory of what Peter had said.

CHAPTER TWENTY-ONE

Holding an unexpected bouquet and flustered by the enthusiasm of the young people, Naomi stood downstage from the bowing actors and refrained from looking for Peter in the clapping audience. She was conscious she had done him credit – that was enough.

The grown-ups sat at the back. Among them Maurice Ellman was conspicuous, not only for the suede jacket and the coloured silk kerchief at the neck of his cashmere sweater. He was tall and bulky, with a wreath of ginger-brown hair surrounding his plump, large-featured face, inadequately lighted by small dark eyes. 'I loved your letters,' he had said when she met him at the station. But first of all he had said, 'I thought you were an elderly lady.' The eager and matter-of-fact tone, the confident approach suggesting he had come walking into her life, were further reasons for being flustered.

The actors bowed again to the clapping, Barbara and Phil standing up in their garbage tins. Barbara had a bouquet, too, and looked odd cradling it while she watched the audience with an astringent sadness. As the clapping continued, she and Phil looked at each other, he as sad as she, and they sank with a synchronised movement out of sight, leaving the stage to Hamm and Clov. The clapping grew louder. Clov tried to retreat, but Hamm dragged him forward to share the applause.

What a beautiful audience it was: young people laughing and applauding, their flesh as crisp as apple shining against their dark bulky sweaters, hair and skin reflecting more of the dim lighting than did the silver cups and shields and the faded gilt of Honours boards.

The curtain fell. The actors yawned, stretched, climbed out of the skin of their roles and went away to clean off their grease-paint.

At supper in the library, Naomi devoured praise and gratitude with appetite and became elated. She carried a plate of cakes to Maurice Ellman.

'Have a cake. You're in lamington country now, you notice.'

'An extraordinary production,' he said in a tone from which he had tried to exclude astonishment. He had not quite succeeded, but she appreciated the effort. 'He's a professional, surely?' He looked at Cec, who was talking to Cathy at the other end of the room.

There was Neil, on the other side of the room, with that big fair girl from Foster's. Odd.

'A local chemist. But he did a lot of serious amateur stuff when he was a student.'

She returned a wave from Peter as he passed by with two of the girls from the convent.

'My son.' Since he seemed to be looking a question at her, she added. 'I'm divorced. One child.'

She was sorry then she had said it. Why would he be interested?

'Barbara is wonderful, too, isn't she?'

He had taken against Barbara from the first moment, when she had introduced them, saying, 'Barbara is going to look after you and introduce you to a couple of people who might be useful.' One would expect a man to be delighted. Instead, he had closed his petals like a great ginger-brown tulip.

'Yes,' he said without enthusiasm. 'Marvellous timing, that pair. Clov was rather . . .'

'Tss.'

Brian was arriving with the headmaster, who wished to thank Naomi for her work, on behalf of Sixth Form.

'But I have a stake in it,' she said. 'Parents are single-minded.'

There was no need to tell that to the headmaster, of all people. He hoped, just the same, in view of the success of this year's effort, that they might look forward . . .

Brian had taken possession of Maurice and was looking for insights into the works of Beckett. He looked round to say, 'Not for me, I'm afraid. That was positively my last appearance on the stage. I'll have to give up the

251

play-readings, too. Into second term and the work is mounting up.'

'Oh, Brian!' Naomi's cheerfulness was extinguished. 'Phil will be leaving. We won't be able to carry on.'

My own doing, she added to herself, though Brian sounded really regretful.

'Very sorry, but there's no help for it.'

Counting heads, she looked across at Neil, who was still beside the girl from Foster's, and despaired of him. Catching his eye, she smiled kindly.

Neil nodded without smiling. He had brought Bonnie reluctantly, since she had taken it into her head that she wanted to come. Now he was sorry, because everyone was too kind. The headmaster had come and asked Bonnie, kindly, what she thought of the play. Luckily she hadn't told him.

'What crap,' she was saying now, setting a cake-fork elegantly at a slice of cream sponge. 'Imagine wasting your time putting on stuff like that!'

'Well, you would come.' Though he regretted her presence, the happiness of his flesh in being close to her made him smile affectionately. Gawd, but he's handsome. The thought shone for a moment on her face. 'I knew you wouldn't like it.'

Let them smile their kind smiles. The walk home would be worth it.

Naomi apologised to Maurice, when Brian and the head-master had continued on their round. 'They're ferocious exploiters, these educators.'

252

'I think it's to their credit.' His voice was not as deep as his bulk promised. 'I must say – I know it's impertinent to be astonished, but I can't help being astonished at the standard of culture in the town. For the size of the town.'

Naomi decided to tolerate the impertinence. 'It's only just crept up on us. The drama group first, then Brian dragged us into doing the play. Then Fitzallan. We're pretty possessive about him, you'll find. Brian pushes that, too. He thinks it's good for the young people to know that the town has a link with literature.'

'You seem to be very much in the centre of it yourself.'

'But I'm the librarian. Culture's hireling!'

He met this with a look, not of amusement, but of inward satisfaction, as if some small enterprise had turned out well. She feared now and then that he was absurd; but when Robert and Barbara came to fetch them he turned his serious, attentive expression on Robert, saying, 'About your grandfather . . .' Seeing him at work, she was glad to decide he was not absurd at all.

Neil lay with Bonnie on the river-bank in the harsh, cold grass. He kissed her slowly and joyfully, working down from her mouth to her breasts, lingering at the firm, petal-textured neck, but never ceasing to advance. He controlled the harsh breathing of excitement as he felt her relaxing against him, passive but approving. As his hand slid farther down she rolled her thighs away from him, with warm, quiet laughter.

'You just keep that till we're married.'

Chasing the fluorescent, palpitating butterfly that filled the screen of his mind, he moaned, 'When?' He lunged after her, helpless. 'When?'

Bonnie sat up and brushed her dress. In a wakeful tone, she said, 'I'm not in favour of long engagements, are you? What about just after Christmas? Then we'd still have time for a decent honeymoon before you go back to school.'

In the starry darkness, a ghastly daylight was dawning in his brain. No! Oh, no! It was Cathy! Cathy was the one! How had this thing happened?

'We're engaged,' said Bonnie, awed by her own happiness. 'Oh Neil, I am so happy. I do love you so.'

She lay down again and drew him close to her, glad to be able to yield to her own excitement. She kissed his face gently, while he forced himself not to struggle. Under promise of marriage? Never. Besides, the word had made him impotent. He must plan his future: a move – he must get a move, secretly, get away to the city alone – first of all, put off the marriage – write a letter from Sydney.

She wriggled closer to him and held him tight. Christ, if she would only let him go, get away this moment . . .

'Neil?'

'Yes?' He asked heavily, 'What is it?'

'Can we get the ring tomorrow? After school? I'll get an hour off work.'

He said with difficulty, 'What about Friday? I'll have to get to the bank.'

He felt wretched, thinking of his savings and his hopes of travel.

At this worst moment of his unhappiness, he got a vision of Cathy's face as she stood on the station, smiling at him with indifference. He hated her. It was all her fault. She had done this thing to him.

'I'll pick it out tomorrow then and you can pay for it Friday. They've got some lovely diamonds in Reynolds'. Neil?'

She was stroking him. Now her hand slid downwards and she offered a most disturbing caress. He leapt away and said, in a shaky attempt at playfulness, 'You're the one who said to keep that till . . . we're . . .' He turned aside, swallowing the last word, and began to get to his feet. 'Come on, home!' He hoped he sounded gay.

'Funny old thing, you!' Bonnie hid her disappointment.

He could never touch her now, of course. He had so much decency in him. As they walked back to the boarding-house, he was composing his letter already: '. . . have decided . . . discovered . . . realised that the kind of sexual . . . physical attraction . . . no basis for marriage . . . swept off my feet by your . . . something, something . . . better to face this now than . . . do not think I am the one to make you happy . . . wish you every (lay it on thick) . . . I will always remember something, something . . . I would like you to keep the ring as a (sweetener) memento of . . .' It had better be a good diamond. Oh, hell! Oh, hell!

At the gate she said again, with horrible sincerity, 'My darling, I am so happy.' Instead of kissing him, she took his hands in hers, with dignity, and held them tight.

Walking home, he sobbed quietly and shed tears of anguish in the darkness.

CHAPTER TWENTY-TWO

'I had just seen that old French film, *La Ronde*,' said Maurice to Naomi. It was the kind of remark, made in his flat and earnest tone, that had made her fear at first he was ridiculous; but now she understood, by his mannered gestures with cigarette and wineglass, that he was laughing at himself. Instead of a sense of humour, he had a serious perception that life was comic. 'I'm sure that had something to do with it.'

The remark fell oddly among the cruets and the silverware of the hotel dining-room, where Maurice looked odd enough. He wore a reprehensible tieless shirt *that buttoned down the back*. It had upset the waitress, but she had not dared to speak, seeing that it was defended by a well-cut black jacket and an air of taking her approval for granted.

Naomi wore her good black sweater with Peter's pendant and a long skirt of printed jersey which Barbara had made in a hurry the day before. She had felt conspicuous appearing in evening dress in Bangoree, which to her was a long social day-time, but now, lulled by the wine, she had forgotten the suppressed grin of the waitress and the glances of the commercial travellers who sat at the other tables.

'A married woman?' Danielle Darrieux with a figure like a bud-vase and a horizontal load of hat tied on with veiling.

'Oh, very much so. To her, I suppose, a lover was one of the ingredients of marriage. She would enter into such an affair very easily and keep it within strict limits. The limits were what I couldn't endure. I tried, you know, to . . . so to speak, to upset the applecart. It became my fixed idea to make her leave her husband. I had very little to offer, of course. In the wordly way.'

'How did she react to that?' Naomi wondered whether the woman had had children, but was feeling too amiable to look for knowledge that might make her disapprove of him.

'She fobbed me off with lies and false promises.'

'She must have had some feeling for you, then. That would be going outside her limits, I should think.'

He squinted thoughtfully at that suggestion, then said, 'Or I was unmanageable', with a small grimace of shame which made her like him more. Even more. She drank a little of the very good claret. 'Looking back – I do rather a lot of looking back –'

She nodded, 'Oh, yes, one does.'

'I see that my faults were involved quite as much as my virtues, such as they are. Yet there's this tendency to see it

257

all as a noble enterprise, no matter what a curse you are being to the object, and a bore to your friends.'

'Because it is stronger than self?'

'But is it? That is precisely what I'd like to know. I was so impressed, secretly, by her wealth and her life-style' – his mouth puckered as at a disgusting taste, as he interpolated, 'I hate confessing that – I used to carry on like an eagle trapped in a boudoir, pretending to despise it all; but I wonder whether I wasn't simply measuring myself against it when I tried to get her to leave her husband. Whether fundamentally it isn't an ego play, with the other person cast as second lead. It's a journey to the centre of oneself, in the end.'

'Even if you're lucky, it's a journey to the centre of the other person. That could be worse.'

The way he had of laughing, throwing his head back silently, showing good white teeth in a grin, seemed like a calm acceptance of the attempt to amuse.

'You know, if we don't finish soon, that waitress is going to attack us.'

'Oh, is that so? We'll have coffee in the lounge, then.' He raised his hand in a gesture that caused resentment but ended by getting coffee brought to the lounge.

'So that was what drew me to Fitzallan,' he said when they were sitting in the deep leather lounge chairs, and the waitress, with a speaking look, had set the coffee on a low table in front of them. 'The killing passion, you know. The martyrdom. One does suffer like a martyr. It quite put me off love. I took to eating instead. Which has obvious disadvantages.'

She suggested, 'You had better try love again.'

He met that with a sleek, unreadable smile.

'I must say, I'd have liked to find the girl. It's been a profitable trip in every other way, but I am disappointed there.'

'She'd have told her own story, not Fitzallan's. Everybody does. Brother is the one you ought to talk to.'

'Her story I'd like to know. Old Mrs Ferris was a great help, but I drew a blank with the love affair. Oh, well.'

Once in bed, Naomi slept straight away, heavy with drinking. A few hours later she came wide awake, tense with horror, hearing her own voice say, 'You had better try love again.' Coyly. The words sounded in her brain again, illuminated with simpers and ogling glances, dropped eyelids, glimpses of teeth, rags of a conventional vision of a sex-starved huntress. Again and again. Desperate glinting smiles swooped like bats from the roof of her dark private cave.

The devil was awake again. One whiff, one whiff of cooking and the taste buds went crazy. She rolled over, whimpering, and buried her face in her pillow. Fear set her mind swimming, drowning, far from shore. Worse now, at this age. You meant it, you meant it, don't lie. If you hadn't meant it, you wouldn't have said it. That was always your story, you didn't mean it, meant something different, you can't think what. Using all your energy pushing reality around.

A series of grotesque posturings and screeching indiscretions – memories embellished by self-hatred – passed through her mind, it seemed with great speed. She dared not summon up his smile, even when reason had begun its counter-arguments: he does not know, he does not judge you by one phrase, he has no cause to condemn you. When at last she let herself remember the smile, there was comfort in it. Her self-contempt could not deform it or read condemnation in it. It made her calm enough to put on the light and see that it was ten to four. She was not surprised at that, knowing how this passion devoured time.

She got up then, swallowed two tranquillisers, smoked a cigarette, wrote a note for Peter and left forty cents on it for lunch money, then went back to bed, limp with exhaustion, worn with suffering, thinking, 'Peace. I must stay away from situations that destroy my peace.' Such peace as she had.

Just before he fell asleep, Maurice realised why he was feeling so cheerful. Naomi had said, 'You had better try love again', speaking of him as of one whose love would be acceptable. That gave him heart – curious phrase. Heart of one kind he had already, and how it wanted occupation!

CHAPTER TWENTY-THREE

Through the open door of the attic, Barbara heard the old woman's slow tread on the stairs. She continued to squat, gazing at the page of the old album, as the steps came closer. Suddenly she slapped the book shut, keeping the place with a finger, sprang to her feet and ran down the attic steps, calling out in a hard, lively tone, 'Mother! Mother! Just look at this!'

She caught her at the top of the stairs. 'There's something here I want to show you.' The old woman shrank from the book that barred her way. 'Look,' Barbara continued in an odd, sprightly tone, 'this photograph here. Do you know who that is, standing right next to you? That's the poet Fitzallan. Roderick Fitzallan. So you did know him, you see. Do you remember him now?'

Looking up from the book and finding absence where she had expected a face with an interesting expression, she clucked bad-temperedly.

Raucous breathing as loud as a cry came from below her. The old woman had sunk to the floor and sat huddled on the top step with her head against the banisters.

In the same artificial tone she said, 'Whatever is the matter? Do get up. You can't sit there.'

The breathing grew louder. The old woman rocked backwards and forwards, hands pressed to her chest. Barbara stooped and looked into her face, which was grey.

Terror whipped the shell off Barbara. The book fell to the floor. She ran down to the telephone and lifted the receiver, which slid in her cold sweaty hands. She wiped her hands on her dress and tried again, dialled Grosvenor's number and while she listening to the burring dial tone said to herself, 'I knew. I knew all the time. I did that on purpose.' Her voice telling Molly Carey that her mother-in-law was very ill sounded false and was genuine, this time. Molly Carey's sympathy was a reproach.

'Dr Grosvenor's on holidays, Mrs Somers. Dr Truebody will be there in no time. You take it easy. I'll just get through to him and see if there's anything you can be doing. Now what sort of attack was it?'

Murderous, said the voice in Barbara's head while she talked about difficult breathing, hands pressed to chest, collapse and pallor.

'Doctor says get her into bed and he'll be right over.'

With the grey colour and the gasping, her mother-in-law looked like a beached sea-monster, the only human thing about her the hands clutching her chest.

'The doctor's coming. I'll help you to bed.' She was frightened now, having done so much harm, of doing more, and tried to pull her upright without violence, taking her weight. It was easier than she had feared. The old woman even pulled herself up a little, holding the banister, and walked, stumbling, leaning on the rail.

Barbara lowered her onto her bed, thinking of the photograph album lying conspicuous on the carpet.

She went back and picked it up, looking round flustered with guilt for a hiding-place and finding none. 'How could I not have known? I knew she wasn't in Grafton. Every time she annoyed me I said something about Fitzallan.' She carried the album back to the attic and pushed it under a pile of books as if it was blood-stained.

She went back then to the bedroom. The old woman was still alive, sitting huddled on the bed, her breath moaning harshly through her gaping mouth. She let Barbara undress her and put on her nightgown without appearing to notice the change.

Now she was breathing differently, in great sobbing gasps, which renewed Barbara's panic. If she lives I'll look after her for ever, she prayed.

The doorbell rang. She hurried down to open the door for Phil, feeling a little better, thinking it was less of a murder if she lived till the doctor came.

'Where is she?' He set off upstairs, quickly but with a controlled movement that reproached panic. When he looked at the old woman and heard her choking search for breath, his face relaxed. He said, 'Get me a paper bag, will you?'

'A paper bag?'

Memory brushed against him, disturbing him like a perfume, causing him intense sadness. He said impatiently, 'A paper bag. It's air hunger. I want her to breathe into it.'

When she came back, he was sitting on the bed beside the old woman, with one arm round her, murmuring reassuring phrases. Barbara had come to herself enough to open the bag, and she helped him to hold it over the frantic mouth and nose while he coaxed, 'Come on, let it go now. Huff and puff and blow my house down. Come on now', talking nonsense in a cheerful and affectionate tone, till the old woman's breathing steadied and her face came to life with a flushed, tired look.

'That'll do, now. Down you go, under the bedclothes. You have to keep warm. Now you'd better tell us how all that started.'

'Send her away.' She gave Barbara a mean, childish look.

Startled, he grimaced at Barbara and suggested she go and make herself a cup of coffee. 'You could certainly do with one,' he said, dissociating himself from the dismissal.

When he came into the sitting-room, she got up and walked towards him, looking remote.

'How is she now?'

'Asleep. I gave her an injection of Valium. She'll sleep for about four hours and wake up feeling normal, I hope.'

'It was my fault. I did it.'

He frowned at her, thinking this out of character. 'It's nothing very serious, you know. I don't think her heart's involved, but we'll run some tests. It was an emotional collapse. I know it can look frightening.'

'It doesn't make any difference, really.'

She yawned.

264

He said, 'Oh, God, don't you start.' He laughed at her, stepping out of his role as doctor to fetch her back because she was so remote. Having stepped out of it, he should never have put his hand on her, never. He seized her by the elbows and was saying, 'Don't take on!' when lust started in the palms of his hands, ran over his skin like a bushfire, and set off an explosion that picked him up and hurled him against her, defeated, dismayed, and crying out for help: 'Barbara! Barbara!' He felt the animal tense with life and thrusting for home against her thighs, but his mouth brushed past hers, shyly, and stopped against her neck.

It was the appealing, alarmed note in his voice that reached her. She had not thought there could be any comfort, ever, for what she had done; no sympathy, for who could believe she could do that without meaning to, as if she had turned into somebody else for the moment? But Phil, too, did what he could not help; he was like her. With the relief of meeting a friend in the middle of a nightmare, she put her arms round him. He was unbuttoning her shirt, then she felt his mouth burrowing between her breasts. She looked down at the top of his head and thought, 'It would be the end of him. I could not be expected to do that to him.' She tightened her hold and they shuffled like a monstrous dancing bear out of the sitting-room across the hall into the spare room with its divan bed.

The peak of sensation came for him with the meeting of skin. He was no sooner engaged, occupying that unimaginable tender bony acid-gold territory, than the climax came.

'Oh, damn it. I'm sorry.' He mumbled, 'Not my usual form, I assure you.'

265

He searched his trouser pockets, found a handkerchief, and began to clean up the mess. While she lay without stirring (and how beautiful, a pale winter sun that burnt his eyes), he dressed quickly, then said uneasily, 'Barbara, you'd better get dressed.'

He gathered her clothes and dropped them on her body, regretfully.

'If it had been a heart attack,' she said, seeming casual, 'I would have been to blame. I might have killed her. Fancy it being so easy to kill someone!'

He saw then that she could not move, that she was knocked silly with shock, still.

'Where's the bathroom, darling?' He was amused himself at the endearment, seeing that he meant to have every moment of his time with her.

'At the end of the hall.'

He found a face-towel, wet it, brought it back and bathed her face with it, then started to wash her sticky thighs, with grotesque memories of Eleanor intruding. She stirred then and finished cleaning herself.

'Do, for Christ's sake, put your clothes on. How old is she?'

That question was a mistake. She had begun to pull on her pantyhose, now she paused. It might take her five minutes to decide how old her mother-in-law was.

'Sixty-eight, I think.'

There was something like love in her indifference to her nakedness. They might have been married for years. But in years he could never begin to take it for granted.

'Then she's in remarkably good nick, being able to stand a turn like that at her age. Not that she doesn't need attention. I'll give you a scrip for some tablets for her. Is there anyone you can send with it?'

'Peter will take it. Peter Faulding. He comes in in the afternoons.'

'What time does he get here?'

'Any time after school. About ten to four.'

He looked at his watch and began to feel frantic.

She was standing up now, zipping up her slacks. He fastened her brassiere on her, held her shirt for her, buttoned it, and said, 'It's serious for me, you know. I really love you.'

'Oh, yes,' she agreed, though he never knew whether she meant that she knew that already, or that she loved him too.

'Is there any chance, if I can fix things with Eleanor?'

'No.' She had sat on the divan to put on her shoes. 'No, you see, Robert . . .'

She woke up completely then, turned dark red, shuddered, and put her face in her hands.

'We're not the first,' he said with pity. 'My dear, I have to go, and you must pull yourself together. I'll write the scrip and leave it for you. You had better take a couple of the tablets yourself when they come.' As he was about to leave her, she clung to him, not from love but because he was a companion in helpless guilt; but he took it for love and was happier.

'You had better ring him.' She took her arms away when he mentioned Robert, though he had avoided the name. 'Tell him she had a nervous collapse and I've given

267

her a tranquilliser. No need for him to come home if he doesn't want to.'

He would never see her again. At the end of the week Grosvenor would be back and he would be gone. He would never see her again and never forget her.

When he had gone, Barbara did her hair and sponged a stain off the divan cover. That, she recognised with a beginning of stoicism, was as much as could be done. She went then to ring up Robert, wondering what effect his voice would have on her, feeling some interest in the nature of guilt, this burden she had taken on. This guilt rather than the other.

Robert's voice did not make her feel any guiltier, but it represented an innocence she must defend for ever.

'You sound tired,' he said. 'Are you sure you don't want me to come home?'

'There's no point. She's asleep. I got a terrible fright, but I'm all right now.' As all right as she would ever be again. 'I'll ask Peter to get the pills when he comes. I think I can hear him now.'

She put the phone down, glad to escape the temptation of telling him everything. Would that go on for long? Was there any hope of forgetting, ever, in her old age perhaps? No use thinking like that.

Later she said, 'It was my fault. I gave her a shock, showing her this old photograph. I thrust it under her nose. I was excited, I suppose, because I'd found a photograph of Fitzallan, and I thought it might make her remember him.' Critically she considered this version of the facts. It would have to do.

268

He looked uneasy. 'She doesn't like to be contradicted. She's made rather a point of being in Grafton at the time. I think we'd better keep off the subject.'

The uneasy look that used to make her hostile roused her sympathy now. Why had she expected Robert to cope with his mother, Robert who had suffered from her no doubt more than anyone else? Longer, at least. He survives by dodging. So he survives. One does the best one can.

He looked at the clock. 'More sherry? I'll go up and see if she's stirring.'

This was like being a new person and having new feelings – like sympathy for Robert, she thought, as she drank her sherry alone in the sitting-room. The sympathy for Robert had replaced a deference that seemed to have been an evasion.

A roar from above spilt her drink and set her running. She stopped at the bottom of the stairs because Robert had appeared at the door of his mother's room, but was shouting still towards the bed.

'This is Barbara's house and while you're living it it you'll treat her with respect and keep your sordid suspicions inside your own nasty mind, that's all. I want to hear no more of that. And don't bother to say any more either about going back to Lionel and Ivy, because Ivy won't have you there. She won't put up with you any longer. And from what I've seen of you here I don't blame her. If I hear any more insinuations about Barbara you'll find yourself with nowhere to go. Do you hear me?'

269

The question was so superfluous that Barbara had to wait till the shocked giggle died out of her mind before she spoke, and by then Robert had begun again.

'I assure you that Ivy did not go away to look after anyone. She left home and refused to come back till you were out of the house. So think it over.'

'Robert, don't talk to her like that. She's sick.'

Robert had started downstairs, still directing his voice towards the bedroom. 'Don't judge others by yourself.' He said to Barbara, looking upward with fury, 'Sick in her mind, the nasty old devil.'

With various coughs, shufflings, and a self-conscious air, he began to divest himself of his anger, which left its colour in his face.

'What on earth did she say?' The shocked giggle made itself heard this time.

'Oh.' He shook his head as if bothered by flies. 'Don't bother about that.'

'But I must know.'

'I suppose so.' He resigned himself to mumbling the words. 'She said you were deceiving me, unfaithful. Barbara darling,' he cried, putting his arms round her, 'don't look like that. Don't. I knew I shouldn't tell you. I didn't want to. I shouldn't ask you to keep her here after that, but what can I do? I swear she'll never . . .'

Barbara having moved out of his embrace, he looked at her wretchedly.

'Who?' She shaped the word but could not say it. 'Who?'

'Peter Faulding.' Naming his rival, Robert looked foolish and knew it. The moment was destructive of dignity.

They looked at each other and slowly gave way to laughter. Barbara laughed and laughed till she began to be afraid she could not stop. She managed it, reminding herself that now she was living in a harsh world and could not afford weakness.

'Still,' he said, 'silly as it is, there's malice behind it. She'll have to change her attitude.'

Too late, thought Barbara. I'll change mine, but she'll never change hers.

At the dinner-table she said, 'She was always coming to look at us when we were working upstairs, just putting her head in and going away again. I suppose it seemed crazy to her, having someone like Peter coming in to clean, unless there was something sinister behind it. And he was never here when you were. I can see how she started to build it up.'

Robert looked overcome. 'If you don't mind, love, I'd rather not think about it. It's very good of you to be so forgiving, but . . .'

Later, in bed, she pleaded, 'But don't you see, if your mother really believed it –'

'What a moment to talk to a man about his mother! Enough to cause impotence, I should think.'

She agreed that that would be a pity.

The other thing had not been sex, really. An indiscretion, but not sex. Nothing like this.

Afterwards, lying wrapped in his arms, she said to him, 'What do you think about adopting a baby?'

He answered happily, 'I've been waiting for you to suggest it. I didn't think I ought to be the one. It would affect you so much more than me. There's nothing I'd like better.'

He tightened his arms around her as they both recognised that was not quite true.

CHAPTER TWENTY-FOUR

Naomi arrived at the kitchen door while Barbara was washing the breakfast dishes.

'Peter says the old lady's ill. Anything serious? I'm going over to town if you want anything.'

'Come in and have a cup of coffee. Have you got time?' She went on putting plates in the drying rack with some doggedness, looking pale.

Naomi took the tea-towel. 'You don't look very well yourself.'

Remorse was proving to be not the steady burden she was prepared for, but a wind that blew in gusts, unsettling and frightening.

'There's been hell to pay, here. She's not ill really, I suppose.' She added flatly, 'It's not my fault she isn't dead.'

'Oh, Barbara!'

273

No matter how she accused herself, she could not relieve her mind by confession, but she would go on trying.

Naomi went on, 'You sit down and tell me all about it. I'll make the coffee.'

Barbara sat. 'Did you ever think she might be Fitzallan's lover?'

Naomi became a statue holding an electric jug. 'Maurice thought so.' Now the stiffness came from saying the name, which might make her wince. 'But I told him she was in Grafton. That was a lie, was it?' she asked, amazed.

Barbara's mind took a short holiday. 'How is he? Have you heard from him?' All troubles apart, she was hoping for some return, on Naomi's account, for the dinner she had given, the skirt she had made, and the time she had spent driving Maurice about.

'Just a note. Sketchy. Thanks for the hospitality and he was off to visit Brother Joseph. Never mind Maurice – go on. Isn't it a curious thing, about lies? You tell them yourself and you're astounded that other people do.' She played for time talking about lies while she admitted to her mind the idea of old Mrs Somers as Fitzallan's lover. That disagreeable old harpy! There was no justice in life, none at all.

'I don't blame her for that one. After all those years – what terrible luck!'

'There is that.' Naomi grinned, swallowing the sour information. 'How did you find out, then?'

'I found a photograph of them together. In an old album in the attic.' It was difficult to speak of the album. 'It's not that.' She proceeded to allow herself all the confession she could afford. 'I did such a shocking thing. I knew. I think

I knew. I would have known if I'd put it all together. My mother had told me things. I knew she wasn't in Grafton. When Lionel was a baby she was here. And then I found the photograph, and . . . I don't know what came over me.'

'She's been driving you round the bend, I know that.'

'I just waited there till I heard her come upstairs and then . . . I sprang at her with it.' She was trembling as she talked. 'I pushed it under her nose. She collapsed, and I thought I'd killed her. The way she was breathing, I thought she'd had a heart attack. Oh, my God. I got the doctor. Phil came. He said not to fuss, it was all right. They think her heart's all right, she's got to have tests.'

'But you haven't killed her, my dear.'

'Nobody understands. I could have. She could have had a heart attack and it would have been my fault.'

Naomi looked at her, intent and sober, and said, 'I do see. But isn't it exactly what she's been doing to you all this time, by inches? There's so much of that goes on, much more than anyone knows, I think. And you did just that one thing, in self-defence really. Somebody else might do it and not know or care. And it turned out all right, so forgive yourself, love.'

'And that's not all.' Barbara had grown even paler. 'Oh, what a day! What a day we had yesterday. Phil gave her a needle to put her to sleep and then when she woke up Robert went up to see her . . . oh, you'll laugh.'

'It will need to be pretty bloody funny.' Naomi's voice was heavy.

'Well, it is.' Barbara was unamused. 'She told him I'd been carrying on, deceiving him.'

'The mad old wretch!' Naomi snapped, and sent Barbara's heart down like a stone in a pond.

'Well, you're never to tell him, never, but she said I was carrying on with Peter. Your Peter.' As Naomi shouted, she added, I told you you'd laugh. She and Robert had a terrible row, and he told her Ivy wouldn't have her back.'

'I would have said that was yesterday's bright spot.'

Barbara shook her head. 'Not yesterday, after the other shock. I went to take her her breakfast and she looked right through me. Well, I'm used to that, but it was different. She wasn't doing it at me, you understand. Just staring at the wall like an image. I'm afraid she mightn't come out of it, ever.'

'Does Robert know about her and Fitzallan?'

Barbara considered. 'I suppose he's the way I was. He could know if he liked to put two and two together.'

'Sometimes, of course, one uses all one's strength keeping them apart.'

'He said a funny thing to her. He said, "Don't judge others by yourself." Of course he was in a rage.'

'I didn't know Robert could get into a rage.'

'Neither did I, till yesterday. Naomi, how can you judge people? How do you know what makes them do the things they do?' She took up her coffee cup, which rattled on the saucer. 'You don't control everything you do yourself, so how can you blame them?'

Naomi took advantage of that, quickly. 'Forgive yourself, then. If you're prepared to forgive other people.'

She had won a little smile. 'It doesn't seem the same.'

'It never does. But it is the same.'

276

'I don't know what I would do without you. And I've held you up when you've got your shopping to do.'

'Not for nothing. It's all right. I've got time. Actually –' She paused because compared with Barbara's troubles what she had to say seemed trivial, but to her it was not. 'I want to call in and ask Cec about getting the readings going again. What do you think?'

Somewhere she could be herself. How she missed that! With Maurice she might be too much herself, and would never again risk those agonies of self-reproach. With Peter and Barbara she was too eager to be what they wanted. The play-readings seemed to her like a fenced garden where the poor idiot might be allowed out for an hour.

'Brian won't be in it, of course,' she said glumly, thinking, 'My fault', forgetting entirely what she had just said to Barbara, knowing it was her fate to destroy anything she cared for. Just as well Maurice had removed himself out of that danger. 'And Phil will be leaving. I don't know about Neil. I think Cathy would like to go on.'

'Robert would join, and it looks as if Laurel Prescott might. Cec and Laurel seem to be getting together again.'

'What is it about the Prescotts?'

'That marriage has been washed up for years, over a love affair of Cec's. One of the teachers. She was moved, but they went on meeting, I think. He used to go away without Laurel, and everybody thought he was going to her. They only kept the marriage going because of Beth and Alan, and everybody thought, now Alan's got his degree, they'd split up. But it doesn't look like it. It might be a help if they were in the play-readings together. Only I don't know, seeing how we're placed . . . Everyone would have to come here, that's all.'

'You wouldn't mind?'

'Not a bit. I could show off my nice clean house.' She had put the milk back in the refrigerator; now she leant against the door, looking stupefied, saying, 'I got the house cleaned. What a long way round to go, to get the house cleaned.'

After a moment, Naomi saw with shock that she was not clowning.

'You mustn't fret about it so. Nothing happened. And so many things would have had to be different. For one thing, she'd have to be half as tough, and have more to lose – a husband and a family, for example. You just couldn't have done as much harm as you think.'

'No, that's right. You have made me feel better about it.'

But there was a guilt that could not be argued away, or even spoken of.

After all, Cec did not want to go on with the play-readings.

'Leave it a month or two, Naomi. Playing Hamm was satisfying, but exhausting. I don't think I'm up to it.' The excuse was hollow; he could not admit that he would miss Phil too much and would not come without him. Naomi guessed his true reason and forgave him.

She came home disappointed, but observed that the poker machine was working, for there was a letter from Maurice in the box, as stout among letters as he was among men. After all, the insufficient thank-you note had meant the

278

carelessness of friendship, not of indifference. She opened
the letter as she went inside, so eager to hear his news that
she hardly noticed the knot of shame loosening as she read.

Dear Naomi,

You were right about Brother Joseph. I had a long
talk with him and felt close to Roderick for the first time.
You must have stirred memories that have been developing. Most illuminating, all of it. All that for the book,
of course. I won't make you read it twice! I take it quite
for granted you'll read the book. I feel you are so involved
with it now I shall bore you with it incessantly.

Fitzallan and religion: Brother J. describes the
connection as a beggar taking up his post on the cathedral
steps. Uncharitable? I don't think so. It sounded more
like forgiveness. What was R's own god, I wonder? Some
pagan type who brought the rain and the corn and could
if he liked bring the poetry.

She skipped to the end of the letter, keeping the rest of it
for slower reading.

Of course I am grateful for your help, but even more
for you company. The thought kept recurring, while
I was in Bangoree, that if poor Rod had come forty years
later he would have been very much happier. I feel quite
exiled, since I left . . .

She had got away with it, been spared. He had not
noticed. She was not going to run any risks, just the same.

279

But a correspondence – she could manage that without exposing herself.

How wonderful to give her opinions, to talk about books, to be herself without fear. Better than the play-readings in being quite her own, a novelty that astonished her. Unconsciously she picked up the letter and held it pressed against her breast.

CHAPTER TWENTY-FIVE

'This term is certainly flying,' said Brian in a fine-weather tone, without looking up from his corrections. He knew that Cathy, sitting behind him at the centre table, had been weeping quietly and steadily for some time, for long enough, in his opinion. 'Three weeks from Friday. Thank God for holidays.'

Since Cathy did not pull herself together enough to answer, he was obliged after all to turn round and say briskly, 'What's the matter with you?'

Premenstrual tension, a painful head cold, an unpleasantness with the headmaster about noise in Second Form, and a spiteful remark from Neil, had all contributed to Cathy's breakdown. She chose the last, which had been the last straw.

She snivelled angrily, 'You heard what Neil said, about that result sheet. "Give it to Cathy. She's got nothing to do in the evenings.' It's not the first time, either. He's always got something nasty to say. My clothes don't suit me, everything I say is rubbish, and I ought to do something about my hair. I'm sick of it.'

'You don't want to pay any attention to Neil.' Brian spoke with irritating lightness. 'Nobody else does.'

'He doesn't attack anybody else.'

Brian was astonished at her sharpness, not having expected anything of that sort from Cathy.

'Come on. It's not as bad as all that.'

'It is to me. In fact I've had enough of it. I'm going to apply for a move. I'm going to see Mr Marriott about it today.'

Two birds with one stone, she thought, and what birds. Liver-picking vultures. 'All things considered, Mr Marriott, I think it would be best for me to apply for a move.' So find somebody else to be the staff mug. No, no pique. Leave him guessing. Just ask for the application form casually, with a friendly smile.

She was enjoying the composition exercise so much that her tears dried up at the very moment Brian began to take them seriously.

'Don't do that!' With moderated tone he continued, 'You shouldn't give him the satisfaction.'

It's myself I'm giving the satisfaction, she thought as she answered, 'I've quite made up my mind.' She went to the sink and began to splash cold water on her face.

'You ought to think it over. It's not the sort of thing you should decide when you're upset. You might be sorry later.'

282

'I have been thinking it over and now I have decided.'

Angrily, Brian watched her paint her mouth.

'You needn't tell me you have any feelings for that twerp. If you cared about him I'd sympathise with you. But you don't. It's nothing but ego, that's all.'

She looked round at him thoughtfully. 'Don't you knock ego. It invented the wheel.'

Brian considered that in silence while she combed her hair. When she turned round, he was wearing a meek, astonished, enlightened air. He said in a friendly tone, 'Cath, I don't want you to go. You're a good teacher. You're going to be first rate. What about those exercises in essay writing you're doing with the Fifths? If you don't take them on to Sixth Form it will all be wasted. They'll get the benefit, but you won't. If you've got a real gift for teaching, it's up to you to develop it. God knows it's not common.'

'You never told me this before.' So far had he been from telling her this, she could hardly speak for wonder.

He passed over her words, hastily.

'I was planning to give you the top first form.'

'No, thank you, Brian. It's very nice of you, but I can't stand another year of Neil and that awful boarding-house.'

She had reached the door when he called, 'Cathy! Come back a minute', and she came.

'Look, I'll have to tell you something. But it's a secret and you'll have to swear not to let it out.'

'All right.' She had her own troubles, but who ever refused to trade an oath for a secret?

'Neil's applied for a move. But nobody is to know about it. You don't have to worry about Neil.'

Cathy gaped. 'But Bonnie would have said! That can't be right! She was talking last night about a house to let on the east side. She wanted Neil to rent it and live there, to hold it till they're married. It's not possible.'

'She's the one it's a secret from,' Brian said drily. 'As I understand it.'

Cathy sat down suddenly. 'Oh, that poor girl!' She gasped with anger. 'The poor thing. How could he?'

'If she finds out,' Brian said silkily, 'I'll wring your little neck on the off chance it was you.'

'Why should I tell her?' Cathy was venomous. 'Why should I save him the trouble?'

The old trade union at work, thought Brian. He felt some sympathy for Neil. There sat Cathy, who had given him a knock-back so that the other one caught him on the rebound; the other one had sprung her trap before he could get clear, and Cathy was rigid with rage because the poor devil was trying to wriggle out. It was the wriggling out that made them join forces, always. He hoped he could trust her.

'But I can't stay there! I can't stay there, knowing!' She said angrily to Brian, 'You never should have told me.'

'You would have applied for a move and I didn't want you to. Let them work it out for themselves. It's nothing to do with you.' Not much it isn't!

'Oh, the poor girl.' She saw Bonnie working at her luncheon mats, opposing a brave confidence to the sly questions of Mrs Martin, who had begun to sniff disaster. 'I thought he hadn't been round much in the evenings lately.' She found gossip steadying. 'Bonnie said he was studying

284

for a higher degree, to make sure of promotion. Oh, dear. You shouldn't have told me, just the same.'

Another test for her social nerve, and the last one she had expected.

Brian answered meekly, 'You had me in a spot.' The bell rang at that moment. He gathered his papers, thinking, as the children were accustomed to shout at such a moment, 'Saved by the bell!'

He had to admit to himself that Cathy was coming on.

CHAPTER TWENTY-SIX

As the months passed, Barbara thought often about social disgrace, which she had supposed to be another country, inhabited by foreigners like Eleanor Truebody. It had instead turned out to be a clod of filth one stepped in hardly noticing and walked into the house, where the stink of it would cling for ever.

Much too late, she realised that people who really care for respectability must put it before everything, certainly before happiness, even before life. That was where she had been mistaken, in thinking anything else could matter as much. As for the baby: she should have concealed the pregnancy, fled to her sister Rene, had an abortion, and lived childless but respectable.

She hadn't had any chance to conceal the pregnancy. The second morning she retched into the bathroom basin Robert had come in.

'Barbara, is it? Is it? You've missed your period, haven't you?'

She had said, bad-tempered, 'Don't build on it.' But he was gasping with the laughter of joy.

He sat down on the edge of the bath. 'No, I won't. But you must admit it's a step in the right direction. Poor girl, do you feel rotten?' Too excited to be still, he had got up and put his arms around her. 'It looks as if we only had to say the word adoption, like a charm. Adoption, adoption, adoption.'

It was terrifying to see him so possessed by happiness.

'What are you after, quintuplets?' She had sounded cold and strained, knowing she was acting the role of herself, that she would have to go on doing that.

'You poor kid. You are feeling rotten. Go back to bed and I'll bring you something to eat.'

She had invited miscarriage, carrying heavy lunch trays upstairs to the old woman's bedroom. 'If it happened,' she argued reasonably to the listener who seemed to be always beside her, 'I could bear it. I couldn't bear to do it myself. I couldn't be asked to do that.' She remembered with misery having thought such a thought before.

Robert stopped her carrying trays. He coped with his mother now as if she was an awkward client with whom there was to be no beating about the bush. She had not left her room since the day of the photograph. Dr Grosvenor was called in to persuade her.

'The day will come when you can't walk,' he had said to her, 'if you don't make an effort now. It's a terrible thing to lose your independence.'

She had stared past him woodenly, a woman who had lived in her power over others, to whom the word independence had no meaning.

Mrs French was hired then to take up the lunch tray and help in the house. She was thin and dark, appeared quiet, but was talkative and uncharitable. Barbara noticed with dismay that she took it quite for granted old Mrs Somers was mad.

'Lucky she's one of your quiet ones. Better than violent. Gives me the creeps though, I must say. Does she ever say anything?'

'She talks to Robert, but she only says she wants to go back to Grafton.'

'Pity she doesn't go, then.'

Barbara went on vomiting, violently, as if she could vomit the future away. Her appetite failed, she grew thin and as her belly grew bigger she looked as if all the flesh of her body was draining to that one spot.

Robert's joy was diminished. That was the best thing she could do for him, to destroy it little by little, to prepare him for disaster. If it's not his child, she thought, he won't have to bring it up. I won't do that to him. The first time she felt the child move she amended that thought, silently. So long as it could pass for his child, she would do that to him. There ought to be pre-natal tests for that, she thought, and startled herself with a vulgar snigger.

It was nowhere near ovulation time, she told herself firmly. Nowhere near. But that didn't always count. Face it, you never got pregnant before. But it was nothing,

288

nothing . . . Perhaps it was enough. There was a laborious unmerry merry-go-round in her head where she circled, carried by fear, by hope, by doubt, by attempts at common sense. Calculation of probabilities became hypnotic, so that she circled without being able to stop.

Robert looked for the source of misery in the house and found it in his mother. He talked to Lionel by phone, making plans to move her to a nursing home.

'Robert, no!' Barbara cried out in such panic she had to justify it. 'She could never stand that!' The old woman had to stay: Barbara must defend her, to expiate, so as not to be punished, and punish Robert.

'Face it. She couldn't be any worse off than she is now.'

'Mrs French is no good to her. She needs friends.' Her voice failed. Her mother-in-law needed not friends, but victims, who were denied to her. Mrs French indeed was bad for her. She allowed her opinion of her to appear in her voice, imposing senility, idiocy, invalidism.

Next day, on her regular morning visit to the wooden image, she said, 'You're very welcome to stay here as far as I'm concerned. I wish you would come downstairs, but I don't mind if you want to stay in your room.'

In a panic, she made suggestions: buy her a little television set, fix a table to eat at, try to get her to stay up a little longer every day. Robert thought it hardly worth while at this stage. The decision it seemed was taken. Looking with fear at the future, she told herself Robert was ruthless.

Naomi did not like Mrs French either. She grumbled, 'I can't talk to you while she hovers about', but she knew that Mrs French was not the trouble and that Barbara was

289

isolated by a private misery. She wondered whether she was tormenting herself about the old woman's condition. 'You know she could get up if she liked, my dear. You can't blame yourself for her illness when she isn't ill.' Barbara had answered calmly, 'Oh, I know. She's just sulking, really.'

Naomi made up her mind then that Barbara was filled with dread of childbirth. Because she was abstracted in company, other women had the same thought, and tried, according to their nature, to comfort her or to frighten her further. She gave up going out, finding it too much effort to listen to such boring talk. She was not at all interested in childbirth except as the end of indecision.

A place was found for old Mrs Somers in a nursing home in Grafton. Ivy, asking herself wistfully how Barbara had managed to alienate the old lady, promised to undertake visiting duties so long as she did not live in the house.

'It's a very nice place, Mother,' Robert said firmly. 'You'll have company there. It will be much better for you.'

The old woman had only taken in the word Grafton, which illuminated her face so that even Robert was troubled.

Barbara said to her, 'If you don't like it there, you can come back', and was horrified at the triumphant little smile that met her, the first reaction her mother-in-law had shown to her since the day of the photograph.

She said to Robert, 'She thinks she's going back to Lionel and Ivy, doesn't she?'

Robert was near exhaustion. 'I told her. I don't know what she thinks. Surely the baby's more important than she is?'

'She's not affecting the baby.'

'She's making you unhappy and that's affecting your health. So Grosvenor thinks. I can only try to do what's best. I thought you wanted this child more than anything else on earth. I know I do.' He added, unexpectedly, 'Anyhow, I can't put up with it any longer. It's driving me mad.'

'So long as it's not on my account.' Barbara was listless, but glad to lose a minim of her burden of responsibility.

As she bent over a suitcase packing the old woman's belongings, the baby stirred and kicked. She straightened up, thinking that if she could ever have looked into the future and seen this moment, it would have been a vision of utter happiness. So it might still be. All at once, her fears seemed absurd and the momentary meeting with Phil nothing beside her marriage to Robert. She remembered the old woman was in the bed behind her, awake and watching her. Perhaps Robert and the doctor were right; perhaps that situation weighed on her and accounted for her insomnia, her lack of appetite, and her morbid anxiety.

The moment of remission did not last long. She began again: If it's not his child he won't have to bring it up, I won't do that to him. How did this happen to me? I didn't intend it. It was nowhere near ovulation time . . .

When the old woman left, Mrs French left too and she was alone with her thoughts. They ran through her mind now like a ticker-tape machine that never paused.

One day in the ninth month they drove her out of the house and across to Naomi's flat.

Naomi on the balcony saw her at the back gate and put down the letter she was frowning over. She waved and smiled, thinking that was what conversation with Barbara was like, these days: waving and smiling across a distance. She said, when Barbara came slowly up the back steps, 'You shouldn't have walked in this heat. I was going to call in this afternoon.'

Barbara paused on the landing to look at the view. 'I wanted a change.' The river like dark quartz bore along its buried treasure of colour and light, but she did not see it. Change was not possible; she saw only the ticker-tape machine in her head: If it isn't Robert's child . . .

Naomi looked with annoyance at her thin, reserved face. She set a chair for her in the shady corner of the balcony, brought her a glass of lemon squash, then said, 'What I would like to know is why aren't you happy? Your mother-in-law has gone and you're having a baby. I would have thought all your troubles were over.'

Seeing the alarm on Barbara's face, she was sorry, and said quickly, thinking to change the subject and cheer her up, 'Cec had a letter from Phil the other day.' Phil's face appeared in Barbara's mind, acne scars and all, framed in a baby's bonnet. She noted coldly that to anyone else this would be a comic vision. 'Eleanor is still off the drink. She's doing this course in teaching mentally handicapped children, and she's been promised a job in the home Linda's in. She's doing voluntary work there at the moment. Phil says she's on the way to becoming a saint. I don't know what tone he said it in.'

'Are they together?'

'I don't think so. I think that marriage just fell apart. For her it would be like living with the past, wouldn't it? Though perhaps she'd like that, wearing it like a hairshirt, you know. Poor Phil!'

Barbara agreed. 'It would be grim living with a saint.' How boring other people's lives were! How little she cared what happened to them. But she had ten more days to live through and they must be filled. If she kept on reading the ticker-tape machine she would go mad. Meanwhile there was Naomi's frightening remark about her unhappiness, to which she must find an answer.

'I feel sorry for the old lady. They were hard on her. I didn't imagine Robert could be so hard.'

'Well, I think Robert did the right thing there. It was doing her no good and upsetting you. Besides, I thought she said she'd rather.'

'Not really. She told Robert she'd rather go into a home than live with me; she thought if she kept it up Lionel and Ivy would take her back, but they took her at her word. She still didn't believe it when Lionel came to fetch her. She said, "Didn't Ivy come?" and you could see it beginning to dawn on her that they meant it. Poor old thing. I felt so sad.'

'You're being rather saintly yourself. There'll be no living with you, soon.'

Barbara chose a safe subject. 'How's Peter?'

Naomi's face brightened, but not as much as usual. She, too, had something on her mind. 'Fine. He's sure of his university entrance now and he's got a job. He likes living with Rick. So cheerful for them both.'

'And how's Maurice?'

The worry on Naomi's face came into context. 'He's asked me to marry him.' She sounded scandalised, almost indignant.

'Oh, Naomi! How wonderful.' Her old smile lit her face, giving the measure of its thinness and its ageing. She was glad to think that in the world she inhabited happiness might still occur.

Struck by the difference in Barbara, sorry to disappoint the smile, Naomi said in distress, 'I can't marry him.'

'I thought you liked him.'

'Like him?' Her distress intensified. 'Of course I like him. He's just the same sort of fool as I am. He makes the same silly mistakes.'

'Like wanting to marry you? Is that such a mistake?' Barbara was almost laughing. She found that a strange sensation.

'Oh, it's my letters he loves, not me.' Naomi was indignant at having to explain herself. She would have supposed her unfitness for marriage was plain to everyone.

'Well, it was you that wrote them, wasn't it?' Barbara would not let this happiness go. It was not hers, but she needed it and would fight for it.

'It's not the same thing at all. Not like living with another person.' She said with regret, 'It's rotten luck. That correspondence meant a lot to me, and I suppose it's gone. You never can go back to what you had before.' She sighed. 'I never loved a dear gazelle.'

If she had hoped to escape from Barbara with a reference she would not understand, her hopes were vain.

Barbara might, indeed, have recognised the manoeuvre, for she was looking at her with Mrs MacFarlane's shrewd and pertinacious gaze.

'I don't follow you.'

'Barbara dear,' Naomi said frivolously, 'I can't marry anyone. I talk to myself.' If that was all.

'Perhaps you wouldn't, if you had somebody else to talk to.'

It seemed to her wicked and perverse in those who might be happy to prefer unhappiness, and there was an unconscious wickedness in Naomi's look of abject complacency and in her frivolous tone. This was Naomi, dispenser of wisdom, giver of advice.

'There may be something in what you're saying. Do you know, I used to get frightful wind pains whenever I was working in the library. People make me pretty tense, usually. Then we gave that talk on Fitzallan and the play for the school, and so many people came to thank me and say they'd enjoyed them it quite cured my wind pains.'

Suddenly she looked beyond what she was saying in a silly childish tone to a prospect . . . if it could be so. If happiness could cure . . . But what an act of faith that would have to be, a step into darkness and space.

Wind pains. Barbara was full of hatred for people whose troubles were so trivial, and had solutions.

By this time she felt she was entitled to an explanation. She had worked hard enough for it. 'Is it sex? Do you . . . are you against sex?'

'No, I am not.'

295

'Then I don't follow you. Not at all.'

'Barbara dear, I wish I could make you understand.' Now she was red, flayed, naked too under the skin. 'I can't . . . really can't . . . stand rejection. Can't run the risk. I'm sure I could never make a success of it, and I can't endure the idea of failure.'

'What about him?' Barbara's voice was hard and high. 'What about him? He's going to be rejected, isn't he? Just because you think he might do it to you, and you can't bear to run the risk. And you're supposed to like him. Well, I don't think it's right. Why don't you take your own advice?' she asked with seasoned resentment. 'Make up your mind what's right and do it.'

Skinless Naomi gaped, and said at last, 'Those are the very people who do give advice, the ones who've made a mess of their own lives. People like me. You'll never know, you can't imagine, what a mess. After my marriage broke up . . .' She pressed her lips together and shook her head, but she went on, 'Dear me, the things I did. How I did carry on.'

'Fifteen years ago?' Barbara could not hide her astonishment. 'Everybody gets a bad reaction when a marriage breaks up. It's just normal.'

'Don't you dare to call me normal,' said Naomi with hauteur.

Barbara laughed. They took advantage of the moment to hug each other.

'Don't pay any attention to me,' said Barbara. 'I'm on edge.'

'No, you are right. Only . . .'

296

She sighed. Fifteen years. But to the neurotic, time never passes, she said to herself. As soon as she had said it, the clock-hand jolted a minute's space forward and she recognised the gloomy, settled satisfaction of her inward tone. I choose this, she thought in astonishment. I prefer it. I cling to my neurosis with love, or at least with loyalty. It's my home ground.

Now she looked at it like a stranger, thinking, 'Why torment oneself so? What a strange way of spending time!'

An odd tale she had read somewhere, of horses left with their halters trailing on the ground, not escaping because they thought themselves tied up – was that perhaps her situation?

The moment passed. Saying to Barbara, 'Are you worrying about the labour pains? They are really not so bad –' she was her imprisoned self again, but with a difference. She could make time stand still; but she could not make it run backwards to abolish the thought that she was a prisoner by choice.

CHAPTER TWENTY-SEVEN

'I never saw a baby boy who looked so like his father.'

The remark drew a loud moaning wail from Barbara in her half-lit world of drugged pain and exhaustion. Finished. Finished. Ruin. The face she dreaded popped out of its garbage tin wearing a fierce, innocent grin. Done for. No hope.

'Well, I must say! What a way to go on!' Sister Grant rarely tried to please, and expected to be appreciated when she did. Disappointment made her rowdy. 'When I think what some poor mothers have to face! And a perfect little boy. You should be ashamed. If there was something wrong with him there'd be something to cry about.' Wanted a girl like herself. These good-lookers were all the same.

'You might have a girl next time,' said the proba-tioner, trying by the gentleness of her hands to make up for the harshness of the sister's voice. 'Now you're nice and comfortable,' she lied as she lifted the basin away. 'If he takes after Mr Somers, he'll be a very nice-looking man, I think.'

Robert. They did not know. They did not understand. They thought it was Robert. But then, if they thought it was Robert, it was Robert, wasn't it? Lucky. One could be lucky. Oh, what heaven! Robert's son.

The probationer said, 'Have you picked out a name for a boy?'

Jackpot. Jack Pott Somers. The ugly little joke belonged in the distorted world which was dwindling behind her like a pierced balloon, disappearing even from her memory. She opened her eyes fully to the daylight and said, 'Edward, after his great-grandfather. Old Mr Dutton, you know.'

The sister was mollified by this proper answer. 'I suppose you want to see him, do you?'

She nodded and smiled as was expected, but she was in no hurry. She took more interest in the probationer's offer of a cup of tea and her talk of the lovely roses that had just arrived. Cups of tea, roses, and sunlight on the river. Before she faced the intense light of joy she must accustom her eyes to daylight in the temperate zone.

After the roses came Robert, brimming with joy, and silent.

'They say he's the image of you. I suppose his eyes will go brown.'

'Like that photo of me as a baby, I think.' Robert was murmuring, for fear of creating a harmful disturbance in the air around the crib, which stood at the foot of the bed.

'I'm just astonished that he's there. That he exists at all. He seems like a stranger, you know. Not the child I was carrying.'

'Well, he is. No mistake about that.'

Robert went to look at him again, and, like Barbara, could make no comment, except that he was there.

Naomi came later, bent over the crib, and studied the baby closely.

'He's the image of Robert, isn't he?' She had to conceal a little disappointment, having looked for something, some sign – perhaps a frogmouth. It was too early for Roderick's good quality stare, but that might come.

'So everyone says. I suppose he must be. He just looks like a blob to me.'

'A very promising blob. Full of potential.' Still looking at the baby, she said, 'I haven't said No to Maurice. Not Yes yet, either. I just told him I'd like us to see more of each other before we made up our minds. So you remember that I took your advice, and we're even.'

'Oh, Naomi, I am so glad. It will work out. I know it will.'

Naomi looked away from the baby to smile at her.

'Are you trying to tell me that all the poker machines aren't rigged against us all the time?'

She chose to use Barbara's favourite metaphor, to renew old affection, and was dismayed to see her start and blush.

Barbara controlled her embarrassment, and said firmly, 'Yes. That is what I mean.'

'You may be right. Who knows but I might decide to try my luck again.'

Text Classics

textclassics.com.au

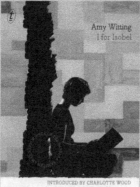

Amy Witting
I for Isobel

INTRODUCED BY CHARLOTTE WOOD

Text Classics

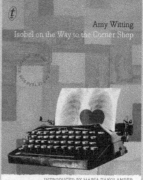

Amy Witting
Isobel on the Way to the Corner Shop

INTRODUCED BY MARIA TAKOLANDER

Text Classics

Amy Witting
The Visit

INTRODUCED BY SUSAN JOHNSON

Text Classics

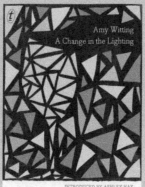

Amy Witting
A Change in the Lighting

INTRODUCED BY ASHLEY HAY

Text Classics

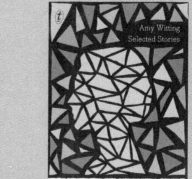

Amy Witting
Selected Stories

INTRODUCED BY MELANIE JOOSTEN

Text Classics